DEMONIC ANTHOLOGY VOLUME VI
A Dark Humor Short Story Collection

DEMONIC MEDICINE

TAKE YOUR PILLS!

DEMONIC ANTHOLOGY VOLUME VI
A Dark Humor Short Story Collection

DEMONIC MEDICINE
Take Your Pills!

Edited by SL Vargas

Jackson Arthur	Alexis Aurol	Rohmann Barisoff	Christopher Blinn
NM Brown	Amy Coles	Lydia McCann	Madison Estes	John Haas
James Harper	Julie Kathleen McNeely-Kirwan	Ziaul Moid Khan
Axel Kohagen	Erika Lance	Jay Mendell	Devin Oldham	Paul Wilson

4 Horsemen
Publications, Inc.

Table of Contents

Introduction

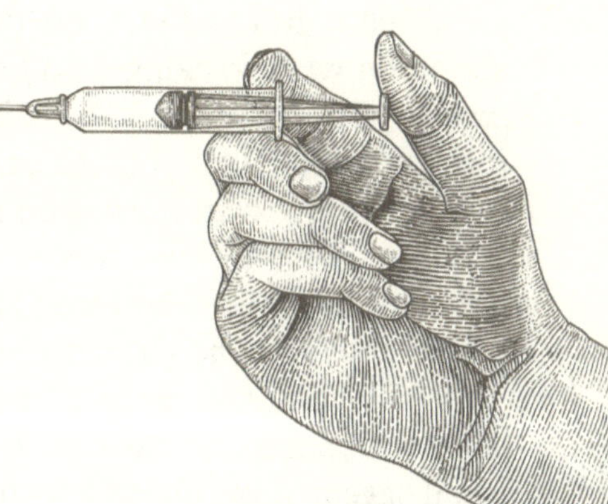

There is very little difference between a hospital and a haunted house. "Now Beau," you might say, "surely that's hyperbole." I'd counter that there's a reason many horror stories take place in hospitals.

There's a certain heaviness to the air that can induce panic, especially when coupled with the fetid stench of antiseptic. Our sense of smell is inextricably tied to our memories, and who among us *doesn't* recall hydrogen peroxide being poured over a scraped knee? Whether the walls are painted a sterile white or an institutional green, the labyrinthine corridors can seem endless. Every turn is a gamble. Will the hallway be empty, or occupied by a lone wheelchair that seems to move under its own volition?

The fluorescent lights buzz and flicker, casting long shadows that trick the eye ("A Simple Brain Scan"). Through parted curtains or cracked doors, the gamut of human suffering is on display: from broken bones and obstructed bowels to grief so overwhelming it burns ("Tears of Fire"). You duck your head to avoid making eye contact. You hope it'll make you invisible.

Seemingly disembodied voices echo. Try as you might not to listen, you become a voyeur. Perhaps you'll hear your neighbor beg to be made beautiful, no matter the consequences ("Bells & Whistles"). Or the clatter of the mop in the supply closet, as your doctor—the one with the thousand-yard-stare—slams the door ("Good Medicine"). Maybe it'll be the couple leaning over the incubator, jabbing their fingers at the squirming *something* inside ("Baby Shop"). The chirp of machines never ceases, no matter how hard you clap your hands over your ears. You'll try not to think about how your neighbors can probably hear you too. Maybe you'll wish they could ("Fresh Start"). *Why won't anyone help?*

"Does it hurt when I do this?" your doctor asks, palpating your abdomen with freezing cold hands. *Yes, but sometimes pain is transformative* ("The Patent Trial"; "Rainbow Rock"; "Brian the Brain"). At least that's what you'll tell yourself to keep from screaming. You certainly don't tell him he's grown horns and leathery wings ("My Brother's Keeper"; "Malpractice") because there's another floor for patients who see the unbelievable ("The Haunted Curtains"). Besides, his bedside manner is impeccable—and he's in-network ("Midnight at the Opal Public Library").

When you're discharged, the pills rattling in your pocket, the horror isn't over. Someone has to take care of you ("Noseblind"), or perhaps, you'll have to take care of someone else ("Your Obedient Servant"). Lord help you if you find yourself in the middle of a pandemic ("Patient Zero"). When you finally forget your harrowing experience, a bill will arrive. *Who knew a number could have that many zeros?* Or perhaps you'll find that when you wake up, you never left the hospital at all ("The Scan").

In this anthology, you will find eighteen tales ranging from the horrifying to the irreverent. There are pustules a'plenty, and even a few that will break your heart. Make sure to consult with your doctor before reading.

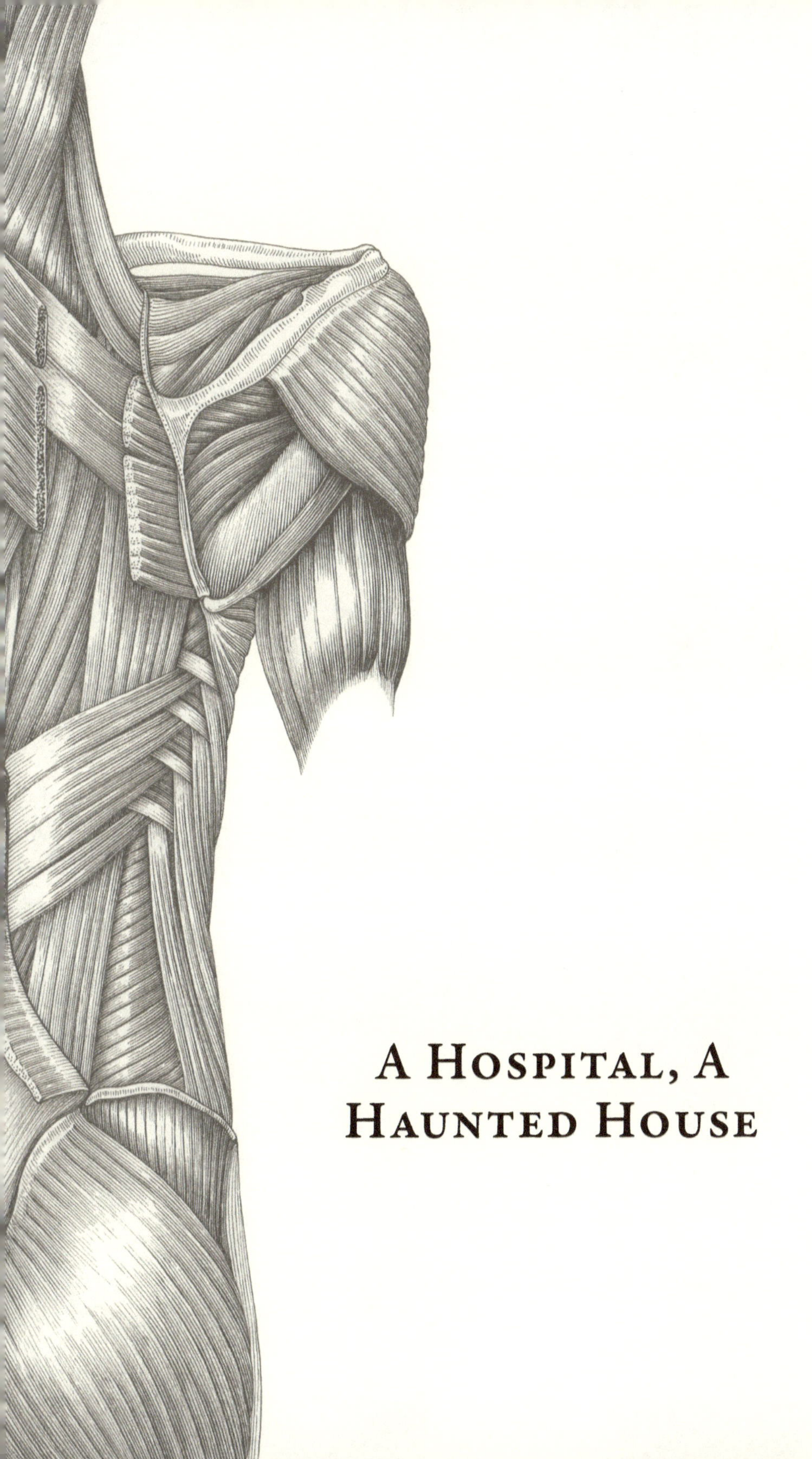

A Hospital, A Haunted House

A Simple Brain Scan

Jackson Arthur

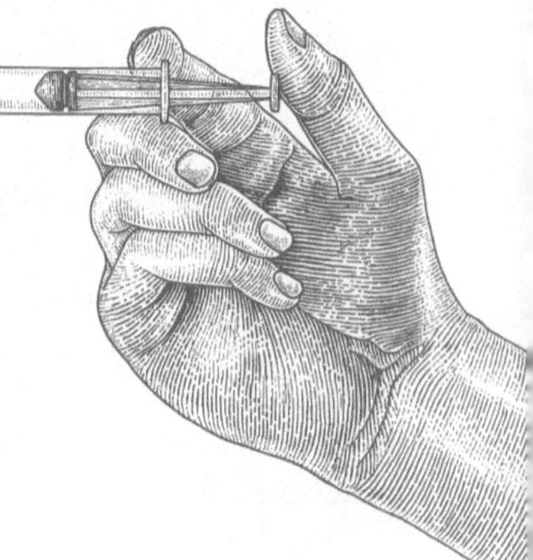

As Judy patiently waited for transport to show up and roll her off to a lower level, she was struck with a brief bout of full-body shivers, her skin and muscles trembling and shaking. Her room on the fourth floor felt even colder than usual, far colder than her last stay, if that were possible. Two white blankets and a single white sheet smothered her from the neck down, but they simply weren't doing the trick. A river of ice still flowed through her veins. Why were hospitals always so freaking cold, anyway? Simply being there wasn't torture enough? They wanted the patients to be as uncomfortable as possible, too?

An ancient, oval clock hung from the wall opposite her bed, the second hand running lap after lap after lap, *tick tick ticking* away the day. Her CT scan had been scheduled for 11:30 a.m. It was nearly 2:30 p.m. Her energy and patience were in short supply.

In Judy's vast experience, nothing rarely happened on time in a hospital. Everything was always ... hurry up and wait. Nurses disappeared whenever she actually needed them. Doctors ran hours behind while on their daily rounds. However, if the hour grew too late, they would end up rescheduling her scan for the following morning. That would mean spending the night away from home.

That simply wasn't acceptable, she told herself.

Ever since being diagnosed as a Hemophiliac with a rare bleeding disorder, Judy has spent far too many nights in the hospital, more than she ever dared to count. When would she catch a break? Or was death the only thing that could break the exhausting cycle? Or would she have to hurry up and wait for the grim reaper as well?

Judy's husband sat in an uncomfortable chair to the right of her bed, partially huddled beneath a pale blanket of his own. In the dim light, he was mostly shadows and vague angles. Within the dark patches on his face, Judy could see that his blue eyes were open and staring blankly into the distance. Slowly, she slid a hand from beneath the mass of blankets and sheets, the movement sending chills down across her exposed skin. Gritting her teeth, Judy reached out from the bed and found her husband's rough hand, which had been resting on the arm of the chair.

"We gotta stop meeting like this," she said, her voice weak.

"You scared me," he replied, his eyes shifting toward Judy. "I thought you were asleep."

"I'm having way too much fun to sleep," she said, and then sighed. "Let's make a break for it. What do you say? My clothes are right over there. We could be at IHOP in 20 minutes. 15 if I just keep this gown on. A full stack of pancakes would hit the spot. Right?"

"Ain't gonna happen," he replied. "Nice try, though."

"They won't let me leave tonight," she said. "I just know it. I'm tired. And I just want to go home."

"I'm sorry," he replied, gently squeezing her fingers. "I know you do."

"Well," she began, "let's get the hell out of here, then. I'm fine. I feel fine. My head feels a lot better now. It barely hurts anymore."

"You passed out and smacked it off the sidewalk just this morning," he replied. "We gotta get it checked out. We need to be sure that nothing is bleeding up there. It's only a simple brain scan. No big deal. If your scan comes back clean, maybe the doctors will cut you loose tonight, or tomorrow morning at the latest. I'm sure you can tough it out until then. Right? And then I will buy you *two* full stacks of pancakes, with a side of hashbrowns. Deal?"

"No," Judy huffed. "Yes. Fine. Deal."

"That's my big girl," he joked.

"Thank you, *daddy*," Judy replied with a fatigued, yet sexy, growl.

"I told you not to call me that," he replied. "It's creepy."

They both laughed and then fell silent again.

Nearly another hour *tick tick ticked* by before a young man, barely old enough to drink, pushed a wheelchair into Judy's room. She considered asking him for a driver's license, but the kid looked worn out, so she kept her mouth shut.

From the chest pocket of his scrubs, the young man pulled a small square piece of paper. "Are you Judy Seaver?"

"That would be me, young sir," Judy replied.

"I will be your ride down to radiology," the young man said. "It looks like you have a CT scan scheduled?"

"Yep. And I am all yours," she replied, and then turned toward her husband. "Can you give me a hand, sweet thing?"

Vacating his chair, Judy's husband placed one hand on her back and one under her arm. Cautiously, he helped her sit up. Her pale legs shifted and poured over the side of the bed. Her sock-covered feet found the cold, tile floor. Her head became momentarily lightheaded, as she put her weight against her husband and stood. Her body, which was running on empty, resisted movement. As always, the strength of her battle-worn husband was enough to transition Judy from the bed to the wheelchair.

"Can you hand me those blankets?" she asked him, once she was seated. "It's colder than a witch's tit in here."

The young man opened his mouth as if to object, but a stern look from Judy forced him to reconsider.

After her husband swiftly shuffled the pile of linen back on top of her, Judy asked, "Are you coming down with me?"

"I'll just wait here," he replied, shaking her head. "You shouldn't be gone long."

"Okay," she said. "But if I don't come back, tell my sister that the hand's off rule still applies."

"Sure thing."

"I love you," Judy said, as the young kid began to push her away.

"I love you, too," he replied. "See you in a few minutes."

The hall outside of Judy's room was a cacophony of hurried voices and beeping machines, which blended into a surge of sound that threatened to fully resurrect her dulled headache. Fluorescent bulbs covered everything in a white light that was unnecessarily sharp, hitting her eyeballs like razor blades. One of the fluorescent bulbs toward the end of the hall flickered and resonated with the buzzing of misplaced electricity. With each flicker, she could hear a familiar *tick tick ticking* sound. As she rolled beneath the flickering light, her sight was attacked, causing her to physically recoil. Her vision jerked and wrenched, and she suddenly saw doubles of everything.

At that exact moment, a short, brunette nurse walked toward them, hastily headed in the opposite direction. The nurse gave Judy a glance and a warm, comforting smile, her body outlined with bright fluorescent light. Resting above the nurse's right shoulder, directly next to her neck, was a dark, shadowy bulge. It was round and bulbous, as if the nurse had a second head.

A second or two after the nurse had turned her head to regard Judy, the shadowy bulge did as well. The black head was not entirely featureless, as a shadow should be. Two crimson eyes peered down at Judy, and a mouth full of jagged, brown teeth flashed her a toothy grin. The glance was neither warm nor comforting. And then, in a flash, the nurse and her second head strolled past them and out of sight.

"Did you see that?" Judy asked the young man pushing her.

"See what?"

"Never mind."

It was a trick of the flickering light, Judy assured herself. She then closed her eyes and kept them shut the rest of the way.

The radiology tech was either new or had clumsy hands, because the insertion of Judy's IV felt like a small, frantic insect had burrowed into her lower arm, ripping and tearing without remorse. She wanted to scream, and cuss, and force the tech to call for her husband. Instead, Judy clenched her jaw and powered through. Once the IV was set, the pain immediately lessened to little more than an annoyance. Breathing in deep, calm breaths, Judy let her head fully fall back against the oversized conveyer belt upon which she laid.

The lights above were the same type of annoying fluorescent monstrosities that had been throughout the hallways outside her room. Judy had been in this hospital countless times, but never remembered the lighting being so intrusive to her senses. Perhaps hitting her head earlier that day made her eyes overly sensitive.

"I'm going to inject the dye now," the short, male tech told Judy. "You will feel a warm sensation going into your body, but that is natural. And it's going to make you think that you have peed your pants. But you didn't. That's normal, too."

Judy wanted to interrupt the tech, to let him know that it wouldn't be her first ride into the oversized, metallic donut. She has taken a trip or two through the tube of sorrow and lived to tell the tale, like a sailor returning after months at sea.

"Are you currently wearing any metal jewelry?" the tech asked. As he began pouring through the preordained list of questions, the fluorescent bulbs directly above Judy rapidly flickered, ticked for two or three seconds, and then stopped. The tech's questions never faltered, as if he never noticed the drastic fluttering of light. "Do you have any tattoos? Do you have any metallic bars, pins, or implants of any kind that I should know about?"

"No to all," Judy replied. "Inject me with that good stuff and let's get this show on the road."

"Sounds good, Mrs. Seaver," the tech replied.

Judy didn't watch, but she knew the instant that the dye had been pushed into her body, because a fire suddenly roared and rushed through her veins. She groaned as the muscles in her arm tightened in response to the unexpected burning. The fire traveled throughout her entire system, scorching everything along the way. A boiling sensation spread from her crotch into her inner thigh, as if she were pissing flames down her leg. Judy resisted the urge to look. Like the tech had told her, she wasn't actually peeing herself.

Once again, Judy wanted to scream, and cuss, and demand that the tech call for her husband. It had never felt anything like this any of the other times. What the hell was the tech doing? Was he incompetent? Or was he purposefully causing her pain? None of those options pleased her.

In less than a minute, the fire had died down into smoldering embers, both in her body and in her memory.

"Are you okay, Mrs. Seaver?" the tech asked. He must have noticed her flushed face. "Are you having any problems?"

Biting back her irritation, Judy grunted, "No problems. Let's just get this over with, please. I'm ready to go home."

"Sounds good. I am going to be monitoring your test from that little cubicle you saw when you first came into the room. It's just right over there, so I won't be far away. You will still be able to see me right through the large window, and I can see you through it, too. Okay? Also, during the test, I am going to need you to remain perfectly still. Okay? Good."

And then the tech rushed off.

For what felt like forever, nothing happened. The silence was awkward and uncomfortable, and Judy was about to protest when the conveyer began to move. Gradually, Judy moved headfirst into the massive, circular machine, until her lower legs and feet were the only thing that wasn't swallowed.

The tech's voice piped in through an unseen speaker. "Are you ready?"

Judy nodded, knowing that a similarly unseen camera was also watching her. She considered adding a thumbs up, but that would further break the no moving rule. The space was roomy enough, but Judy was feeling a little cramped, slightly uncomfortable. The tube no longer resembled a large donut in her mind. It had transformed into a circular vice, ready to clamp down and crush her at any moment.

Good thing Judy wasn't a claustrophobic person by nature, or else she would have been totally losing her shit.

Deep breaths helped. Deep breaths always helped.

"Beginning the test," the tech's voice piped in again, "right ... now."

The machine was soundless. Yet, immediately after the tech announced that the test was beginning, Judy heard more humming and clicking from the fluorescent bulbs, which were obstructed by the metal tube. Nearly rhythmic flickering and flashing created deep, shifting shadows inside and all around the circular machine.

What the hell was with those damned lights? Judy asked herself. *Why do they keep acting so spastic?* She waited a second or two for the bulbs to correct themselves, as they had before, but they only got worse.

Closing her eyes, Judy tried to ignore them, but the clacking grew louder and louder, filling the room with reverberating chaos. *Tick tick tick.* The sharp sound bored against her skull like a spinning drill bit. *Tick tick tick.* The blinking lights conjured phantom images across her eyelids, strange patterns and outlines that resembled abstract people and places, like vague ghosts pressing against the fleshy barrier, desperately seeking a way through. *Tick tick tick.* The large knot on the back of her head, the injury sustained during her fall early that morning, started to pulsate, perfectly in step with the electric clicking of the fluorescent bulbs.

"Will you fix the lights?" Judy asked the tech, her head twisting back and forth hoping to escape the irritating stimulus. "Or can you turn them off? They are really bothering me."

"I need you to remain totally still, Mrs. Seaver," the tech replied.

"The lights!" she suddenly cried out. "You need to do something about those lights!"

"Quit moving, please."

She didn't.

"Stop moving."

She couldn't.

The CT machine seemed to pull in both the flashing and the clacking like a magnet, gathering it around her, wrapping her tightly with it, like she was being swaddled in a blanket of glass and barbed wire. Judy's head wound throbbed and palpated harder and faster, harder and faster, as if a separate living organism had attached to her and was ravenously feeding. The tech continued instructing her to remain still, but his increasingly aggravated voice was noise in the background of her torment. Like a flimsy twig caught underfoot, she was about to snap.

Reaching her limit, Judy exhaled a primal growl. Hastily, she began to shimmy backward across the large conveyor toward freedom, the bottom of her hospital gown riding higher and higher up her thighs. She didn't care if the gown got snagged and was pulled clean off. She was getting out of the room and away from those lights, no matter what. In fact, she was done with that entire hospital, whether her husband liked it or not.

"What are you doing, Mrs. Seaver?" the tech asked, his faint voice coming from the speaker inside the oval machine. "The test is not complete. Please get back into the CT machine, so that we can finish."

Judy didn't answer nor did she return to the test. Even though the exertion made her slightly faint, she somehow managed to slide her weak body feet-first from the machine. Upon reaching the end of the conveyer, Judy sat up and fought to regather her breath. As if responding to her escalating internal panic, the lights flickered and clicked faster and faster, making it difficult to see. She tried to look around, but the strobe-like effect of the lights caused her vertigo. Firmly, Judy gripped the sides of the conveyor and held on with all of her might, afraid that the vertigo would unbalance her enough that she would fall. In an attempt at decreasing the effect of the lights, Judy lowered her eyes and focused on her own body, while blocking everything else out for the time being.

"Are you okay, Mrs. Seaver?" The tech's voice no longer resonated from inside the machine, but directly in front of her, causing her to flinch at the unexpected closeness of it. She looked up and found him standing only an inch or so away. "Is something wrong?"

The short man was difficult to see through the visual onslaught, his thin frame seemingly twisting and bending within the constantly shifting light and sound. He didn't seem affected by anything that was happening.

"Don't you see the lights?" she asked, her voice full of pain and despair. "Don't you hear them?"

"I don't see or hear anything, Mrs. Seaver." the tech said. "Would you like me to call your nurse? Or would you like something to calm your nerves? Some Ativan?"

A black mass moved at the back of the tech's head, and Judy assumed that it was an illusion of altering shadows. But then the black mass moved again, further revealing itself to Judy. It was a head, dark and round like a giant piece of coal. A set of high-sitting eyes peeked at her from behind the tech's head and shoulders. They were bright, glowing red, like the tips of lit cigarettes. Below the eyes, abnormally and unsettlingly close to them, was a grinning mouth filled with jagged, dirty teeth. Other than the eyes and mouth, the creature was featureless. The constantly flashing light rolled over it in consistent waves, causing its surface to crawl and slither, like the skin of a dark snake.

"What the fuck?" Judy exclaimed, physically shuddering away.

It was the same type of creature that had been attached to the nurse upstairs, she recalled. Judy shrieked. "What the hell is that?"

"What is what?" asked the tech, clearly confused.

The black mouth slowly opened freakishly wide, revealing three rows of those nasty brown teeth. Judy expected the creature to speak. Instead of talking, though, it swiftly bit down onto the tech, sinking its nasty teeth into the side of his neck. Somehow, there wasn't any spurting or flowing blood. And the expression on the tech's face remained unaffected, as if some dark creature wasn't latched onto him. As Judy continued to watch, frozen and helpless by fear, the creature's mouth began to gyrate, and it seemingly began to feed.

All of the air was violently forced from Judy's lungs as she screamed in utter terror. After the scream, air returned to her body, but only in shallow, nearly useless gasps. Slamming her eyes shut, Judy tried to regain control of her breathing, but the hyperventilating only grew worse.

She heard the tech say her name.

"Mrs. Seaver?"

She felt his hands touch her shoulders.

"Are you okay?"

Instinctively, Judy reacted by slapping and smacking at him blindly, striking the man several different times. His hands retreated from her shoulders. She then heard shoes frantically tapping against the tile floor, heading away from her. Judy opened her eyes just enough to see the tech rushing toward a phone hanging from the far wall. With his back turned, Judy got a full view of the creature clinging to the tech's backside. Its head was the size of a toddler, but closer to the shape of an egg. Its body was long, narrow, and perfectly in line with the tech's spine. Several short tentacles protruded from its eel-like body and were attached in random places across the tech's upper and lower back. It was made entirely out of shadow, or some bizarre substance that resembled it.

"Hello," the tech rambled hastily into the phone. "I need someone to come to the radiology lab immediately. The patient is..."

The tech's voice faded to a murmur. Judy couldn't take her eyes away from the creature, watching in stunned silence as its long body contracted and retracted like a water hose. It was feeding. What was it feeding on, though? There hadn't been any blood. Yet, the creature was obviously sucking something from the tech's neck. If not blood, then what was it taking? The possibilities gave her chills.

A drawn-out flash of light lit the room, like lightning filling the sky, and Judy's attention was suddenly drawn to the tech's cubicle and its large window. Another exaggerated flash lit the room and Judy could see her terrified reflection in the rectangular piece of glass. Her eyes were as wide as two silver dollars, filled with terror and distress. Another pair of eyes were also reflected in the glass, two glowing red orbs perched right above her shoulder blades.

"Get it off!" Judy howled. "Get it off! Get it off!"

She could suddenly feel it, suckling against her spine like a black slug. How had she not noticed it there before? How did the tech not realize that there was one attached to him? Couldn't he feel it, too? Flailing her arms awkwardly, Judy tried to reach around to the center of her back, to get her hands on the creature. But she only ended up grabbing empty air. It was there, though. She could still see its red eyes in the window. She could still feel its suckers cupping her shoulders and ribs. Why couldn't she get her hands on it, then?

"Get it off!" she continued screaming. "Get it off!"

As she struggled, her arms stretching and twisting, Judy lost her balance and toppled from the conveyor. Her weak legs were unable to catch her momentum and she crumbled onto the floor. When she struck the hard tile, her temporary IV was ripped free. Her blood, abnormally thin due to illness, began rushing from the open vein. The last thing that she remembered before losing consciousness was the sight of her blood splashing onto the floor and the stabbing sensation of the shadow creature biting into the side of her neck.

"Judy? Honey? Are you awake?"

The voice of Judy's husband pulled her back from the darkness, and she opened her eyes to bright, blinding light. It was a consistent, steady light, thankfully. There wasn't any more flashing or gyrating from the fluorescent bulbs. And the only *tick tick ticking* that she heard was from the familiar clock hanging on the wall. Somehow, she was back in her upstairs room.

"How are you feeling?" her husband asked, sliding his hand into hers.

Judy hurt like hell from head to toe but she was safe and alive. Was she, though? She was alive, but was she actually safe?

"Mirror," Judy said, her voice quiet and raspy.

"Mirror?" her husband asked, his tired face furrowing with confusion. "Is that what you said, honey?"

"Mirror," she grunted, her voice carrying a lot more force behind it. "Mirror."

From Judy's purse, her husband swiftly dug out the tiny, oval mirror she always carried with her. She held out her palm and then aggressively snatched it from him. With a shaky hand, Judy held the little mirror in front of her face. She checked her left shoulder. And then her right. She didn't see any glowing red eyes reflected, but Judy knew that the mirror lied. The shadow creature was there, even if she could no longer see it. She didn't need to see it, because she could still feel it wiggling against her spine, possibly readying itself to feed again.

The knot on the back of her head agreed by bulging and throbbing.

"Everything right as rain?"

Judy raised her eyes from the mirror to look at her husband. There was a shadow creature on him too, she just knew it. Did everyone else have one attached to them? Have we always had them on us, feeding on us like parasites? And why was she the only person aware of them? What made her different from everyone else?

At first, a sense of loneliness swept over her. She was the only one who could see them. She was all alone in her suffering. But then Judy considered what her new improved perspective on reality could mean and her hands stopped shaking.

The shadow creatures were parasites, she reminded herself. Not monsters. Not gods. Parasites. And parasites could be exterminated.

"Honey?"

"Yes, dear," Judy replied, a grin spreading over her mouth. "Right as rain."

TEARS OF FIRE

JOHN HAAS

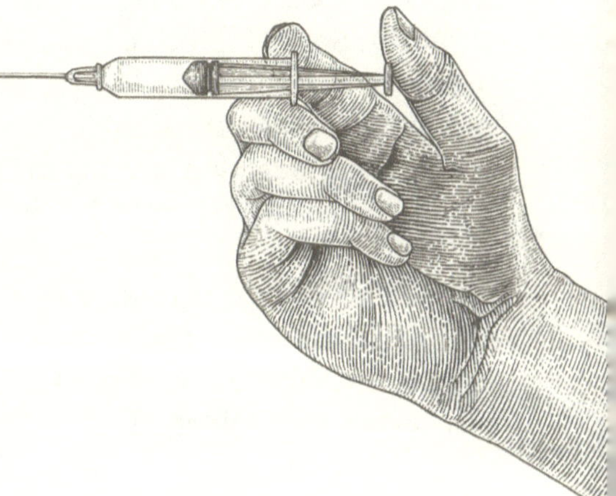

Nancy Peters carried her brother Scott into the emergency room, placing him on one of the waiting chairs. When she was sure of his comfort—as comfortable as possible with one leg in a makeshift splint—she turned and rushed to the check in window. An agonizing ten minutes passed while some grossly overweight lady moaned about a headache.

Fat bitch, eat some vegetables and maybe that wouldn't be a problem.

Nancy closed her eyes, immediately ashamed of the thought and its unfairness. She was hardly a size two herself and never aspired to be. No, those negative thoughts came from concern and fear for her little brother.

That awareness only went so far. Another minute passed and Nancy wanted to plant a foot in this woman's ass and encourage her to hurry up. Without any name-calling though.

Finally the woman turned, and Nancy gave her a sympathetic expression before rushing into the space left behind. The admitting nurse was an older lady with a name tag identifying her as Sheila and eyebrows which had been ruthlessly plucked then drawn back in.

Nancy babbled everything to her in one long, high-speed word.

"It's okay, dear," Sheila smiled patiently. "Slow down a bit and tell me what you need."

Definitely someone's mom. She reminded Nancy of her own. One deep breath and she tried again.

"It's my little brother, Scotty. We were skateboarding ... well, he was skateboarding, and I was watching him. That's my job this summer while my parents work, instead of being a lifeguard or flipping burgers like my friends."

Sheila cocked her head to one side.

"Right. Sorry. I'll focus, I'm just worried."

Nancy was nervous all right. Scotty was only ten years old. Half her age and all her responsibility. At college, she was an adult, paying bills and making her own meals, writing papers on ancient folklore and legend. Once she returned home, it was back to being a child in mom and dad's house.

At least they'd offered her the cushy job of watching Scotty all summer. That was pretty cool, and a hell of a lot easier than the jobs her friends had. Now they would take it back because of a stupid accident that wasn't her fault at all.

"I think his leg is broken. He was skateboarding and twisted wrong and..."

She couldn't finish. Sheila nodded, marking things on a clipboard.

"He's only ten." Nancy heard tears close to the surface. "Please help him."

Sheila continued to write while Nancy envisioned jumping the counter and demanding something be done. That wouldn't help. She remembered her own visit to the hospital for a broken arm around the same age. Weird how that worked.

"Have a seat with your brother," Sheila said. "We'll get a doctor to you as soon as possible."

As soon as possible. A euphemism for an unknown period of time between now and next Tuesday. Las Vegas was giving odds on next Tuesday. Nancy sighed and Scotty groaned. His forehead was sweaty and his skin pale. Should she call mom and dad? They would leave work and rush to the hospital, but all they would see was a crisis dumped into their lap, not her responsibility while taking care of the situation. No, she would see this through and get them home in time to make dinner.

Why hadn't she taken Scotty to a movie instead of the skate park?

Enough. What's done is done and there's no way to change it.

The minute hand crept around the wall clock while Nancy did her best to distract Scotty from the pain. *How could they let a little kid suffer like this?* Urgency and emergency should go hand in hand.

Into their second hour Nancy glared at each new person who came through the door. One guy with stab wounds went to the top of the list. That was fair, she guessed. But that kid with breathing problems? Come on. Aw, man, she should have said Scotty hit his head on the cement and lost consciousness for a moment. Concussions were serious stuff, but she never thought quick enough in this kind of situation.

The automatic doors zipped open again and Nancy cursed inwardly. A man walked in, staggered in really, and sat across from them without even going to see Sheila. He leaned forward, head resting in his hands. His clothes and hair were mussed up, face covered in dirt. Was he alone?

Tears dropped from between the man's fingers to spatter against the floor. Big, fat drops from one eye then the other. Nancy imagined she could hear each one as they hit.

Tss. Tss.

Wait. She *could* hear them. They landed and sizzled, like liquid in a hot pan. Thin wisps of angry smoke rose from where they hit.

Tss. Tss.

Tss. Tss.

The man glanced up. The tears had etched a groove through the grime on his cheeks.

TSS. TSS.

One particularly large tear fell from his face and, just before it hit the floor, burst into flame. The following tears went through the same process, flaming as they fell, each one greater than the last. A small pool had grown at the man's feet.

He groaned, muttering a word. Was it *no*?

Nancy was engrossed watching this spectacle for several minutes, unsure what to do. The fire was worrying. If the pool continued to grow it would surely reach them. Should she move Scotty? Tell Sheila?

Another tear fell and hit the pool of flame with a muffled explosion.

Bam.

Nancy jumped, the spell broken.

She had one arm around Scotty's back and another scooped carefully under his legs.

"Nancy," he said, half in a doze. "What is it?"

She jerked her head toward the man and Scotty followed, eyes growing wide.

The explosions had grown to equal small firecrackers now. Others in the waiting room had turned in their direction, some from curiosity, others from annoyance. No one panicked.

The man glanced up, his gaze locking on Nancy's. "Run."

A heartbeat passed before Nancy did exactly that. With Scotty in her arms, she bolted for the door which whooshed open in front of her. It moved too slow, and Nancy turned sideways to squeeze through the gap sooner. Scotty gritted his teeth against a scream as his leg was repeatedly jostled.

"Oh God," he said.

"Sorry, Scotty. We've got to…"

"No."

Nancy realized her brother wasn't talking about the rough treatment or them fleeing from the hospital. The explosions had grown loud enough that they could still be heard after the door closed behind them.

Inside, screaming started—shouts.

The second door opened as they reached it and Nancy rushed into the sunshine, not slowing for a second, threatening to spill them both onto the hot pavement. She didn't stop until she reached her beat up Subaru.

Surely this was far eno—

Behind her, the emergency room exploded.

A rush of wind and heat threw them forward. Nancy twisted to take the impact as they were thrown into the side of her car. Another twist as they fell to the pavement, trying to ensure Scotty fell on top of her. She was half successful. Scotty howled with pain and Nancy's head bounced off the parking lot with a sound like a melon smacked with a baseball bat.

When she came back to awareness the sound of Scotty screaming her name pounded inside her skull, muffled slightly by the ringing in her ears. Her brother lay on his good side, shaking her.

"Okay," she managed. "I'm okay."

Relief flooded his face in a half smile/half grimace. Nancy struggled to sit up, wondering if maybe *she* had the concussion.

"Careful what you wish for," she muttered.

Didn't matter since there was no emergency room to treat her, only a smoking crater where it had been. Rubble and bodies were visible from where they lay. Debris had been flung as far as the car. In the distance, sirens got closer.

"You two okay?"

A man bent over Scotty, checking his leg. A doctor, just coming in to work, or maybe going home. He wasn't dressed like it but had a key card on a lanyard which identified him as Dr. Miller.

"His leg is broken." It was all she could think of to say.

"What the hell happened here?"

"The guy was crying explosions," Scotty said.

Miller nodded, undoubtedly diagnosing shock. Understandable. How could anyone explain what they'd just seen without sounding out of their mind? Miller turned toward her for a more lucid answer and Nancy opened her mouth, unsure what she could even hope to say. Before the first word tumbled out, a glimmer of movement came from the rubble which used to be an emergency room. Doctor Miller finished tightening the straps of Scotty's splint as a man emerged from the dust and debris.

The crying man.

"That's him," Scotty said, his voice almost a whisper.

The man didn't appear to be crying at the moment. There were certainly no sounds of explosions, no flames.

"Help me!"

Miller turned, drawn by the anguish in his words. This man didn't seem like a terrorist or crazy man or someone who might cry explosions.

"Help me!" the crying man repeated, his voice complete misery.

Doctor Miller rushed across the lot, speaking to the man in a low voice as he approached.

"Watch out for his tears," Scotty called.

The crying man shook his head in response. One tear burst into flames, visible from where they were.

"Shit!" Nancy scrambled to her feet.

Head throbbing, she staggered for the back door, jerking it open. Nancy quickly helped Scotty into the back, then rushed for the driver's seat. Within a moment, she was behind the wheel, car ignition twisted and ready to go, already reversing.

Sirens filled the air.

One police car cut sideways to block the exit while others continued past. A cop rushed over, one hand on the butt of his gun. Nancy rolled down her window.

"It's that guy," she said, pointing. "The one that doctor is talking to."

The cop nodded, but neither went back to his car nor moved his hand.

"I need to get help for my brother," she said.

There was a small clinic about fifteen minutes from here and that would do just fine for them.

The cop looked at Scotty in the back seat, splint around his leg, and nodded again. Then he spun at the sound of muffled explosions. Through the windshield, Nancy could see flaming tears, each larger than the previous, hitting the ground. Doctor Miller backed away as other police officers surrounded the man.

"What the hell?" the cop beside her car muttered.

"Oh god! Please move your car. Please! I have to go."

The cop made no move to do so and gave no indication he'd even heard her. He stared across the small lot at this strange spectacle. Each of the officers surrounding the man held their guns pointed in his direction, stepping closer.

"He's going to explode again," Nancy warned.

The explosions continued to grow, both in volume and intensity. The officers looked at each other, hesitant to shoot a moan who only stood there crying, even if those tears were exploding.

Bam! Bam! Bam!

The cops all retreated one step.

"Get down," Nancy warned the cop beside her, trying to follow her own advice. Her seatbelt prevented it and a random thought of *when did I even put that on?* came into her mind.

BAM! BAM! BAM!

The explosions came in rapid succession, building force.

BAMBAMBAM!!

BOOM!

A white flash filled the world and Nancy's car rocked, throwing her to one side, then back. If not for her seatbelt, she would have rolled into the passenger seat.

"Scotty?"

Vision started to return.

"Nancy?"

Sound.

"I'm here. I'm here."

Could he hear her?

"I'm okay, Nancy," he said. "Let's go! Please!"

The windshield held a spiderweb of cracks. Outside, the crying man stood in a fresh crater, dirtier but otherwise unscathed while the police who had surrounded him, as well as Doctor Miller, were gone. Thrown to god knew where. Vaporized maybe? The cop outside her car was flat on his back, unmoving, and several feet away, closer to his own car now.

Time to go.

Past time.

"Scotty?"

Nancy tried to twist around, but a screech of pain in her left side called a halt to that. Giving up, she glanced in the rear-view mirror and found Scotty pressed against the far door, gaze shooting past her. He shook his head back and forth.

"Help me."

With a jump, Nancy refocused on her open window, and the crying man who stood there. He leaned down closer to her.

Help him? *Help him?*

She wanted to tell him to piss off, to let her and Scotty go, to please not hurt them.

Deep breath. "How?"

This close, she saw how blue the man's eyes were, blue like a clear sky. Without the flames and explosions, he looked normal, but those eyes were welling up again. He looked at her a moment longer before pulling the back door open. He crawled inside with her brother.

"No!" Scotty yelled. "Don't!"

"Get away from my brother!" She jammed the seatbelt release button, but it refused to let go. Again and again she stabbed at it while the man hovered over Scotty.

Tss. Tss. Tss.

"D... Don't..." A dreamy look crept across Scotty's face, his protests dwindling.

"What the hell are you doing?"

Another round of hissing spatters and the man retreated from the car, standing in the parking lot once again. "They can heal, or they can harm."

"They ... the tears?"

"Yes. If they build too much..." He gestured at the carnage.

Nancy glanced in the mirror again, saw Scotty moving, lifting his leg. He removed the splint and flexed his muscles with a laugh, then looked at her with amazement.

"Like a Phoenix," she said, latching on to a legendary creature she'd read about this past semester.

The man sagged against her car door, both hands gripping where the window would normally be.

"Mister?"

"It's okay. I'm okay."

He straightened, a tear falling to the ground with a Tss. Nancy wondered just how okay this man really was.

"I can control them," he said. "Usually."

"Um ... okay."

He sighed, sniffled. Another tear fell with a Tss. "My wife died today."

"Oh," she said, then realizing the impact of that statement, she repeated. "Oh! You can't stop crying."

"I thought maybe I could use the tears..."

He shook his head, looking at the destruction around him. Another tear fell.

The concept of these healing tears whirled inside Nancy's mind. *What a gift. What a curse.*

"I destroyed our home before I could leave."

This poor man. Nancy reached one hand out and placed it over his. She had to get him out of here, get him someplace he could grieve without destroying the world around him.

Could they cure disease as well as heal broken bones? My god, what a—

BLAM!

Nancy jumped.

The explosion wasn't from his tears, though it had come from nearby.

He looked down at his chest and the round, red hole which had appeared there, then back to Nancy. A look of surprise and pain.

BLAM! BLAM!

Two more holes.

"No!" she screamed.

The cop from outside her window was back on his feet, a few feet's distance away. His gun was still raised, a trail of smoke curling from the barrel. His other arm hung uselessly at one side.

The crying man pitched over backward, hitting the ground like a sack of flour.

"No," she whispered. "No!"

He didn't need to die.

There was so much potential for what could be done with those tears. So much benefit to mankind. He had healed Scotty's broken bone and—

Tss.

"Huh?"

Tsssssssss.

Nancy looked out the window, down at the crying man. His tears were gone but blood leaked from the wounds which had killed him, sizzling as it seeped across the pavement.

TSSSSSSSS.

"Oh, no."

Nancy flipped the shifter into reverse and stomped on the gas.

"Hey!" the cop objected. "What are you—?"

"Run!" She twisted the wheel left to maneuver around the police car, ignoring the pain in her side.

A glance back at the emergency room, a smoking ruin that had been caused by a few tears. *What could flowing blood do?*

The Haunted Curtains

Ziaul Moid Khan

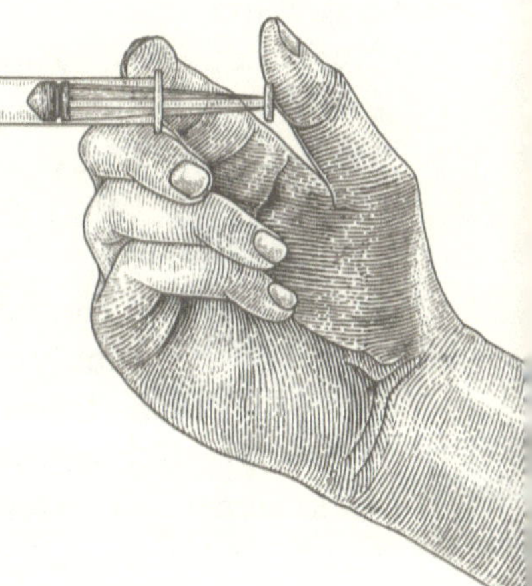

The day my mother was detected with blood cancer, I cried well past midnight. In fact, all members at our home were woebegone, but showed a brave face. Father took a week-long casual leave from his Central Reserve Police Force duty at Delhi Metro. Nidhi, my sister, was sleeping beside me on the other bed. All members managed themselves somehow, but alas I was inconsolable.

All will die one day, and everyone knows it quite well, but Dr. Garg's statement that my Mom was in the second stage of this deadly disease and would hardly live a couple of months, sort of devastated me. I did not want her to die. My mind was not ready for it.

I'd never encountered such a gloomy atmosphere in my life before. None seemed to have any words of compassion to share with me. Speechless, I cried nonstop tears for hours. Still, none thought to wipe the wet salt from my cheeks. It was understandable: all loved my Mom and felt more or less the same sorrow for her when they came to know about her approaching death.

I recalled: a man named Ashok in my neighborhood had shot himself in the temple. Almost the entire village gathered around their house as the news spread of his suicide. I could not dare to visit, despite all my other family members rushing to his house. Though they came back repenting, for Ashok's head after the fatal blow was in a gruesome state. Beggar's description, you know.

I was happy not going to his house, but very sad for his death. They speculated: he'd taken this dire step for a girl whom he loved, perhaps passionately, and she did not reciprocate. I always feared dead bodies, visiting funerals, and mourning. And now my own mother was nearing death. I could not swallow this fact. The hard, harsh reality.

Lying prostrate on my bed, my face sank into my pillow. My chest brushed against the cushion and my tears ran down my cheeks bedewing the pillow beneath. I was helpless, hopeless, and less of all positivity. I never wanted to lose my Mom—not at any cost. Come what may. The diagnosis giving mom only a few months to live stirred my latent emotions. My heart simply didn't accept this reality. Truth's bitter like a gourd, after all. But sometimes—or more often than not—truth is unacceptable.

I reckoned something was wrong in the report, some computer error or the doctor just miscalculated her illness. *She cannot die*, my heart said, *she cannot leave us when none of us siblings are mature and independent enough to survive in the cruel human world.*

No siblings in the family were children, true. The plan we all had to finish college was true, too, and Mom would not be here to help us. Nidhi was doing a master's in chemistry and my brother Dushyant was attending his first semester of B.Tech. and I was a student of B.Sc. in my first year. Mom had said: "Shalu, you should be a cardiac surgeon." And I too wanted to crack the pre-med exam, but suddenly this cancer thing plagued all my dreams and shattered them like anything. I was lost in these thoughts; when I encountered something weird that night which I did not anticipate. The time was one a.m.

First, I thought it to be just a fleeting self-doubt, but upon close observation, I sensed I was not wrong. The curtains suspended at the French window in my bedroom suddenly animated and moved like the pendulum of a wall-clock. It was a February night, so obviously the ceiling fan was off, and the windowpanes were tightly shut, dismissing any possibility of the backstreet winds that could violate the peace of my bedroom. I saw the floral green blinds violently fluttering like the enormous wings of a raven, first right then left and then right again.

I sat up bolt-straight and gazed at them up-and-down, fixedly, trying to comprehend if it was at all possible. The faint neon light from the street bulb, penetrating the crevices of the window, fell onto the side of my cotton-stuffed pillow. Rummaging around on the bedside study-table, I found the switch of my table lamp and the next moment the mercury vapor light illuminated the room.

The blinds were dead-still as if they'd never animated. *It's a mirage or an illusion,* I said to myself, turning off the light again and letting my head sink into the pillow's soft comfort for a nap. After that, a few moments passed in peace, and then the fluttering sounds of the curtains returned again, startling my very fundamentals. Every hair of my skin seemed to have sensed the bizarre, the paranormal. They stood at their ends. Horror knows no logic, no math.

All my rationale was running a riot in the present condition. For a moment, I forgot my mother's cancer and beheld the strange night's happening. Adapting my eyes with darkness, I saw—or I think I saw—a face or rather a portion of a face: a woman, middle aged, with unkempt hair and bloodshot eyes, her hands with their long fingers and even longer nails clutched the blinds tightly. And it was she who was, in fact, shaking the curtains crazily.

As I screeched from the utmost core of my throat, Nidhi woke from her dreams and jumped off her bed into mine. Now she was shaking me terribly like the woman was shaking the blinds.

"SHALU ... SHALU ... SHALU," she said hysterically. "COME ... COME ... TO YOUR SENSES!"

I pointed to the curtains as she turned on the light. But they were drawn with all civility.

"What the hell's there?" she questioned with her voice shivering like someone exposed to extreme winter cold.

"Those curtains ... those cur..." I muttered, still infected with a bad fright.

"Yes, they're curtains," she said, trying hard to pacify me. "Then what...?"

"They were ... fluttering," I said, still shivering and striving to figure out if it was real or my hallucination.

"You must have had a nightmare, kid," said Nidhi grimly. "See, they're just ... just OK, perfectly fine."

Then there was knocking on the door, a persistent rapping followed by a familiar voice. "Nidhi ... Shalu ... open the door!" It was Daddy with Dushyant standing just behind him. They must have heard the screeches and hurried to the door. Opening the latch, Nidhi explained everything to them, wasting no time. They were kind of indecisive to believe it or not. Finally, Nidhi let them in to discuss this matter further. Clueless, I was still looking at the curtains with apparent disbelief.

None believed me. It was sheer madness they thought. Sort of an illusion, I must have imagined: my own brainchild. But I knew I saw it happen, whether one bought this story or not.

"Shalu," said Daddy, sitting beside me and caressing my head affectionately. "You seem to have a bad impact on your mind. If need be, we'll seek a psychiatrist's counseling."

I was sane and not at all abnormal. Still, I said nothing. All other members in the family were clueless about the incident. The door opened again and this time it was Mom who frisked into the room. Sitting beside me, she said that she had heard the ruckus. Though Mom looked apprehensive, she did not say much, only tried to assuage me by caressing my head. My eyes were still glued to the curtains which seemed innocent, and now were challenging my rationality. It was hard for me to justify a point in this abstract matter.

After half an hour or so, all left for their respective rooms except Nidhi. She took hold of both my hands and said, "It's all OK. Now sleep, Shalu. We'll talk in the morning. So, no more discussion about it."

Morning found me cheerful. Last night's ordeal was done away. And I was somewhat feeling relaxed. In some secret vault of my heart, I thought it to be, yes—my own brainchild. Thinking that I would not freak out again, I got normal, but Mom's terrible disease was still so nightmarish I could not forget it, at all. And so, I spent some time in her care during the day.

At twilight, after supper, I went back to my bedroom. It was a starry night and the full moon's beams were easing through the curtains' gaps. Nidhi was watching T.V. in the drawing room. Dushyant and Daddy were with Mom in the master bedroom. I was getting ready to read my book on pharmacology. For convenience, I took two pillows, reclined them against the French window with the blinds down, and supported my back against the windowsill. With it, I immersed myself into learning. Of course, I wanted to score good marks in the examination. That was a priority.

I was striving to comprehend how drugs are chemicals of low molecular masses which interact with macromolecular targets and produce a biological response, when there suddenly appeared from nowhere, a wet crimson mark right in the center of the page I was reading. With a shivering into my spine, I touched it with my forefingers and brought it close to my eyes—it was blood. I wiped my nose with my left hand. It was not bleeding. I double-checked my hands; they too were not wounded. But the little blood splatter was very clear and glaring.

I was frozen to my place as the curtains suddenly revived and fluttered like the wings of a dying bird after a road accident. I looked up and could not believe my eyes: there was the *face*. The same *woman's face*, agonized with a cut lip and bruises all over her bloody countenance, eyes bulging out from the sockets and besmeared with horror.

Before I screeched on my mightiest pitch, one more drop of thick blood fell from the corner of her lower lip. I saw it come like a ball in the game of cricket reaching in slow motion before hitting the wickets. The blood drop fell across the page, dismantling all my doubts.

This time, the rescue team did not have to seek much explanation though, as they saw themselves: the two sizable drops of thick human blood, fresh without clotting. The sentence that the drops had almost covered read: *Most of the drugs used as medicines are potential poisons, if taken in doses higher than those recommended by the physician.* Amid hysterical screeches, I pointed to the curtains, which were still like dead limbs. The agonized woman's face was gone as if (it) might have never appeared from the curtains. Like it was a conspiracy to falsify my justification.

That night, Nidhi slept in my bed with me like a mother sleeps with her child.

But as I slept, I saw her—the woman—in my dream. Or it was a horror flick. This time, I saw her completely. Not just the face: her whole body, unclothed, every inch of it. Not a thread was there to cover it. She stood dead-silent beside my bed. Gazing, with fuming wrath, straight into my eyes, and holding with her left hand—the window curtains. Her sagging breasts were smeared with fresh dark blood. Her belly bulged out as if with seven months' pregnancy. And the bushes of black curly hair between her thighs were too nightmarish to talk about. She was a typical ghost: death-pale, fresh from the coffin, and haunting an innocent girl: me.

Then I heard a ringing. The ear-piercing chimes. Startled, I awoke, It was my 5 a.m. alarm. The early morning sunrays were making a light gold pattern over the window blinds.

Psychiatrist Priya Jhajhariya's cabin displayed more about her personal accomplishments than abnormal psychology. From her scouting days to her casual meeting with Dr. Aruna Broota, (almost) everything was on the walls with citations including her honeymoon pictures—not the bedroom ones, though. Daddy brought me to her for consultation against my will.

She seemed fit for a fashion show, ready for a catwalk or to give away her autographs. Shehnaz Hussain's entire latest makeup line seemed to have been used to partially hide her original appearance. And the thought never crossed my mind that she could be at all helpful in my case. I did not know why, but she could not impress me.

The room shone bright with a pink glow like the casinos shown in *James Bond* flicks. It gave an apparent impression of tappers; instead, it was the effect of the fancy lights in the ceiling. The royal armchair Dr. Jhajhariya sat in gave an impression she did not wish to lose even a single client. No book on clinical psychology I could spot around. Either this branch of science needed more exposition, or she just needed some more exposure to learning.

I took the first chair from the left of her Chinese table and slumped in.

"Kumari Shalu, have you ever been to a counseling session before?" she said, taking a notepad in her hands, her baby-pink nail paint reflecting in the fancy lights giving an aura of acrylic nails. Though they were real, I thought.

"Not at all," I said casually, trying to look calm.

"You claim to have seen a woman's face peeping out of the blinds in your bedroom," she said, emphasizing the word *claim*.

"I'm not *claiming*. I actually saw it," I said, defending myself.

"But you simultaneously say, the lights were turned off."

"Precisely."

"How come you see a face when there is pitch dark in the room?" she said, staring at me like a novice crime investigator.

"As you know, doctor," I said, re-adjusting in my chair, "after a while, eyes adapt themselves to darkness."

"Of course they do," she conceded, "but not so much that one could tell facial expressions, blood and all that, I mean—"

"But the second time I saw *her*, the light was on," I cut a solid point across, "and the blood drops..."

"Anyway," she continued, "do you sleep well?"

"Not anymore, now."

"When did the abnormality ... I mean ... the problem begin?"

"A fortnight before, just after moving to this new house," I replied.

"Shalu," she said, swiveling the chair a little to her left, "do you've an idea about Obsessive Compulsive Neurosis?"

"How do I?"

"It's a complication in which the subject is bound to do or think something, irrationally again and again due to depression, or anxiety, or both. Your mother is the case in point."

I didn't respond, just looked through her as if she did not exist.

Around a dozen more stupid questions she asked. The counseling took half an hour to finish. Then she sent me out and called Daddy in.

Later, on our way home, Daddy told me: the counselor thought my paroxysm was a critical case of somnambulism and hypochondria caused by Mom's illness. She had suggested I needed to come to her clinic for a few more sittings. Apart from it, Dr. Jhajhariya prescribed some antidepressant drugs, too.

I was adamant I would not visit her again, forget about taking the pills. All the same, I was pleased she did not straight away surmise me a Schizophrenic and recommend an asylum, the worst possibility.

Next night's nightmare was no different except that the woman was not unclothed. She seemed to be gazing out, and not gazing right into my eyes like she was doing the previous night. Still, her hands clasped the curtains tightly on both sides. I could not see the woman's breasts, but only the back of her and noticed a blood trail emanating from her neck and dripping off the center of her bum.

She wore a violet top, sleeveless and showing fairly from the sides her armpits and the remnants of the recently removed hair. What made her horrendous was her blood-smeared body that otherwise was pale like it did not have blood in the veins.

Then I heard some weird sounds: as if somebody was retching in the distance. Not this woman, but someone else. The sounds then changed into violent coughing, persistent and too loud to be ignored. I woke up. The woman disappeared. And I found Nidhi, still in deep sleep.

Unhooking the latch, I reached out like a sleepwalker coming back to their senses, as I came to realize my Mom was throwing up. She spewed blood with the half-digested cauliflower she'd had for supper. I was sorry, being paranoid; I almost forgot the cancer that gripped her. But now the glaring truth was bare in front of me, again.

I took Mom's head in my lap and caressed it affectionately. It consoled her. Daddy and Dushyant too reached there, by now. For a moment, I forgot the bloody ghost. Mom's eyes welled up and from the corners of them tears started rolling down, bedewing her cheeks and touching the sides of my hands. Death seemed to be approaching her every moment. And we could not do anything.

I wanted to tell Nidhi my last night's nightmare, but due to Mom's illness, I remained tight-lipped, for I didn't wish to enhance our family's complications. Daddy was already passing through a bad patch. So, I thought it better not to raise this matter at the moment.

Next night, I slept with a bit more fear for reasons unknown to me. In my dream, *she* was there again. Reclined on me from my bedpost. Blood dripped from the corners of her lips and, taking a course to her chin, it was falling on and wetting my abdomen. I could feel its weird coldness. Its thickness. Its living vitality. Now, it was going down my thighs. I could feel it in my lower abdomen, the area every spinster wants to offer only to her husband or lover or both. I could feel the numbness—as if the blood was oozing out of my own body.

Suddenly, I came to realize that if I didn't sit up, she'd lie down upon me and pierce her four incisors into my neck like *Dracula* did to his chosen victims. Now, more and more blood was flowing from my V-part. Stirred, I woke up, panting breathless and found myself bleeding profusely. OH MY GOD! I GOT MY PERIOD!

Dr. Garg declared Mom needed the change of her entire blood periodically: every third or fourth month (if she would live that long). For it, we were at Yashoda Cancer Institute, Ghaziabad. To transfuse four units of blood, we needed to donate the same pints in return. That was the standard process in almost every hospital in our vicinity or in all the medical facilities in India, I guessed.

Nidhi, Dushyant, and I gave each one unit of blood, but, nevertheless, we needed one pint more. Daddy was weak enough physically, his hemoglobin level was so low, we were against his donating a pint. Dushyant suggested the name of his physics' teacher, Rana Sir. He was a Good Samaritan and would not refuse to donate, my brother thought.

And he was right. Rana reached the hospital's cancer wing in no time and our big trouble was solved quickly. Though I knew beforehand that he would agree to donate, for I once cherished a sweet relationship with him that nobody knew about. Yes, we had come close and passed some memorable moments in each other's arms.

And there evolved a romantic relationship we'd enjoyed before we split up, for no other reason than that we could not get married. In India, live-in is still considered a sin. And getting married to your sweetheart is equal to conquering Mount Everest. Thus, all options were closed, and we decided to close our chapter.

Momentarily though, Mom now sparkled with some color in her cheeks after the transfusion, yet her poor health was still reflecting from her face. She would have to stay in the facility for the first chemotherapy. Meanwhile, she suffered a great hair-loss. And now she was bald. Even if the treatment was successful, it'd take a long while to heal and get back her hair.

The day Mom's chemotherapy was scheduled I stayed at home for my exam preparation, while all others went to the sanatorium. I was sure I'd have no problem at all during the day. I made a cup of tea and boiled two eggs for breakfast. As I finished it, I immediately launched myself into hard-study mode and didn't bother about the Ghost of Kamini. Until then, *she'd* never paid me a visit in broad daylight. Ghosts seem to have their own self-made protocols—one of which is, not to venture out in the daylight. Nights, somehow, are more convenient for them. They simply love the solitude of night. They too want peace. Good. God. But I was mistaken today. Every rule carries an exception, too.

It was a late sultry summer and as the day progressed, the blasting sun outside could be felt inside the house, too. I pulled the curtains on the French window to keep the room cool and soothing and free from the glaring sun outside. I reached my wardrobe and took out some clothes to beat the summer heat. Pulled over an opaque floral blouse that revealed a fair chunk of my bosom, but I was comfortable in it. Without a bra, my orbs looked bigger, heavier than they should, and my nipples, protruding.

Strange but true: *breasts are the only part of a woman she both wants to show and hide at the same time. On the one hand, they like to pull over a deep neckline that sufficiently shows their cleavage, but on the other, they hardly like any peeping Toms around.* I sat down on my bed again. For a while, I read the book sitting cross-legged, but then shifted my posture. I laid on my back, put a pillow under my head, and held the book in front of my eyes.

For quite some time, I did not have any problem, rather it was very comforting, but then I felt my eyes getting heavier with every passing second. A strange drowsiness began to possess me. Then my eyes shut. I tried to reopen them. They opened for a couple of seconds and then I could no longer keep them like that. My book fell onto my chest, and I crossed to oblivion.

Unlike a common sleep, it was a queer intoxication: an abyss that could only be created by heroin or marijuana, none of which I ever took in my life. Soon, I came to realize I was not alone—Kamini the murdered woman stood beside me. Her hands held my paperback, and she was peering into it, while mine were clasping my pillow tightly.

Then, I stood up ramrod as if under some ghoulish influence, stripping off my clothes one by one: my floral blouse that left me topless, my breasts hanging loose like two succulent mangoes, off was my mini skirt and then my milk white G-strings, too. Kamini looked at me with a grin, picked up my clothes from the bedpost and wore them piece by piece. The tables were turned. She took my place and I, hers.

Now, she was there reading my book, while I stood naked beside the French window clutching the curtains, my long hair hanging loose, my heavy breasts sagging and my cleavage dripping with blood: crimson, fresh and wet enough to be precisely felt. We—God knows why— exchanged our positions. And then she called out my name, shifting her gaze from the book and focusing it on me: "SHA LU ... S H A L U ... S H A L U ... KID ... SHALU!"

There I stood on my bed shivering, dripping with fresh, warm blood. And then there was a sound slap right across my face and the room's dimensions changed. Kamini vanished and the bedside where she had laid was unoccupied. Instead, Nidhi now stood facing me and shaking me like hell by the shoulders. I came back to my senses. No blood dripping, instead it was my sweat. I realized the electricity was off, so the room was blazing with heat. And my whole body was perspiring.

"Have you gone nuts, Shalu?" said Nidhi, forcing me down to sit on the bed. "Put on your clothes ... hurry up. Thank God! It was me who came to your room, first."

I was, naturally, very embarrassed. Had there been Daddy or Dushyant in place of Nidhi, what'd have been my impression?

Mom's growing illness reached into a chronic condition: the third stage. And the first chemo was, in fact, not very helpful. Doctors at the facility said, *Mom needed a second round of chemo immediately.* Daddy mortgaged Mom's gold jewelry for the sake of her better treatment. We were financially devastated. This time, Naveen, mom's half-brother, and a friend of his, did the blood donation for transfusion. Two more units of blood we bought by paying some extra bucks. We were ready to go to any length to save Mom anyhow. Still, we had but little hope.

Before Mom on her stretcher was carried into the Operating Theater, I hugged her tightly and cried. I feared to let her go, lest she should not come back *alive.* I did not know why, but it felt as if I embraced Kamini and not my Mom. I shivered at the very thought and cried more and more. Daddy signed, as the standard process, the undertaking papers for full responsibility, in case of an untoward happening with Mom during the therapy. He remained strong, carrying a storm inside his mind. Nidhi and Dushyant were woebegone, teary-eyed, and looking flustered.

After a while, the bulb on the top of OT's glass door turned red and that was an indication the therapy was underway *now.* The blinds were pulled over and we couldn't have the inside view. We waited outside impatiently. Daddy had been off to the medicos to buy post-therapy medication. We sat in the iron chairs fixed to the floor facing the O.T.

Nidhi sat on my right and Dushyant on the left, while I sat in the center. None of us took breakfast today. My stomach churned but it was pointless to demand food under the circumstances. And I knew my siblings too must have been facing the same condition. But we were more concerned about Mom's illness than anything else at the moment.

After half an hour or so, Daddy appeared with two packets in his right hand: the first one contained Mom's drugs and the other one having disposable paper-cups and a transparent polythene containing tea. A packet of glucose biscuits was a welcome relief. He served tea to all three of us and then poured the fourth cup for himself. At that moment, the glass door made a creepy sound before it flung open and there appeared a nurse with a green scarf neatly tied to her Eiffel Tower bun. Approaching us, she handed a slip to Daddy after having verified his relationship with the patient.

Some injections were required. Daddy gave her the polybag containing medicines he'd brought and immediately left without finishing his tea. My eyes were glued to the door. The curtains at the glass door revived my fear of those hanging in my bedroom window. For a moment, it seemed Kamini stood there too, holding them with both her hands. I jerked my head in exasperation and the tea from my paper-cup sprinkled over my sky-blue blouse. Startled, I glanced at the glass door and felt relieved: Bloody Kamini was not there. Both Dushyant and Nidhi were staring at me with questioning eyes.

And then came the bad news—Mom died. "The second chemo could not be successful," the oncologist said. I lost my wits and screeched hysterically the way I did when I happened to observe the macabre, the bizarre in my bedroom for the first time. My siblings too joined me in mourning. A few medical students walked past us making grim, sad faces. Death makes its own environment: gloomy and dreadful. The whole graveyard shifts to a place where someone dies.

Some paperwork was done, and the body was handed over to us. Daddy was busy making some phone calls, while we clamored into the back of the ambulance after Mom's body was settled inside by the ward boys in green uniforms. Daddy took his seat beside the driver as he drove home our dear Mom, in fact only the last remains of her.

Cancer killed her eventually or was it something else? The siren of the ambulance was very unsettling. And I saw: the window curtains, inside the death vehicle behind the seat where Mom lay, fluttering violently. I knew it was because the outside wind was getting inside through the windowpane, which was slid aside. Still, I didn't dare to have a second look, for it seemed Kamini sat beside Mom's head. I was baffled. It was like my soul was *possessed*. Was I *cursed*?

As we reached there, we found our house filled with varieties of people: black, white, long, short, and stout, including women, children, the rich and the poor. People came from all walks of life to pay their last tributes. Most of the respect to a person is usually given after their death. The funeral preparations were already underway.

Death is the mockery of human life. Everybody seems to finish up business once someone dies. A dead body is sooner than later to be disposed of. People get stale, stinking after their death. But I feared Kamini was still there sitting beside Mom's cadaver. And in my heart of hearts, I wanted Mom to be cremated at the earliest. So, when they took her away to be burnt to ashes, I took a deep sigh of relief. Because then I could have a look around with no peril of spotting the murdered woman. She was not there. Gone to the crematorium with mom, perhaps.

"I'm sorry for your mother," said Mrs. Nehra, our immediate neighbor. She looked sideways before coming close to my face. "A word's no longer yours as soon as it slips off the tongue," she whispered. "The only favor I want from you is, I should not be dragged into this matter, in case you raise the alarm."

Mrs. Nehra was a typical, well-informed, soap opera sort of woman. She knew her neighborhood to a level where other women in the colony were bound to envy her. She could give sermons over divorces, elopements, split-cases, lost jobs, miscarriages, and teenaged love affairs that happened in the entire vicinity. She could easily update the local radio broadcasting station. It was, though, a mystery how she got to know these facts. But I was sure she must have some sound knowledge about the house we had rented recently.

"Your name won't surface anywhere, Auntie," I said undertone. "I just wish to know what the hell's wrong with this house or with my bedroom, in particular. Or is there a connection between my nightmares and mom's death?"

"Connection I don't know," she said, "but horrible, very horrible things happened in this house. Poor Kamini! Misfortune fell on her side."

"Who was Kamini?" I barked. "And what the hell does she have to do with me?"

"The lady who lived in this house before you," said Mrs. Nehra, still looking apprehensively here and there. "She lived and died in this house ... or ... was murdered to be more accurate."

"Murdered? Who killed her by the way?"

"That ... that I don't know," Mrs. Nehra said, trying to hide the truth. But her eyes told me that she knew it.

"Please Auntie, tell me! Don't cloud the mystery," I implored. "You know everything ... I mean, almost everything."

She came closer.

"My name should not be dragged into this matter," she repeated her restraint.

"I swear, I would never tell a soul that you told this to me," I said. "Now tell me who killed her."

"Rajesh Kashyap, her own husband." Mrs. Nehra dropped the bomb.

"What?" I said, aghast. "Why would a husband murder his own wife?"

"Extramarital relations, you know!"

"Who was the cheating spouse: husband or wife?"

"Husband," she said. "Kamini was only trying to win him back."

"By the way, though it's none of my business," I said, trying to hide my fondness in this matter, "who was the woman responsible for this woman's murder?"

"The witch who ruined Kamini's world was her distant relative," said Mrs. Nehra. "A Shalu Verma."

The last words thundered into my ears like a bolt from the blue. A sudden realization dawned upon me: *The girl responsible for the murder of this woman was my namesake. Could it be the reason the dead woman was haunting me every night?* My fear from the ghoul was now shifting to sympathy for the poor woman. But my hair rose in dread over my whole body.

Irony. It was me who was being dragged into this matter.

Thirteen days had passed since Mom died. As a mark of respect, her head-shot was framed, garlanded, and put onto the wall, suspended from a peg in the prayer room. There was an unending chain of relatives who visited our house, meanwhile. Some of them stayed for a couple of days, some paid a passing visit only. All through this while my room too remained well-occupied.

It was good, because the Ghost of Kamini did not appear for quite some time, at least as grossly and shamelessly as she would. *Ghosts too have their protocols*; this realization began to settle in me. But I wanted to get rid of the bloody curtains in my room. So, I stripped them off the French window and shoved them into the washing machine.

It was only then that I spotted the deep crimson marks over the windowsill. I took a dusting cloth, drenched it in water, and wiped the window frame where the sill was tarnished with dried blood. The bloody stains were too rough to be removed easily. I wondered if Kamini kept a vigil over my frame-cleaning-business. Just to check, I looked over my left shoulder. Nobody was there. I resumed my work, though without much success.

So, I reached over my room cabinet and withdrew a plastic bottle, the label read: *Vanish Liquid Stain Cleaner, ₹62 only*. The spray refreshed the blood. It felt like it fell over there just moments before. I made a picture of Kamini's murder in my mind, but then shook the feeling off my head. I used the cloth rag to remove the stains but could only do so partially. It was a hard nut to crack.

And it was then that I heard a bone chilling, cold voice behind me: "What are you doing, Shalu?"

The dusting cloth and the stain cleaner slipped off my hands and fell to the marble floor. But my squeal stopped midway as I spotted Rana standing very close to me.

"Damn! You terrified me," I said, recovering my breath.

"Are you a chick? Scared so easily?" he said and gave a forced smile. "I thought you to be a brave girl."

"Yes, once I was, but now a slight exertion can stir me."

"Your Mom's death must have a severe impression on you," he said. "I can understand. All you need is rest."

"All I need is some *Ojha*," I said. "Because it's *something else* that is haunting me day and night."

"Something *else*?" he said with curiosity in his tone. "And why do you need an exorcist, by the way?"

"Have a seat, I'll tell you," I said, offering him my room chair.

I narrated my predicament, only holding back Mrs. Nehra's identity, for I'd given her a word.

Rana listened to me with rapt attention, occasionally nodding, and frowning with awe and queer expressions writ large over his countenance. When I was finished, he said coldly: "One more solution is possible to rectify this cas—"

I looked at him with questioning eyes, Nidhi beside me.

"And what is that?" I asked with cold interest.

"—Meditation. And in your case: A séance meditation."

"How?" Nidhi blurted out. But Rana didn't seem to have noticed her and continued.

"Shalu, I'll assist you to do séance meditation and call *her*," he said, eyes focused in some vacuum. "It'll strengthen you to fight against the dark forces. It's a *therapy* I've practiced hard for years in Haridwar. And it'll help you too, I'm dead sure."

"When are we doing it?"

"Tonight," he said, rising from his chair, "provided that you want to get rid of this ghost issue."

Nidhi and I agreed.

Daddy was in New Delhi, back to his duty at Metro Station. And convincing Dushyant was not that difficult of a task. A planned encounter with the Ghost of Kamini was henceforth scheduled.

Early that night, Nidhi spread four floor-mats in my room. On the first one, Rana took his position sitting cross-legged. I sat just opposite, facing him. On his right was Nidhi. While Dushyant sat on his left. The doors were closed. The curtains were back on the French window after having been washed and ironed. Despite the presence of all these people, I still wondered if Kamini would be back to frighten me as I shut my eyes at Rana's cold command.

"Shalu, am I audible to you?" he said in his familiar, cold but husky voice.

"Yes," I said, putting both my hands in my lap.

"Fine. Are your eyes shut?"

"Yes." His own eyes must have been closed. Or he would not ask such a question.

"Let your whole body feel relaxed."

"Okay."

"Feel your mind is a vacuum. No tension. No anxiety. No fear. No past. No future. Just the present moment and that's—pure and blissful."

I didn't respond this time. But tried to assume what was suggested.

"Remember some good moments of your life," he said.

I remembered my Mom giving me a shower, while I was a young girl, so young that I could not even pronounce Mom's and Dad's names properly.

"Recollect some more memories," he continued.

I did. I saw Rana and me, huddled together in bed without clothes. He was holding my tits and I was giggling like a fairy. Then, those arousal moments were there—unforgettable. Sex isn't a sin. Still, it's almost banned in the entire world and considered a taboo that cannot be removed by any stain cleaner.

"How's it?" he asked.

"Beautiful."

"Now come to some difficult level: Try to recall some mathematical equation which you found hard to solve."

Suddenly, I found myself in seventh grade. Precisely thirteen years old or so and at my puberty age. Now I looked like a girl, for my breasts just started getting a round shape. And I recently noticed my pubic hair and the occasional itching in that area. Mr. Rajendra Yadav, our school math teacher was there in the classroom, teaching us Algebra. The blackboard was filled with some equation where X was unknown, and I was trying hard to figure out what the hell he was trying to prove.

Have you got it? Mr. Yadav said after having filled the entire blackboard with his zigzag writing. All the other students replied in unison *Yes, sir,* but I said *No, sir.* He explained the entire equation again, but it didn't reach my head. He did it thrice; still I could not figure it out. Eventually, he gave up and said, *Come later to my office; I'll explain it to you, there.*

And I precisely recalled how I met Mr. Yadav in his office after the school hours that day. As I took permission and went in, he gazed at me fixedly, perhaps at my chest which had taken a round shape in the past few weeks. It seemed he was in a different mood now.

"Remove your glasses," he said as I grasped the situation. He left his chair and came around the table. Took off my spectacles and passed them to the oak table. No Algebra though he taught me there, just pulled me to his office sofa and kissed my moist lips.

I felt his spiky beard with half-gray hair against the surface of the soft skin of my face. It was my first kiss: a dirty one, a forced kiss rather. I could not say *no* to it, but I knew I was against it. I was underage. Was it child abuse? It was like two generations were meeting *forcibly.* Hell, both my relationships were with my teachers. Was it a double coincidence or my fate or both? His eyes tore through me, his fingers did the rest.

My math was no good, but I knew quite well what he was doing was not *Algebra.* The creep was only satisfying his lust with his wooden office door shut, though not bolted; he knew no one would come. All had gone home except me and him. Eventually, he laid me on his office couch and in a nutshell did everything he could.

Sometimes we cannot stand against what is wrong. I couldn't object to Mr. Yadav's exertion. He saw my everything, and I could not say *no* to him. Thus, in the next few minutes, he explored me totally and made me forget *the bloody Algebra.*

Forty minutes later when I came back home that afternoon, my stomach ached. I regretted giving away something precious to the wrong man. Rather I was robbed of something I should have safeguarded.

I started with Rana's fresh command: "Now think of this bedroom. You are alone. Visit your present realities and nightmares, too. It's high time."

"OK!" I said. Still my mind drifted back as I realized my past was no less haunted than present with Mom's recent death and the bloody curtains.

And then I saw *her* again, drenched in blood, naked, loose hair all over her face, sagging breasts, and *she* was…holding…the *curtains*. One more thing: Kamini did not have eyes, just the pupils, peeping through the hair covered face.

"HELL, SHE IS HERE!" I shouted.

"COMMAND HER!" said Rana in a high-pitched voice this time.

"WHAT?"

"QUESTION HER. ASK HER WHAT SHE WANTS."

I didn't need to ask anything, though.

She spoke: *You ruined my family. I'll ruin yours. Fucking Bitch, you lured my husband and provoked him to kill me and my dear unborn child. Oh, dear, dear child!*

All heard it this time. The voice was loud and clear, but weirdly, it was emerging from no other source than *my own lips*. With a changed voice, I was suddenly a split personality.

"Now reveal your true identity," Rana said, "and command her to leave you."

"I have nothing to do with your fucking family," I yelled in *my* voice. "NOR DO I KNOW YOUR BLOODY HUSBAND."

You're Shalu. You instigated Rajesh to kill me, so that you could live in his arms for good, she thundered.

"GODDAMMIT! I'M NOT THE SHALU YOU'RE LOOKING FOR. I'M DIFFERENT. JUST A NAMESAKE. WE MOVED HERE ONLY THIS MONTH. I DON'T KNOW ANY RAJESH."

There was silence for a few moments. Kamini in me spoke again: *I don't believe you. And why should I?*

"You don't have an option, *Kamini*," I said, this time in a soft tone. "And now leave me alone. Don't chase me like HELL. Just … just go away from my life."

And, if I don't go? The ghost bargained.

I was not sure what to say this time.

Rana came to my rescue. "Threaten her to go away!"

"THEN I'LL BURN YOU TO ASHES. JUST GET LOST FROM MY LIFE."

Where should I go? This is my house. I shall live here alone, she insisted.

"This is none of my business. Go to Hell," I said. "This was once your house. Now it's mine. You'll have to go."

No response. Just creepy crying sobs from the ghost. She was melting.

"And why the bloody hell, do you keep holding these curtains? Don't you've any other business?" I almost scolded her, only realizing later how offensive were my words.

Moments passed in silence before her voice escaped my lips again: *You don't know what excruciating pain I felt when he fed me those bloody pills that rinsed my guts and oozed my blood from my nostrils and mouth. I held FOR SUPPORT these curtains and called him for help, but he was so cruel looking at me as if he was waiting for my death.*

"You go or I'll burn you, bloody fool!" I said in a cold voice, imitating Rana. Though I wasn't sure how I could burn her. But the trick worked.

Please don't burn me! Don't burn me! I'll go! I'll go! She sobbed.

"Then get lost from this house immediately—right now," I commanded.

With a change of tone, she began to laugh like they do in horror movies: *I'LL GO, BUT THE TUMOR IN YOU WILL KILL YOU.*

"TUMOR?" I was taken aback.

Yes, the malignant tumor. Do you think your chest's recent extra growth is without a reason? The truth is: the way your mother died, so will you.

I felt drained of all energy. My mouth was choked. My head felt heavy. The entire house seemed to spin around.

I opened my eyes. And then suddenly there was a terrible dust storm somewhere outside. The ghostly winds roared like hell. The bedroom door was flung open. The electricity supply was gone. The windowpanes shattered and the glass pieces scattered all around. The curtains fluttered like they did the first time I'd experienced the paranormal presence. The gusts of wind suddenly filled the bedroom and shook the entire interior. The curtains were pulled off forcibly from the pegs by the tornado and, before we could comprehend anything, they just moved mysteriously out into the alley through the shattered, battered French window.

After a couple of horrible minutes, the blasts of wind stopped as suddenly as they'd started. The tenseness of the eerie environment was shifted to a calm and composed condition.

"Kamini is gone ... for good, I'm sure," Rana said with finality looking at the bare window.

The only light available in the house now was from the blood moon out in the sky. Nidhi and Dushyant were still glued to the fallen shards of glass. I stood up from the floor-mat still looking at the missing curtains that hung at the window just moments before. Then, I left for the prayer room with my eyes burning like hell.

There, I found Mom's framed picture on the floor, its glass scattered all around me in innumerable pieces. I sank down where Mom's battered snapshot lay and heard my own sobs as I came to realize I was crying. The resurrected *ghost of Algebra* seemed less painful now. My breasts ached severely. The entire house was spinning around. The floor beneath my feet was collapsing, giving way to rubble and debris.

And then, there was some severe itching felt in my throat followed by a violent cough. Tiny droplets of spittle came off my mouth and scattered across my hands. Something dark came into view among the salivating particles. A close observation showed what it was: a blot of blood. Was it a death warrant?

The demarcation line between life, death and faith suddenly seemed more and more merged, intermixed. I felt more devastated than vulnerable. Life's as painful as death. Only I realized it tonight. At the sound of some footsteps I looked up. Rana, Dushyant and Nidhi stood surrounding me, probably trying to figure out the right words to pacify me. But no words could do so. Words have their own limitations.

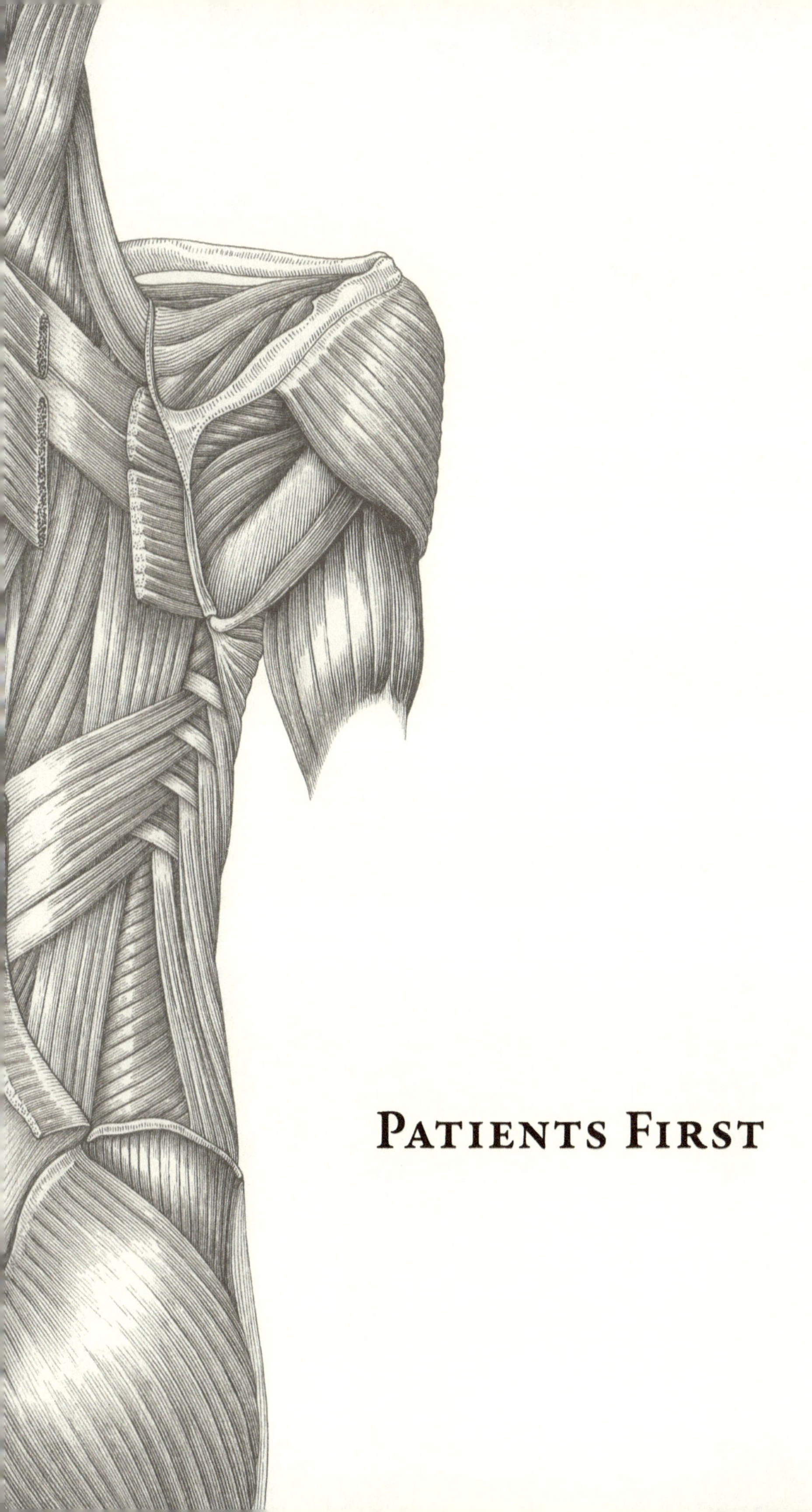

PATIENTS FIRST

Bells & Whistles

James Harper

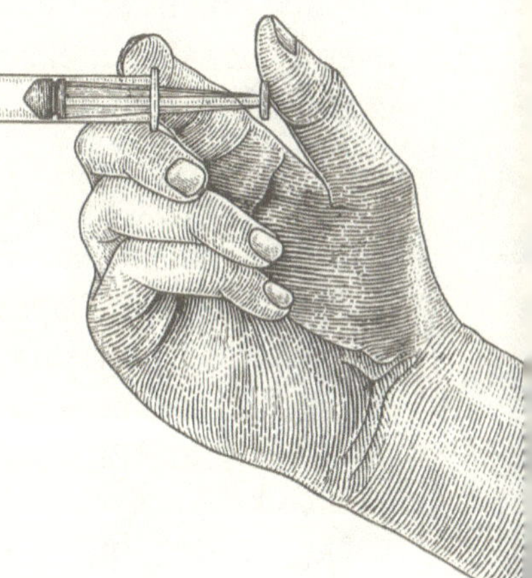

Daphne's struggle with weight loss had reached critical mass; she had lost control of the spiraling pounds that had packed onto her body. Glaring at her bathroom scale, she watched as it taunted back 366—a number she'd promised herself she'd never get to.

"Enough's enough," she said to the empty bathroom before stepping off the scale. Grabbing her bathrobe, she put it on as she descended the stairs.

"That's it," she said as she entered the kitchen. "I'm taking that weight loss system."

Her sisters looked at her as she stood, fists on hips, at the threshold. Spatula raised, Lara turned from the stove to smile. Daphne watched her move about the kitchen in her faded paisley housecoat, her white-calloused feet inserted in bed slippers that had long ago given their pink over to gray.

"What's different about this one?"

From the kitchen table, Moria said, "Yeah, what makes this 'weight loss system' any more special?" Using an air quotes gesture to piss Daphne off (she knew she hated that), she adjusted her thick red glasses on the bridge of her nose, smiling at her sister as though she knew something Daphne didn't. Daphne knew what she thought, but at this point, didn't care.

"I'm done," Daphne said, her palm to the floor as she moved it in a parallel cutting fashion. "Quite simply, I've had it. I'm 366 and I ain't getting any lower. I'm joining that Weight Aweigh system."

"The one from TV?" Nana said. She stood by the sink, running water over dishes. She looked ready to head out to work, dressed in her black vest uniform and white blouse.

"Right."

"Well, it's expensive," Moria said. "You seen how much it costs on the internet when we saw it on our shows the other night."

"I don't care," Daphne said. "I'm using Daddy's money to pay for it."

"Oookay," Lara said. "You know—"

"No, no and no. Don't you even try and talk me out of it."

Nana said, "But Daphn—"

"No."

Moira said, "But you always—"

"*No*," she said with force. The echo of her voice bounced off the kitchen walls. They all went wide-eyed. "I said no. And I'm done talking about it. I'm gonna do it." She turned to march toward the stairs.

As she pivoted, Lara said, "It's your money to do with as you please."

"Right."

"But you know you always drop out of these diets. What was the last one you did? The Hallmacher Diet?" Moria asked.

"Yeah," Nana said.

As Daphne climbed the steps, Lara walked into the dining room to call up after her. "You always give up!"

From the top landing, she said, her voice rising, "I'm not giving up this time! I mean it!" She went into her room to get dressed.

The television blathered as she entered, dropping her robe to the floor. The commercial that had prompted her decision played; the local station had it in heavy rotation.

"Dr. Gregoire's Weight Aweigh Plan is a new procedure developed especially by him to remove fat and excess weight at the source—in your body. The state-of-the-art formula will melt away body fat.

"No dieting.

"No pills.

"No plans.

"A simple series of injections will eliminate all the fat from your body in as little as three weeks."

She stood in front of her full-length mirror, attempting to study—in an objective way—her form, the way her body looked. She frowned as she saw the bulges and flab.

She was fat. No way to sugar coat it, ain't no lying here and now. Fat. She whispered to the mirror. "I'm doing this today."

As if to answer her declaration, the television said, "And if you act now, you'll receive twenty percent off your plan. But hurry, spaces are limited."

Daphne went to her laptop.

At Weight Aweigh, Daphne sat with Pamela Mitchell, Dr. Gregoire's counselor at the practice. "The course will be ongoing. Twice a week, we'll monitor your weight loss. If more injections are necessary, we will make that determination and give you the shots." Pamela said, nodding for emphasis.

"So you'll be injecting into my belly?" The potential pain worried her.

"The abdomen. Yes, and other areas. Directly into all the areas that need addressing."

"And this will get rid of all my fat?"

"If the procedure works the way it has so far, yes."

"And no dieting?"

"No. No dieting, no exercise, and no pills. Just like we say in the commercials. Dr. Gregoire's specialized method does it all with a few simple series of injections. It's all you need.   Ithasallthebellsandwhistles."

"Bells and whistles," Daphne whispered, smiling. "Where do I sign?"

The painful injections went on for an hour that seemed as if it took a day. The first course was a grueling affair where the doctor chose five different sites to apply the treatment. Her whole body felt raw and sore by the third shot.

"Just another," Dr. Gregoire said.

Why do doctors think that we don't know they're lying when they minimize like this, Daphne thought. She grimaced at the shot in her buttocks. The injection, slow and measured, lasted for the eternity of a minute. Or at least it felt like it did to Daphne. She closed her eyes, ground her molars, and breathed through her mouth while reminding herself that this would all be worth it in the end.

In the end, ha, she thought.

"Now, you're going to want to double your intake of water every day," the doctor said. "The most important aspect of the treatment is that you flush away the serum as it becomes inert."

"Inert?"

"Gets stale," his attending nurse Charlotte said. She smiled with warmth throughout Daphne's ordeal. "Goes dormant."

"Yes, the serum—which is actually a suspension—undergoes a deadening process once it's completed its task," Dr. Gregoire said. "The suspension performs its function then goes dormant, dead. So, it's very important to flush it out of your system as it does."

"Wh-what is the serum?"

"Oh, it's a new development I've helped pioneer," said Dr. Gregoire with obvious pride. Once the Trump administration came in, the regulations for the kind of treatment we knew would work but could not develop fell away. We had experiments that showed this would really help a lot of folks who had faced little or no success in the arena of weight loss. We knew it would work; we just needed a government that would be helpful, not restrictive."

"Well, hail to the chief," Daphne said. Then, "Ow" as another injection filled her abdominal cavity.

Returning home, she swung by Stella's for one of their famous chocolate mousse cakes. Daphne decided to get an extra-large as a treat for her sisters.

After dinner, she made a big show of bringing it into the dining room for dessert. The girls clapped and laughed upon seeing the masterpiece.

"Oh my, what's the occasion?" Nana said.

"Yes, what? We only get Stella's on birthdays and holidays," Moria said.

"Yes, yes. What's the occasion, dear?" Lara said.

Daphne displayed the cake on the table, then reached for the cutting knife. With a flourish, she sliced and served the rich cake.

"Well, I want to think of this as a new beginning. Today's just the start of a new path and a new way of life for me."

"Ain't this gonna ruin it?" Lara asked.

"Yeah, won't this blow your whole diet for the week?" Moria said.

Daphne laughed. "No, silly. And that's the point." She dug into her cake to eat with glee.

She saw results after only three days. Not believing her eyes, she thought she saw a difference that Friday.

"Nana, Nana, come up here," she called from her bedroom. Nana came to the threshold.

"What?"

"I think I see a difference."

Nana shrugged. "You think so?"

"Yes. Yes, I do." She turned to study her figure in the full-length length mirror.

"What does the bathroom scale say?" Nana said. She adopted a playfully ominous pitch to her voice. The bathroom scale stood as the implacable arbiter of all such judgments.

"Let's see." Daphne scampered to the bathroom, taking Nana's arm as she passed.

Standing in their cramped bathroom, Nana pressed her back against the turgid green wall as Daphne dragged the scale out of its corner with her big toe. The metal on its bottom scraped the linoleum as she pulled it closer.

With a quick look at Nana, she stepped up on it. The red LED flashed twice before revealing 361.

"I knew it."

"How much were you before?"

366."

"Wow. Nice."

"I know, right? I knew it!"

Daphne could not contain her eagerness to relay her progress to the clinic. he ran out the door to jump into her Civic. A smile broke over her face, one she could not stop, not that she even wanted to. She stepped on the accelerator, pulling out of her street then down the highway, speeding over to the offices on the appointed day for the first week's report.

Her cheeks ached as she continued to grin, thinking she must look like a lunatic. She didn't care; she felt like one. As she rushed through the doors, she almost ran into Charlotte.

"Oh, excuse me."

"Why, hello Daphne. What's the rush?"

"I can't wait to show you what I've lost."

A smile blossomed on Charlotte's face. "Well then, we should go straight to it." She led Daphne to the weighing room. The scale showed that she had lost ten pounds.

"Ten pounds in the first week," Charlotte said. "Your progress is quite remarkable."

"Really?"

"Oh, yes. Would you like it if we shot a video?"

"Are you kidding me?" Daphne giggled. "Of course."

Over the course of the next several months, as she lost a record amount of weight, the clinic shot video of her progress and posted it on the Weight Aweigh website. Daphne became a hometown internet sensation, recognized wherever she went. She could not shop for groceries without drawing a cluster.

During the Week 14 weigh in, Charlotte recorded her numbers then pressed her clipboard against her chest. "I have a proposition for you, Daphne."

"Okay."

"How would you like to work here?"

"Are you kidding me?" Daphne clasped her hands as if in prayer.

"Not in the least. You've shown such great progress; we think you'll make a fine asset to our organization."

"When can I start?"

The next Monday, she reported for duty at the Weight Aweigh clinic, spending the morning in orientation before her desk assignment where Charlotte showed her the weight loss process. Charlotte scooted her chair beside Daphne, leaning close to point to her monitor. Daphne winced, inhaling her perfume.

"The secret to Dr. Gregoire's process is that he's developed a serum that's extracted from this." She stroked some keys to bring up the image. A wasp appeared.

"A wasp?"

"Not just any wasp. The tarantula hawk."

"Tarantula hawk?"

"Yes, Dr. Gregoire has synthesized the venom of his mutated tarantula hawk to bring the results you, and many others, have experienced."

"That's amazing."

"Yes," the pride in Charlotte's voice could not be mistaken.

"Let me show you." She stood to walk toward the back rooms of the clinic, leading Daphne. Soon, they stood before a vaulted steel door.

"In here, we keep the wasps for harvesting." She opened the chamber. Inside, Daphne saw a large room lined with Plexiglass floor-to-ceiling cages. She thought it must hold hundreds of cages.

"In each of these, a female tarantula hawk lives its life. The doctor has worked out a way to raise a specific species of the wasp that he has specially mutated. Its genetic structure now fosters the weight loss you've seen after the injections. The extract of the venom from a healthy wasp promotes rapid success."

"Wow," Daphne said. "Can I see one?"

"I'd love to show you," Charlotte said, shaking her head. "But they're very dangerous."

"Dangerous? Really?"

"Yes, believe me. I've been accidentally stung by one of these bastards. The pain shot through my arm and paralyzed me. It felt like an electric charge had been sent through my body. All I wanted to do was lay down and die. The pain persisted for the whole day."

"Oh my god, that's horrible. I'm so sorry for you."

"I wanted to die. I really wanted to die." She took a step closer, looking Daphne in the eyes. "I threw up for two days."

Turning to face Daphne, Charlotte said, "So what's your background?"

"I used to manage a security firm. We'd do the coding and installs for labs just like this one."

"Oh, great. Management skills are exactly what we're looking for."

"Well, as you know, when you manage, you end up learning how to do everything. And that's how it was at my old job."

"I think you're going to be great here."

More video shoots started soon after, almost twice a week. With an eye toward marketing, Dr. Gregoire wanted Daphne shot as much as possible around town, at monuments and local sights. One day, she modeled at a shoot at a park close to the clinic office where a small crowd gathered. Daphne smiled at her new notoriety.

After the shoot, a woman approached her. She wore a three-piece business skirt suit, navy with black pinstripes.

"You're Daphne from Weight Aweigh, aren't you?"

Daphne's heart jumped a beat, the first time she had been recognized as a celebrity. She beamed back at the woman.

"Yes. Yes, I am."

"I need to talk with you." Her expression showed concern.

"Well, sure."

The woman motioned for them to sit on a nearby bench. As the film crew packed up their gear, the two women sat facing one another.

"I'm Sandy Burns. I work in a lab near yours for the Smithsonian. We do entomology research."

"Ento—"

"Bugs. We study insects."

"Oh, that's nice. Our clinic probably used some of your research for our treatment."

"Well, if they did, they didn't use all of it. Or, at least, they didn't use the important part."

"Wha—what do you mean?" Daphne held her hand to her mouth.

"Let me ask you. We've learned that Gregoire uses tarantula hawks in his treatment."

"Right. Yes, he—we use the venom from the wasp in a formula for injection."

"Are you *sure* it's the venom?" Sandy asked with authority.

"Why, yes. I think so. What else could it be?"

"I need you to come with me." She stood.

Daphne looked around her. The film crew had vanished. "Where are we going?"

"My lab. Don't worry, it's not far."

Daphne marveled that the lab stood within a half-mile of her own office. Sandy led her inside, taking her straight to a vault room not unlike the one at Weight Aweigh.

"Here we keep our tarantula hawks for research and analysis. How much do you know about the wasp?"

"I know that its sting is like the second most painful in the world."

"That's true. But you should also know—or learn —about how it breeds."

"Breeds?"

"Yes, breeds. We've been monitoring Gregoire's methods for some time now. He's used the recent drop in regulations brought on by the new administration to roll out his method." She shook her head, eyes closed. "He'd never get away with this otherwise."

She led her to a series of Plexiglass cages in the vault room. Inside each, Daphne saw a large tarantula. As she looked closer, she saw a wasp in each cage too.

At the first cage, Sandy said, "We've just introduced a wasp into this cage." She touched Daphne's arm. "Watch."

The wasp dove straight for the spider. The spider, sensing a mortal enemy, attacked the insect, batting the wasp with its legs. The wasp hovered then swooped toward the tarantula. Moving to avoid the onslaught of legs, the insect found its moment, descending atop the arachnid. It stung the spider.

Daphne took a breath as the tarantula became paralyzed.

"The wasp will now drag the spider back to its lair." Sandy moved to the next cage. "This is what happens next."

As Daphne watched, the second wasp inserted its stinger into the lower abdomen of the spider. "It's laying its eggs," Sandy said.

"So?" Daphne looked at Sandy. "I mean, gross. But so?"

Sandy motioned for her to come over to the third cage. Within, she saw another tarantula, still alive but motionless and shriveled. Sandy said, "The larvae eat the spider, consuming all of its internal organs."

Charlotte turned from the cage to catch Daphne's appalled stare. "They save the vital organs for last," Charlotte said. Daphne felt her jaw drop to her throat.

They moved to the final cage. "Until—" She presented the last sequence. Inside, the larvae, having eaten the spider into a shell of itself, burst through the skin to pupate.

Early the next morning, before going to work, Daphne stood in her bedroom studying her new figure in the full-length mirror. Somehow, her skin did not seem right.

"Nana, come up here please," she called.

Her sister stood in the doorway, arms folded. She gave a soft whistle.

"Are you sure you haven't lost too much weight?" Nana's voice dropped a register.

"Ya think?"

"Definitely." Nana took a step inside. "Look. Your skin is just hanging on your body. It's gotten to the point where it's draping on you in folds."

Daphne saw it too. The outer surface of her form now looked like a bed with sheets piled upon the mattress top.

"It doesn't look healthy," Nana said in a low tone.

"I'm going to find out about that right now," Daphne said with determination. Descending the stairs, she left to head to Weight Aweigh.

Rushing to the office, she drove with a vengeance. While the commute took a mere fifteen minutes, she meant to make it in ten.

She drummed her fingers on the steering wheel at a stop light. "Come on."

At that moment, pain erupted from her belly. She gasped as she reached for her stomach. To her surprise, she felt wetness.

Am I bleeding? she thought.

She lifted her fingers to see blood on them. Blood and more: the larvae she had seen yesterday—a dozen squirming maggots— twisted in her upheld fingers. She pulled the car over to vomit her breakfast into the gutter. She drove to her clinic in seconds, getting to the office before anyone had arrived.

She took the time before the office opened to prepare the lab. Knowing Gregoire arrived before anyone else, she called him on his cell.

"Yes, Daphne?" he answered.

"Doctor, I think there's a problem with the wasps. Can you meet me now in the vault room?"

Gregoire sighed. "Can't Charlotte handle this?"

"No, sir. I think this deserves your attention."

"All right."

When Dr. Gregoire arrived, she met him with a grim smile. She handed him a file then said, "Doctor, I think you should take a look at a wasp cage that's malfunctioning."

A look of alarm crossed his face. "Yes, at once."

At the vault room, Daphne opened the security door to allow him to enter. Once inside, she sealed the vault behind him. From the Plexiglass observation window, she watched. She had set all the wasps free. Now, they attacked Gregoire.

Daphne watched Gregoire scream without sound at his fate. The wasps swarmed him, stinging him again and again. Their anger unparalleled, they came at him in repeated attacks, stabbing his skin over and over, each sting the equivalent of a 220-volt electric line.

Daphne watched him cry in pain and rage as the wasps crawled over his body. His face was a swollen ruin from the incessant stings, his red skin bloated and gushing blood from the poison. He slowed in his swatting of the insects, his energy draining as the venom took hold.

A great, sharp pain rocketed through her abdomen. Daphne fell to her knees as the larvae within her finished their work. She sensed the worms, the moving larvae, as they squirmed and crawled within her, writhing and eating her internal organs. They had already evacuated her internal muscle tissue and most of what was left of her digestive system, now they began to devour her liver and lungs in earnest.

Then Daphne heard it. Her eyebrows knotted as she listened, making an effort to hear what she thought could not be possible. Then she confirmed it: she could hear Gregoire's screams despite the soundproofing, his pain so great that his cries broke through the baffling.

He collapsed to the floor, no longer capable of swatting or brushing the insects; he just dropped, his arms dangling at his sides. The wasps continued their assault, diving at him again and again to pump his body with their venom. She watched as he died writing on the floor of the lab.

Pain bolted through her gut. She realized that the advanced progress the larvae had made was due to their proliferation, a fact that would not have been possible were it not for Gregoire's mutations. Her skin and muscles rippled beneath her touch. She could feel them crawling inside her, carving her from within. The larvae, perhaps sensing their imminent release from the confinement of Daphne's body, had sped the progression of their eating to a prodigious degree, chewing away at her pulmonary tissue before proceeding to the heart.

The pain was beyond endurance as the maggot-like creatures bore through her abdomen and thorax at a rate that left her without strength. The agony of the destruction of her internal organs was more than she could bear. She collapsed on the floor of the lab, sobbing and screaming at the anguish the nascent insect life brought upon her.

The larvae burst through her skin, blowing a hole in her navel the size of a grapefruit. They streamed out, spreading across her skin.

Another eruption broke through her chest, blood and pus matter clouding her vision as the larvae punched out of her ribcage cavity. They began consuming her from the outside as well as the inside.

In a gushing flood, the larvae spilled out of her, leaving a cascade of blood, pus, and insect matter to stream from within her. Unable to even think now, she watched as the larvae ate her whole.

Staring at Gregoire's body twitching on the concrete floor, she realized her choice: a quick death full of pain or a slow one in agony. No choice at all, really.

She opened the door to the vault room to allow the wasps to escape, to roam about the larger complex with freedom. They swarmed around her to sting her as well. Again and again they stung, the pain causing her vision to blur then blacken.

The pain felt as though she had clutched an electrical line allowing the current to run through her, a hundred thousand pains cataloged into an overwhelming agony that made her cry then scream. It electrified her skin as if ten thousand knives stabbed her all at once, inflicting the sensation throughout her form, her tissue alive with fire. Then it moved to her brain.

Those thousand pains were multiplied a thousandfold again. She died as the pain overcame her, the darkness spreading through her senses. The final convulsions wracked her now-decrepit body, collapsing under the wasps' onslaught.

Good Medicine

Madison Estes

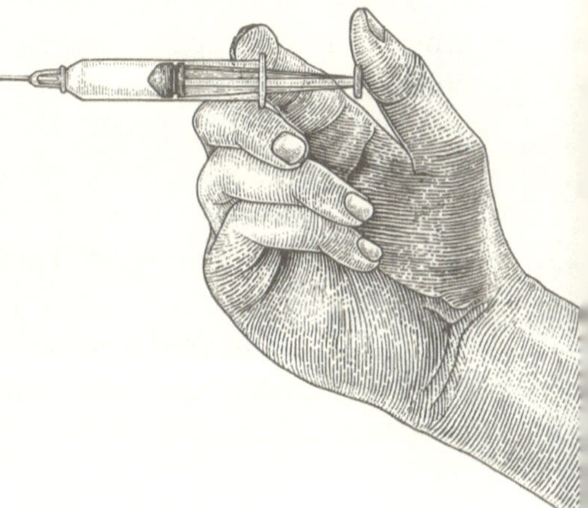

She made an uncertain incision into the dying woman's abdomen. She heard the voice of her supervisor guiding her on her cell phone as she worked up the nerve to plunge the scalpel in deeper despite the screams of her patient. She had performed the procedure before, but never without anesthesia. She did what she had to though. The crying child in her arms was proof of her determination. Her supervisor checked in with her.

"This is a miracle," Dr. Nashimi said as he examined the baby. "No signs of CR-26 even though both parents were infected. Take him to neonatal care." He added, in a softer voice, "I know that was rough, but you did well, Sarah. Good medicine is about perseverance. That's why this baby is alive."

Dr. Nashimi's praise was as rare as it was brief, so she accepted the compliment with a smile even though she could still hear the mother's screams in her head.

Two days later, while standing on the roof of the hospital waiting for a helicopter he told her, "A doctor's work is never done. The CDC needs me to care for patients in their temporary quarantine. You're in charge during my absence."

"In charge of what?" she asked, the wind blowing her bangs in front of her eyes.

"The hospital! Don't let those soldiers boss you around. And don't forget the code word. I'll contact you as soon as I can. And check on Mr. Holland."

She went to his room and discovered Mr. Holland had died in the ten-minute time span between leaving and returning. She sighed as she checked him for a pulse.

"Time of death is 10:48." She pulled the white sheet over his head and nodded to the soldier in the gas mask who had been waiting off to the side to retrieve the body. He wrapped the patient in a plastic tarp and loaded him onto the gurney. Sweat trickled down his red face and he coughed.

"You might want to look at the patient in room 210," he rasped.

"Are you sure you don't want me to have a look at you?" She put a hand on his shoulder, and he shrugged her off. He readjusted his protective gear, trying to make what was heavy and burdensome a little more comfortable.

"I'm fine. It's just this gas mask and suit. It's so damn HOT." He kept trying to shift his mask around, but no matter how he adjusted it, it continued to suffocatingly press up against him.

"Why don't you rest for a while? Go get some water. You need to stay hydrated."

"You just worry about yourself and these patients."

"I'm fine. I had the vaccine when it first came out."

"So did I," he said. He opened his mouth again but whatever he was about to say was lost to another fit of coughing. Instead, he motioned for her to follow him with a hand wave.

The patient in 210 was shriveled up in a ball, barely conscious.

"Mrs. Bosman? How are you feeling? Can you hear me?"

"Great. Another lost cause," the soldier said. He walked out of the room. Sarah sighed. After this patient inevitably died, it would just be her, Sergeant Barcroft, and Daniel, the baby she had cut out of a dying woman two days ago. The ER had overflowed with people merely four days before. The army evacuated several people to the CDC camps for quarantine and treatment. There had been only two doctors at the hospital, but there wasn't much more they could do that the nurses couldn't.

Most treatment revolved around providing comfort measures. They were waiting for more instructions from the CDC.

When Mrs. Bosman finally succumbed to death's beckon, they went to the neonatal unit to monitor Daniel who was resting fitfully in an incubator. "You're wasting your time," Sergeant Barcroft said. "It's infected."

"'It' is a boy. His name is Daniel."

"Well, Daniel is going to die. Newborns have weak immune systems."

"I know. You do remember I'm a doctor, right?" Sarah snapped.

"Don't get snarky with me! I'll leave you here to deal with the rest of this mess on your own." He pointed toward Daniel and the incubator.

"Why don't you leave then?" She put her hands on her hips and glared at him. He coughed especially hard as if his body wished to demonstrate why he was unfit for travel. "Never mind. You're too sick to leave."

"Watch me. You can dispose of Daniel yourself, can't you? It's easy. Just wrap him in plastic, put him with the others, and set it on fire." He gestured toward the window where piles of burned bodies were stacked together.

"I am aware of the disposal methods. If it becomes necessary, I can handle it."

"When." He loosened the black strap of his gas mask and wiped a line of sweat off his forehead with his hairy arm. "When it becomes necessary."

Sarah didn't reply. She watched Daniel through the glass. She could hear Sergeant Barcroft gathering his supplies, but she didn't look up to say goodbye. He headed toward the door. Part of her hoped he would leave, and she'd never have to see him again.

"I'll contact you if I reach the camp. I'll tell you what the conditions are like, and if you should even bother coming."

"When you reach the camp, not if, Sergeant."

"Let's not pretend. We both know I'm a dead man walking. Only question is how long I've got left."

"Miracles can happen." She smiled as she looked at the baby she never thought would live.

"Yeah, sure. Take care, Dr. Enoch."

"You too."

The cafeteria food expired long ago, so she survived mostly on junk food and a hidden stash of protein bars in one of the break rooms. When she got to the point where she had to break into the vending machines, she discovered that smashing the glass with a waiting room chair had been fun. It made her feel wild and rebellious, not at all like a prisoner in an almost empty hospital, cut off from all communication with the outside world.

She shook some of the remaining fragments of glass off the Lays potato chips. As she ate the pathetic meal, she told Daniel about her days as a sleep-deprived medical resident. She told him how brave his mother had been when she had to perform the emergency C-section, even though his mother was dying of whatever fucked-up plague the CDC wasn't curing. She told him how special it felt that he was still there with her; that his warm, breathing little body gave her hope. She told him how scared she was of the supply room and how she would go out of her way to avoid walking by it. She talked to Daniel more than she had ever talked to most people. He was a good listener.

Sarah fell asleep next to the bassinet, her head cradled in the crook of her arm. A single bright light irritated her enough to wake her. The sun peeked through the slot in the blinds where the cord ran through. Startled, she realized it was silent. None of the monitors showed any life.

"No!" Looking into his incubator, she saw that his tiny face had turned blue like all the other babies in the neonatal unit. When she took him out, he felt cold. "No, no, no!" She fell to the ground and held him tighter. She coddled him, trying to warm him up. She placed him on the table and performed CPR on what she knew was just a body.

She kept up her futile actions until she couldn't physically go on. She collapsed onto the floor screaming. She felt equal parts despair and frustration. After everything she'd done to save him, she so desperately wanted him to live. She almost resented him for dying when she'd worked so hard to keep him alive. How dare he leave her all alone when she gave up everything for him. She might as well have left with Sergeant Barcroft for all the good she'd done.

After her tears stopped and the snot quit bubbling out of her nose, Sarah went to the supply room and stared at the leg sticking out from behind the shelves. Only medical personnel had access to this room. That part of the situation made sense because there had been many nurses and nursing assistants inside the building up until the end. What didn't make sense was the fact that the scrubs were green. Only doctors and surgeons wore green. As far as Sarah knew, all the doctors had left early, either to help with patients elsewhere at the CDC camps or to be with their families. Only she and Dr. Nashimi stayed until the brief military occupation, and only she remained after he'd left. Dr. Nashimi got on the helicopter and was currently helping the CDC. He was going to come back after things settled down, or else he would send someone for her. He was in Atlanta, so he couldn't be in the Constance Memorial Hospital supply room on the fifth floor. He certainly could not be the dead body that was lying on the ground. He was fine when she watched him board the helicopter. At least well enough to travel.

Except, now that she thought about it, she actually had not watched him get on the helicopter. She still had a dozen patients back then. (*That reminds me, I need to check on Mr. Tumbleson, he wasn't looking so good that last time I went in, all blue in the face, and when was the last time I saw him breathing?*) She had been in a hurry to return to her charges, so she turned around and ran back inside after they'd said good-bye. He was still standing on the rooftop when she last saw him. The rooftop was not the helicopter. Then again, the rooftop was not the supply room either. What business would he have had in there?

Sarah knew that Dr. Nashimi was in Atlanta, busy helping the CDC administer life-saving vaccines and provide aid to those already infected. He was busy and should not be disturbed. She wished he'd send someone for her though, or just call and let her know how he was doing. *But he's very busy*, she reminded herself. *He is doing important work. I should try working. He'd be disappointed if he knew I was idle during a crisis. He would criticize my lack of initiative again.* There wasn't a single other living soul in the hospital. It didn't matter though. Good medicine is about perseverance. A doctor's work is never truly done.

Their code word was "owl" because that was the Rice University mascot, and they had both attended there. Dr. Nashimi would use it if he really wanted her to come. If she didn't hear that word, she needed to stay where she was, either for her own safety or other reasons.

She really wished Dr. Nashimi would call her, so she could stop thinking about that damn leg with the green scrubs—that impossible leg—and so that she could focus on her work. She was getting sloppy. Just because the patients were already dead, it was still no excuse for careless work. She placed the stethoscope on Mrs. Bosman's chest and could not detect a heartbeat. Sarah expected that. She patted the patient's back with a gloved hand. "I recommend bedrest."

"For how long?" Mrs. Bosman's corpse asked her, with those hollowed-out cheeks and stiff hands bent in unnatural angles from rigor mortis.

"A really, really long time. Maybe, forever?" Sarah laughed at that, because it was truly funny, this whole business of treating patients who were already dead. It was a relief. No more worrying about pesky surgical complications, no need for monitoring vital signs, and best of all, no listening to patients complain about their aches and pains. Why hadn't she treated dead patients before the apocalypse?

"Maybe their insurance didn't cover it," she said, chuckling. "Well, Mrs. Bosman, you might be dead, but at least we finally stopped that awful cough once and for all. Wasn't that what you were most worried about? Well, you don't have to worry anymore." She laughed again, in a fit of hysteria. Her hand clutched her side as she doubled over, laughing. Wasn't laughter truly the best medicine, even in dire circumstances? It was always best to keep a sense of humor about things. It created resilience.

She laughed until she cried.

That night, Sarah dreamed of the leg with the green scrubs. In her dream, she summoned the courage to look further, but it was just a leg: a bloody appendage with no body attached. When Sarah woke up, she almost felt relieved. She wanted to go to the room immediately and see if her dream had been prophetic, but her body felt too heavy and her head too light. It was probably a side effect from the junk food diet. She stayed in bed and just stared out the window, looking for owls. Instead of flying vermin, she heard someone walking down the hall outside her room.

"Sarah?" he said.

"Sergeant Barcroft, is that you?" She squinted. "Wow. You look good." She looked him up and down, appraising him and his healthy appearance.

"I wish I could say the same. What happened to you?" He looked genuinely concerned, and he extended a hand toward her shoulder. She jumped before he made contact, so he retracted his hand.

"It's a long story," she said.

"Well, I've got time."

"Okay, but first I have to go check on a patient of mine. Please wait." Sarah went to the storeroom and filled a hypodermic needle with tranquiliser. She walked back to the military man and, before he could react, plunged the needle into his shoulder. She'd practiced medicine enough to know it wouldn't take effect immediately like on TV so she ran. Sarah avoided him for the three minutes it took for the drug to work on his system. When he went limp, she dragged him into the psych ward where she strapped him to a bed for psychotic patients.

Sarah waited. When his eyes opened and registered the world around him, she said. "Well, Sergeant, tonight we're having protein bars and Doritos for dinner. For dessert, we have a wide variety of candies. Unfortunately, no Snickers or Milky Ways though. I ran out of those a few days ago." She watched as he struggled briefly with his straps.

"I have rations in my vehicle. Canned goods, MREs. Why don't you let me go get them?" he offered.

"Because you're my patient, silly. The first living patient I've had in a long time. I can't risk you going out and getting sick. Do you know how fragile living patients are? They are a lot more difficult than my other patients, that's for sure."

"I'm your first ... so you have dead patients?"

"Yes." She smiled.

"And you are treating them?"

"Yes." Her smile grew bigger.

"Why? Do you think if you take good care of them that they will come back to life? Because I'm pretty sure that's how you get zombies."

"Don't be ridiculous. They can't come back to life. That's what makes it so appealing. It can't get worse because they are already dead. It makes the job so much easier." She laughed a little in relief.

"Do you understand how insane you sound right now?"

"Oh yes, I know. I didn't understand how I could do it either until I didn't have any choices left and I had to find some way to continue my practice without living patients."

"You could have just left the hospital, got in a car, and drove until you found someone who needed help. You could just help me."

She looked at him as though he'd suggested she jump off the roof of the building to see if she could fly. "I am waiting on the CDC. They are supposed to send me instructions. I was given full responsibility for this hospital. I can't just leave."

"There is no CDC." Barcroft tried to grasp the buckles on his straps. His reach was too short.

"What?" Her eyes widened.

"There is no CDC anymore. Some of the people who worked there are still alive, but not many. The vaccine didn't work as well as they thought it did."

"Well, we're both alive."

"We're miracles."

She rolled her eyes, crossing her arms across her chest. "You scoffed the last time I mentioned the idea of a miracle."

"Well, maybe I've come around since then. I'm still here, aren't I?" he said with a grin. She wasn't smiling, and he had enough sense to guess why.

"How's Daniel?"

"He's about as good as you predicted he would be." Sarah looked out the window.

"I'm sorry."

She could sense his sincerity. She shrugged. "A real miracle would have been if Daniel lived. We're just statistical anomalies. Excuse me; I have to go check on my other patients now."

"Oh God," he muttered.

When she came back an hour later, she brought snacks and a water bottle. Her bun had collapsed into a messy half up-do with hair bursting out everywhere. Her eyes possessed a faraway look, and her body odor was so strong his eyes watered.

"How were your other patients? Still dead?"

"Yes," she said flatly.

"I'm sorry, but I've got to ask. Is what happened to Daniel ... is that why you decided to start . . . giving medical care to the nonliving?"

"It might have had something to do with it." She was looking at something shiny in her hands and playing with it absentmindedly. A few beads of sweat trickled down the side of the sergeant's forehead.

"Well, why are you doing this? You're wasting your talent, wasting both of our time—just let me go." His voice cracked a little, and he craned his head upward, trying to see what Sarah was holding.

"You have some lacerations on your head. I'm going to apply some ointment and treat your wounds." She showed him what was in her hands: a pair of scissors, a tube of antibiotic cream, and bandages. He sighed in relief.

"Well, thank you. I would appreciate that."

She set the supplies on the table closest to him and looked at the patient board on the wall. "Who is going to assist me later today? Perhaps Squires. Oh, wait. He's gone ... maybe Johnson." She glanced over the soldier at Johnson's dead body sitting out in the hall. His mouth hung open. Flies were congregating around his face.

"Bynes?" She tilted her head thoughtfully.

"I saw Bynes upstairs earlier," he said. "I don't think she'll be assisting in surgery anytime soon." Sarah didn't catch his sarcasm, so he added, "Or ever."

"She's dead too?"

"She's very dead. They're all dead, Sarah. And you don't have any patients. Not any real ones." She looked around as if it had never come to her attention before that they were alone. Her eyebrows scrunched together in confusion.

"They're all gone," she said at last. Her wistful tone quieted them both for a moment.

"We need to leave."

"Where?"

"The radio said Huntsville is a safe zone. There are people gathering there."

She didn't look interested. Her hand grazed one of the tables.

"They might need you," he said.

"No one needs me. I couldn't save any of them. They all died."

"That wasn't your fault."

"All of them died, even the babies." She shrugged. "None of it mattered. They say touch is the most powerful form of healing ... but it didn't matter."

"It mattered to them." His kind tone of voice brought her comfort like a reassuring hand on her shoulder. Her face took on a distant, lost expression. Her mouth softened, and her eyebrows furrowed as she thought back on the days after the outbreak.

"Some of those babies were never held before I held them," she said. "Some of them weren't named. Weren't loved. Like Daniel. I couldn't let him die like that."

"You did the right thing. I was wrong. I should have never pressured you to leave. But what you're doing now is wrong. There are people you can be helping. People who are sick from other things, people who get hurt from accidents. We don't have a lot of medical help these days."

She took a deep breath and said in a tiny, scared voice, "But they could die."

"I think their chances of living will improve if you're there."

"But I'm not ready to try again." She wrapped her arms around herself protectively. She stood several feet away from her patient and avoided eye contact, as though she were afraid of him.

"You wait until you're ready to do something important, and you'll die never being ready. Some things you can't be ready for until they are happening. You just have to prepare as much as you can. You can become prepared; you can't always become ready. But I'll be with you. I'll help you. We can do this."

His earnest tone promised her an optimistic future as his eyes locked with hers. She maintained a neutral expression until she finally looked away from him and sighed. "I can't leave. What if Dr. Nashimi comes back and I'm not here? I'll be in so much trouble."

"OH, WAKE UP!" he yelled, spit flying from his mouth, limbs pulling against the restraints. "THE WORLD IS IN TROUBLE. FUCK DR. NASHIMI. FUCK HIM. HE'S DEAD!"

Her eyes went wide and her posture rigid. Before Sergeant Barcroft could even regret losing his temper, Sarah left the room and took off running down the hall, away from him. She exited in such haste that she did not register his groaning or cursing echoing in the hall, nor did she notice that she had abandoned the scissors on the table next to the ointment and bandages—just within his reach.

She had to know. Hearing another person say out loud what her greatest fear had been all along made her fingers tremble, made her trip and stumble into a crash cart on her way to the fifth floor. She could no longer tell herself she was waiting for what she suspected would never come. She had to know right away.

She opened the door and hesitated. The whole hospital reeked of vomit and death, but in this small, enclosed room, the stench was extra potent. She covered her nose with her hand and approached the body as though it were a wild animal she was trying not to startle. When she saw Dr. Nashimi's face, she wasn't really surprised. Despite her ever-present suspicion that he was dead—had been dead all along—she still fell over and sobbed. She bumped into a shelf and knocked over medical supplies. An IV bag burst open, spilling all over the floor. The IV fluid sprayed on Dr. Nashimi, mingling with some of the corpse's crusted blood. A faint red streak spread, reaching for her. It saturated her scrubs and lab coat. As soon as she inhaled, she choked on the decaying scent. She coughed, but it still lingered, crawling into her throat, and gagging her. She scuttled, trying to get away from the truth, and all she saw was him getting on the helicopter, even though she knew she never really saw that. The fake memory replayed itself over and over again in her head, trying to make itself real.

"You aren't coming for me. You never were." She had no idea how long she stayed in her stupor, but when she came out, she decided that she needed to let Sergeant Barcroft go. Maybe she would even go with him. This place wasn't good for her. This whole place was a lie, a series of false hopes. A moment of repulsive clarity came when she thought about the dead patients she had been "treating," and she wanted to die too. What a sick, sick little girl she had been. Maybe Sergeant Barcroft was the message Dr. Nashimi was trying to send. Maybe he was her owl. She had just begun to wrap her head around this when she was tackled from behind.

"Nooo! Nooo!"

"Hang on, I'm not trying to hurt you! I just need you to come with me—oh, God." He saw the body on the floor, and the distraction was enough for her to slip out of his grip.

"Wait a second!" He chased after her. She ran without thought, operating on adrenaline and fear. She reached the staircase and stopped, leaning against the wall, leaving a trail of intravenous fluid and some of the good doctor's blood behind her. She anticipated his fall before he even got to the stairs. The image of a bright yellow sign flashed in her mind—the words **CAUTION: SLIPPERY WHEN WET** appearing in bold block letters—and then he tumbled down the staircase before she could open her mouth to warn him.

Looking back at it now, she honestly thinks that falling down the stairs might not have killed him if he hadn't hit his head on the handrail, yet his sudden demise did not come as a complete shock. Living patients are so fragile, after all.

A few hours later, after she has rested, she drags his body downstairs and puts him in one of the patient rooms. She sighs with sadness and regret. She was starting to like him. He could have taken her to the safe zone. She could have helped living patients there. But it is what it is. She puts a medical wristband on him and begins to incorporate him into her daily schedule. She's going to clean that head wound on him that she never got around to earlier, plus all the new ones. It will take a long time, but that's okay. Good medicine is about perseverance. A doctor's work is never done.

Baby Shop

Paul Wilson

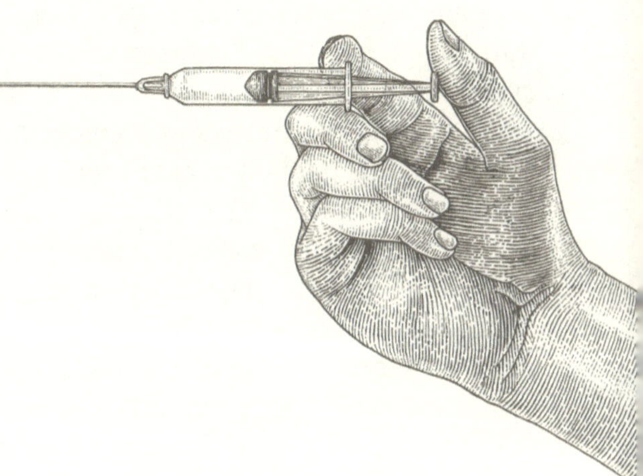

"I'm a little scared," Helen said, clutching her husband's shoulder. He looked up from the medical form's monotonous lines of type and noticed her nails. Helen had taken to gnawing her fingers since finding out she was pregnant, and while John could have used this opportunity to call her on it, he didn't. He felt the same unease. He took her hand and kissed it.

"I'm here."

Something was different about this doctor's office. What exactly he couldn't pinpoint, but they had been assured The Baby Shop could take the greatest care of Helen's needs. For his baby's sake, John ignored his worry and focused on the beauty he found in his wife, giving her his best smile of reassurance.

Helen's hair was a light shade of brown, almost blonde, and as thin as corn silk. It was pulled back today, the humidity being too much of a bother to wear it down. Her eyes were fawn-colored and a little dewy, set above a mousy nose. John loved her parts, even her bony shoulders and bee-sting breasts. Her voice was her best trait. It was velvety—even if she did use it to talk on the phone too much. Before he bent to the medical forms again, he looked at Helen's face. She wore what his mother would have called *God's spit*, but what Helen's gynecologist said was a CHLOASMA, a word too damn chewy for John to get out of his mouth. It was the mask of pregnancy, or more simply, brown patches on her face. John liked that phrasing better. Call it what it was instead of some fancy title.

John bent to fill in his height, weight, and other statistics he didn't think was any of their business here at The Baby Shop. Wouldn't they be examining Helen? She was the pregnant one.

Doctor Bigley, Helen's gynecologist, said she would receive the most advanced care here—the best there was—and for once in his life, John could afford the best. He wanted to take care of his son from the very beginning, even if it meant coming to a strange place. And unless it was his corn field, his workshop, or trading on the dusty town roads, it was a strange place for John. He yanked on the choking collar of his best shirt, flipped the first form over to its back side, and plodded forward.

He hated filling out forms, but at least he understood *how* to fill them out: pen to paper. He didn't have to sit behind one of those aggravating computers like over at Doctor Bigley's office: name, plus a dot-com-something, then a mouse click to save, *but oh, you didn't end with a period or a semicolon or some other frigging thing so you have to do it all again Mr. Nesbitt.* Just give him a pencil, for crying out loud. In the few times John was forced into using computers, they never did what he wanted. Unless it was tilling soil or finishing furniture, he didn't feel in control. You never got dirt under your fingernails from a keyboard, but most people didn't understand that.

"Did I tell you that Shorty over at the Feed Store is gonna start using computers next month?" John asked.

Helen looked over with a grin and shook her head.

"He's had that clunker of a cash register since he opened that store. Every time you buy something, you're supposed to hear a solid *thunk* and then a *ding*. Not the damn clacking of a printer."

"Computers are everywhere," Helen soothed. "They're taking over. Shorty's just trying to keep up."

John snorted. "He said he was gonna *assign* all us regular customers a number to help with order processing. I'm not a number; I'm a man who helped him paint that store, who pulled his truck out of the mud during the floods two years ago."

John bent to his forms again, muttering about the world. He tried to put the aggravation out of his mind. His concentration belonged here. How long had he and Helen been trying to have a baby? John measured it by the harvest. The corn grew and multiplied in six months, but Helen took six years. Now they were seeing a baby specialist. The Baby Shop, indeed. And what a frigged-up name that was! A shop was where you worked on cars. His shop was where he stripped, finished, and hammered furniture for his neighbors. It wasn't right to associate that word with the soft flesh of babies.

"Shit," John muttered. "What's my blood-type, Babe?"

Helen told him. He asked why in the hell they needed that. She listened with a smile, noticing his hands. They wore calluses. The backs carried deep pink scars from days gone by, as well as fresher cuts scabbed over. John's knuckles were permanently stained from the oils and paints of his shop. But they were good hands, loving hands that cared for her. John had killed with those hands: chickens, cows, rabbits, and the occasional squirrel so she could eat. They were hands unafraid to do the right thing in their master's service. She let her eyes wander over the man who loved her for the past seven years. His skin was like the sole of an old army boot. His eyes were acorn-colored, his hair black and oiled down for this trip into town. He showed some age in crows' feet. His jaw was a rock shelf. He was a good man, a strong man. Her man.

How she wanted this baby with him! No more nights of hearing the phantom crying of a newborn who never laid in a crib. She often woke in the rocker John made for her, holding a bundle of blankets or a stuffed animal because she had dreamed of picking up her child to love or console.

John wanted a baby, too, and though they tried (most often twice a day), she grew impatient waiting. John hurt with her over the disappointment, but he couldn't understand the loss, the *emptiness* inside where life refused to grow. Helen felt a physical ache throbbing with its own life, often driving her to the bathroom to cry—or if John wasn't close by—to scream with the frustration of repeated failures.

Her moods darkened. She aimed her frustrations at John. Helen fought with him just to relieve the pressure threatening to blow apart her empty body, but also so they would make love after. She begged him each time to make her pregnant, but her period always returned. Helen began to hate her body.

In desperation, she went to see the voodoo lady over in Shy Town. Her best friend took her, sitting beside as the stinking nag quizzed Helen in a whisper.

"You 'ant a child, dearie? Old Rose can 'elp you ... Do you 'ant that?"

Her hut smelled of manure and soil, that funk of growing that was Helen's atmosphere for the last seven years. Rose brewed a drink from corn leaves and less identifiable things. It tasted of spices. Had it helped? It hadn't hurt.

Some would brand Helen a heathen for thinking of another in the sight of what God so plainly gave. As for God, well, Helen would praise His name every day for her baby's health if her child were healthy.

Rose told Helen to wish for her baby. When she caught pregnant, Helen called her best friend who, instead of sharing her joy, was quiet. No matter. The baby was coming, and if it was born of Rose rather than God, then this modern place with its tests and computers and lights could make it right.

John was on the front side of the last form. Good. He would focus on her again soon. For his part, John noticed her looking and dotted her hand with the pen. Helen giggled, leaning into him. He was thankful for the distraction.

Four weeks ago, John and Helen learned they were expecting. The crops they sold last season were the best their land had produced in four years, so John was able to pay all of Helen's medical bills up front, an accomplishment in which he felt no small pride. Maybe that was why Dr. Bigley, Helen's gynecologist, sent them here.

"I'm going to send you to a specialist," Bigley conferred through his thick mustache. "He's a compatriot of mine." (John took that to mean friend or at least someone Bigley worked with). "His name is Dr. Weaver. One of the top baby men in the biz."

"Why do we need a specialist?" Helen asked, clutching her dress top.

"There's nothing wrong." Bigley chuckled to show how foolish the notion was. "These folks take special care of babies. And the parents. I assumed you'd want to go all out. The Baby Shop can do things I can't."

Well, they'd see about that.

"Five years from now he'll be starting school," John said, turning over the last form.

"He?" Helen pinched him. "You mean *she*. A little girl with my eyes, your ears, and a full head of black hair just like my brother Orin." She stared across the room at an old television set. The color was off, so all the actors were green and purple. Helen spoke low, almost to herself, her smile shrinking.

"I hope she's all right."

John followed her gaze. The television took up most of the far wall, a low and wide floor model. John didn't look at the screen, but at the figure on top. A short, chubby baby-doll was propped against a dusty set of plastic flowers. The doll was naked. Its smooth, plastic skin glowed under the fluorescent lights. John's flesh humped in goosebumps as the oddity of the doll set in on him. The paint that made up its face was stripped away. It was blank.

John looked around the waiting room. It was dark and decorated in tones of brown and orange that reminded him of barren fields after a drought. The front doors were pushed back down a long hallway so sunlight never reached the waiting area. Rows of orange plastic chairs were bolted together along the wall. There were no other couples in the waiting room. A single receptionist window was greasy with fingerprints.

Paintings decorated the walls, prints consisting of one-color backgrounds and a dab of another color; red over black; blue over gray; green over vomit yellow. The splatters made John think of blood.

Thunder rumbled outside, in another world. It had been hot and humid all morning. A storm was waiting to start just as they were waiting to be called into the doctor's office.

"What do you think he'll do to me?" Helen asked. "With the computers and all, with that ultrasound like we saw on television, they'll just point a camera at my belly, right?"

John smiled at her, but it felt cold and small on his lips as if he were carrying a slug with his teeth. He spoke through it.

"You'll be fine. Quit looking for ill omens."

She *was* looking for ill omens. She couldn't help being superstitious. But look what good finally came from that nature. Rose's magic had seeded the barren field of her body. Helen fingered her lucky pendant, thinking of her little girl and how she would grow up, but John coughed suddenly, bringing Helen back to the reality of the waiting room.

"Hon?"

"Fine. Just the smell," he said.

John stifled another cough with the back of his hand. The room's stink of antiseptic brought back the memory of having his appendix out when he was eleven. But this was a twisted smell. Changed. Soured. Then he was a child, now he was a man who had learned to trust his instincts, and they were telling him to run, to grab his wife and run. He wanted the best for his family, but this wasn't it. The feeling grew to a shout. Sweat broke under his shirt. John reached, meaning to take Helen's hand and go. The desire was sudden and hard and loud. He would invent some excuse or just tell her he didn't want her in The Baby Shop if it came to that, but before he could rise, a shrill voice asked:

"Mr. and Mrs. Nesbitt?"

The nurse, a short round woman with flabby arms, appeared beside them. John could reach out and touch her if he so desired—but he didn't, God, no. She was holding open an orange door painted to look like part of the wall. It had been hidden from them.

"Yes," Helen replied before John could stop her.

"This way."

They followed the nurse—who never turned to look at them—down a cramped hallway. Her bulk swayed. She glided from right to left as if drunk. John was reminded of the time one of his cows wandered to the far corner of the pasture to die, moving in the same uneven way toward death.

She stopped at a small brown door, pushed it open, took their forms, and told them to wait inside. Then she walked away without so much as a nod or smile. That was just as well. John had no attention for her. It was all consumed by the room.

It was small, painted in the same two-tone orange over brown, and it was an abomination. Paintings hung on the walls, dark things with sinister suggestions just beyond John's comprehension. He stepped around the exam table and its crinkling butcher's paper to look at the largest one. It had a black background with a red-skinned baby waving a chubby hand. Its head was tilted up. But it had no face. Its face was suspended in space to the baby's right. Blue rays of light extended from the head to the face, which had squinted eyes and laughing lips.

To the right was another. A baby knelt in the foreground lit by blue light. It had dozens of faces superimposed on its head. The crowded effect hurt John's eyes.

There were more: long, short, big, small, wide, narrow, some with blank-faced babies as the focus, some with only pink, bloodless pieces. A triangle-shaped oil painting showed parents sitting at a picnic table where various arms, legs, and heads were displayed. John was sure the couple were drooling at the selections before them.

Above the art, at the top of the wall, was a gold plaque: WE BUILD BETTER BABIES.

"John!" Helen grabbed his shoulder, but voices claimed his attention. He could hear the conversation next door. One voice was deep with knowledge, the other two high.

"We can—" One voice started, but Helen's cry drowned out the rest of the sentence.

"JOHN! The pictures!"

"Hush!" He commanded, something he hadn't done since their first year of marriage when Helen ran to the tractor from the back where he couldn't see her. John pressed his ear to the wall.

"We will take your nose off the baby, Mrs. Brendell, and put on..." The rustling of papers. "...your great grandmother's. Correct?"

"Yes, such a cute button nose."

"Now, Mr. Brendell, you want a boy, and have both agreed to that. I see here you also want a..." The quick flapping of pages. "...an eleven-inch penis for him. Correct?"

"No, Richmond, I told you that was too big."

"Nonsense, dear; do it, doctor."

"Won't it hurt him?"

"No Ma'am, we simply rearrange the genetics. We build a better baby."

John turned to Helen. "That isn't a doctor's place," he said. Once wasn't enough.

"This isn't a doctor's place." John's face was a bleached smear.

"They mess with its body?" Helen asked.

"They're making babies. They're—"

The door opened. A man entered, reading from a clipboard. He was tall with steel-gray hair. His clothes were neat and pressed. His shoes gleamed. But his nose—his nose was red and caved. The right nostril was missing completely. A scar twisted down the bridge and he wheezed as he breathed. *Cut off his nose to spite his face*, John thought.

"Ahhhh, the Nesbitts. I'm Dr. Weaver."

John heard the doctor in the next room discussing the baby's feet as he stared at Dr. Weaver's outstretched hand.

"Who's in the next room? Who is that doctor?"

Weaver looked hurt. "You want Dr. Conners? But Dr. Bigley said—"

"What's going on in this place? What are you people doing here?"

Dr. Weaver's face bloomed. He understood. "You don't know what we do here at The Baby Shop." He looked John up, down, and smiled. "You don't know."

"It sounds like butchery."

"It's genetics, Mr. Nesbitt." The smile reappeared, the same one used by slick-talking salesmen trying to convince him to buy supposed bigger and better tractors.

"Men and women make babies. You should stay out of it."

Dr. Weaver bared his teeth. "*We* have advanced in technology. Men and women make the raw materials that *we* shape. Men and women make imperfect beings." Weaver fingered the deep red pit of his nose. John suddenly understood this man polished everything he could: his shoes, his belt buckle, his buttons. He made everything about him as perfect as possible to make up for the crater in his face.

"We build better babies, Mr. Nesbitt." The words rang with rehearsed conviction.

"Children receive cleft palates because a mother is too selfish to stop smoking during pregnancy. Down Syndrome, retardation, cancer," Weaver's tone rose sharply, making John's seem dull by comparison. "*Cancer*! Cancer, Mr. Nesbitt." He jerked his finger away from his nose and licked the spit from his lip. "Those are your *human* results. What we do here is correct the mistakes. We boost immune systems and cure diseases. We make athletes, writers, race car drivers, leaders, soldiers; we make people—"

"God makes people!"

"AND WE FINISH THEM!" His eyes blazed. "We determine if you have a boy or a girl; whether it will have red hair, or black, or brown; curly or straight; freckles or china-white skin. Name it and we can do it here. Can you do that with a God who throws out diseases and imperfections like Santa Claus tossing candy at a parade?" His finger went back to his nose. Weaver did not catch the motion this time and stroked it roughly. "Computers tell us what your child will look like—boy or girl." He looked at Helen. "How badly do you want a little girl, Helen?"

She gasped. John shoved her behind him and balled his fists.

"How bad do you want it, Helen? I can make it a reality."

Helen's voice was ragged and torn: "How do you do it?"

"How? We punch holes in the genetic code. Science mapped out the strands. It was only a matter of time before we learned to control them."

He walked to the sink where boxes of rubber gloves were stacked. Weaver took out a black pen, closed it in his fist, and punctuated each word by stabbing it through the cardboard box top. "We." POP! "Punch."

POP! "Holes." POP! "In." POP! "Their." POP! "Genetic." POP! "Code." POP! POP! POP! He smiled as he stabbed. His forehead gleamed with sudden sweat. His cheeks turned the pink of baby fat. "We can give you a girl, Helen."

And Helen thought it would be … what? Right? She thought of the drink the voodoo woman gave her. If she had soiled their child, it could be made right here. Isn't that what all this advancement was for?

"We plug whatever we want into the holes. We know where to punch, how to punch, and what to put back. We know, so we act."

"I can make explosives out of pig shit and kerosene, but don't. You're crazy."

"We can give you what you want."

John had fantasized about sitting on the porch with his boy while they looked over the land they had farmed together. Now, he saw that land tilled by machines with no sweat or blood invested in the soil. He saw them growing fat and lazy while the machines did their work. "Not what I want," John said.

"How long will you sow in the corn?" Weaver asked.

"No," John said, shaking his head. "No!" He grabbed Helen's hand, meaning to pull her out the door, but it was not the grand exit he intended. Did she resist him? John jerked her, pulling her out of the room, determined to get them as far away from the blasphemy as possible. He pulled Helen down the hall, never turning to look at her or Weaver whose voice followed them out the door.

"The world has moved on, Nesbitt! You can't stop it!"

As Helen's first screams of labor began, the sun slipped away, not wanting to see the coming events. A bloated moon took its place. John delivered.

It was a girl.

He saw his nose, Helen's eyes, and a head of black hair just like she had hoped for in The Baby Shop's waiting room. John trembled as he studied the creature. His vision doubled from sweat and fear of what Helen had done. She moaned from the bed, raising a wavering hand.

"Wanted a girl ... I wanted. I went back. It's not so bad. Really." Helen wasn't confessing but convincing herself.

The thing pulsed in his hands.

"They made it. Clean. Right."

Blood drooled down John's arm. The baby-thing was silent. Patient. It stared, eyes wide and much too alert. Its skin, though soft, was a broken promise. Helen killed his son for this creature that came from a tube and technology rather than their love. How in the hell was he to live with this alien? With his traitor wife? The answer came with clear authority: he was not.

John raised the child over his head and slammed its soft skull into the bed's wooden footrest. The baby made no sound. There was a thud, a splash, and he raised it again. He drove down the dripping mass in a muscle straining blur. Helen screeched, her velvet voice now cheap cloth. A final swing and John was finished. His hands and face were pink with blood, mimicking Helen's own CHLOASMA. He wiped his away.

A knife lay on the bedside table in case the baby came feet first, but of course, it did not. The Baby Shop didn't make mistakes like that. The knife was also for the umbilical cord. John realized he hadn't separated mother and child yet and as Helen twisted herself out of bed, the wet pulp of the little corpse dragged on the hardwood floor.

The blade sliced down, catching Helen in the eye, the cheek, the nose. Flesh tore. Blood flew. Her screams turned to wet gurgles. She raised her hands. John hacked them. Her index finger clung by a strip of flesh. Her ring finger plopped to the floor. Finally, one of his blows went wild and caught her in the throat. Blood exploded, her voice warbled, but still John continued until he cut off her face, just like the babies at The Baby Shop.

John dropped the knife. It landed beside Helen's foot, her nose, and a glob of her left eye. He stumbled out of their bedroom, through the house, and the front door. The night air cooled the hot blood on his face.

Since the day he dragged Helen away from The Baby Shop, John rejected all things mechanical. He adopted a creed for their life. "A man's labor has got to be his own." He told Helen this time and again. He repeated the words to himself as he stood on his shaggy lawn, looking at his home and land. His family had been swept away in the current of time. They had drowned.

His tractor was an unfamiliar hump before him. The metal gleamed dully. Angry. Had his ancestors used one? No. What of the truck parked by the house? His forefathers walked. Was he a traitor like Helen? The thought nibbled at John with sharp rat-teeth. What of the house? The barn? How many of his forebears weathered the elements in huts? Caves? In just their skin? It all had to come down. A cleansing was needed here.

John kept extra gas cans in the barn. He chose the largest and strode outside, walking lopsided as the can's weight sloshed, eager to set to any work. Had it been bored with no machines to power? No matter, John had work for it now.

John splashed the barn's red hide. It hadn't rained in weeks and the wood sucked the gas greedily. John threw it against the window where it cut the pollen in greasy tracks. It puddled on the windowsill. John reached in his pocket for a matchbook. It came from the bar where he spent a lot of time lately, preaching against the evils of technology, where Shorty Robinson finally told him he needed help. John struck the match and flung it.

Flames bloomed. The glow raced up, out, its heat sudden. John's eyes watered. He backed up. There were many cans of stain and polish inside the barn likely to explode. The heat baked his back as he crossed the yard. Grass where his son should have played parted.

John raised the gas can and charged his home. He slung gas onto the downspout, down into the central heat and air unit which he had not allowed to be turned on despite the heat. He tossed gas high, so it dripped from the eaves. John splashed it against the kitchen window where Helen looked out when cooking. He flung it against the den where their days wound down, where they planned their future. John made a trail onto the front porch, through the front door. He covered the carpet, the curtains, the walls. He walked the entire house, then back to the grass, and tossed the empty can away. He pulled a new match, struck it, tossed it. His home caught fire.

Technology had beaten him. John saw all the places computers would settle. Maybe the firemen would be robots, his judge, jury, and executioner merely cold, faceless machines.

John turned in circles, trying to look everywhere at once. He found his plow at the edge of the cornfield. Had his ancestors feared it as he feared computers? Did the other Nesbitt farmers see them as meddlesome machines?

John heard sirens. The neighbors had seen the fire. The authorities were coming to get him. He'd be photographed, jailed, part of the system. He'd be a number. A number instead of a man.

No. No. Never that.

John walked up the porch, closed his eyes, and entered the flaming doorway. Fire licked his gas-soaked shoes. As his pants caught, John entered what would have been his son's room. He sat in the middle of the floor and watched the flames race toward him like a child coming to play, like his son would have run to the fields to tell him supper was ready. John spread his arms, welcoming his boy, lips pulled back in a grin. The child came. John's hair caught fire. Flesh peeled back from his forehead. His eyes sizzled, boiling in their sockets. Finally, John screamed—not from the pain, but as he collapsed, he heard a metallic laughter in the approaching sirens.

Fresh Start

Christopher Blinn

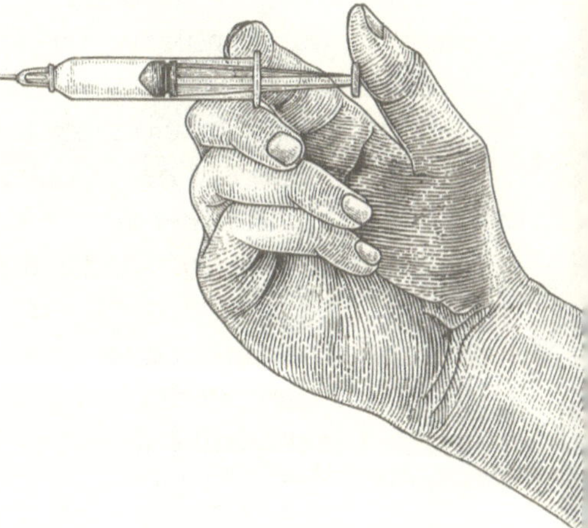

She woke to clanging. Squeaking. An uneven wheel sent tremors up the legs of a metal table, jostling the stainless-steel tools on top.

Tom pushed the table, humming a tune he made up as he went. His patient stirred. "Ahh, you're awake."

The woman groaned.

Tom parked the table, grabbed a stool, and sat bedside. "Let me clean you up a bit," he said and dipped a washcloth in a small pink basin.

"Aarrghh, what the … who…" the woman muttered. She tried to move, but her arms and legs were restrained.

Tom wrung the washcloth and dabbed her forehead.

The woman squinted and blinked out tears. Her vision unfocused, she could only see a blur of the man who spoke.

"It's alright," Tom said, adjusting the woman's pillow. "Everything's going to be fine."

"Did I have an accident?" the woman croaked.

"In a manner of speaking." Tom answered.

"What does that mean?"

"Nothing, dear. Try to relax."

"Why am I strapped down?"

"You have an injury. A sudden movement could worsen it."

"Can you undo me now? I won't try to get up," she promised.

"I'm afraid I can't. Doctor's orders," Tom said.

"Could you ask the doctor, please?" Her voice weakened. Still groggy.

"Well, I am the doctor." Tom snickered.

The woman sensed something wasn't right. She squeezed her eyes shut, hoping to improve her vision. She might feel better if she could at least see where she was.

Tom rinsed the cloth again, passing it over her cheeks; he moistened her lips and cooled her neck. "How's that feel?"

The coolness was nice. "Good. Thank you," she managed.

"Great," Tom stood and bumped into his table. The instruments clanked. "Oops," he apologized. "Try to rest, you have a big day ahead of you."

The woman tried to speak. She was exhausted and rest sounded good, but her instincts were setting off alarms. A big day ahead of me? What the hell did that mean? What was the last thing she remembered? Showering. Dressing. Walking to the dumpster at the back of her building to get rid of some trash. And—and nothing, that was it. Maybe she'd been in an accident. Fallen down some stairs and injured her head. Maybe it was the fog of drugs. No, something wasn't right. She diverted all of her energy to clear her vision. The silhouette of the doctor sharpened slightly. Tall. Thin. Balding. Awkward stance. She recognized the man. Pulled on her restraints.

"Now, now," Tom said. "You're supposed to be resting."

Her brain matched the voice with the shadow.

Tom pushed more sedatives through her IV. and watched his patient drift away.

Consciousness returned like a television effect. Whites and grays drifted off the edges, the center of the screen forming a picture. She heard the doctor's voice.

"Welcome back." Tom said.

Her vision wasn't perfect, but better. She tested her arms and legs, Still secured.

"Are we feeling better after our nap?"

The voice stabbed her. Her eyes shot open with shock giving her away.

"I see you recognize me."

She scanned the area. A basement. Cement walls. Exposed beams. Clean, except for a few cobwebs. "You're that creepy barista from The Coffee Attic."

"Creepy barista. Perfect. It's exactly why I brought you here." Tom sat. "You left out 'hard-working medical student trying to make a living.'" Tom folded his arms across his chest and stared at the woman like a defeated parent whose beautiful fruit had rotted inside. He recalled her rejections to his dinner offers. The first wasn't so bad. *Sorry, I have a boyfriend,* she said. A lie, he learned. It wasn't that she didn't have a boyfriend, she did. And she had another and another and another. He could never share her. The refusals worsened. Spurns, shuns, and snubs. She threatened violence from her latest beau.

"So, I wouldn't go out with you, you're gonna tie me up and rape me?"

"Oh no, I could never do that."

"What then? You're gonna keep me chained in your basement like a pet?"

Tom said nothing, watching and listening.

She tested her bindings. They held, but she felt a bit of her strength had returned.

Tom's mind was still somewhere else. Daydreaming.

"Say something for God's sake, ya freak. Just like at the cafe. Staring and staring. How many times did I have to say 'no, I don't want to go out with you?' They call it stalking, you fucking weirdo."

"You're really in no position to be hurling insults." Tom returned.

She couldn't believe she was glad to hear him speaking again, but she was. She'd learned enough through police dramas to know she needed to personalize this. Make him see her as a person with friends and family and not just an object for his sick fantasies.

Tom reached under the bed, dragged out his victim's backpack and held it up for her to see. He unzipped it and foraged inside.

She watched. Waited. Gathered strength.

Tom removed item after item and placed them aside. He fished out her diaphragm, smiled, and frisbeed it across the room. "Ahhh, here we are." He held a small clutch. "Louis Vuitton, of course. Now, let's have some fun. I heard your friends calling you Franky, I think it's short for Francine, so let's see if I'm right." He slipped her license from the purse, closing his eyes. "This is exciting, don't you think?" He created more anticipation for himself. "I find that sexy: a beautiful woman with a male nickname."

She rolled her eyes.

"Ready? One, two—"

"Frances," she blurted out.

"Wha ... why'd you do that? You ruined it." Tom jumped from his stool. Paced. Angry.

She knew poking him would make things worse, but she couldn't help herself.

Tom calmed down and returned bedside.

"Look, my Dad's rich. I can get you whatever you want," Frances said, testing his resolve.

"What I want is you. Gorgeous dark hair. Green eyes. Smoothest skin I ever seen. And your *figure*. I've never seen anything more perfect."

Franky fidgeted. "Let me go and I won't tell anyone. Maybe we can have a bit of fun before I leave." She tried her feminine charms.

"No, it's too late for that," Tom laughed. "Besides, it's not just about your rejections to my offer. That, I can handle—and you're right, I did stare. That was rude, I admit. I did not mean to make you uncomfortable. But after a bit, I noticed that I wasn't the only one you treated like shit. Which, oddly, made me feel a bit better about myself." Tom paused.

"Please," Frances tried to recall her captor's name. She focused. Thought of his Coffee Attic name tag. Christ. Maybe she could reverse that stupid personalization thing. It was on the tip of her tongue.

"Nose always in the air," Tom continued. "Like you were better than everyone else. I couldn't believe God would put such a black heart inside such an otherwise perfect creation."

Black heart. She felt the punch of the words. *How could she let anything this nut job said bother her? But it did. Was she really that awful of a person? What was she supposed to do? Date every Tom, Dick and Harry who asked her out. Tom. That was it. His name. Tom.*

"I contemplated forgetting about you when I saw you race a pregnant woman to the last empty booth one day. Too far gone to be redeemed. I figured karma would catch up to you one day and save me the effort." Tom paused. "But—"

"What? Tom. But *what*?"

"Tom," he laughed. "Very clever. In the past, I dreamt of hearing you say my name but now it just sounds, I dunno, fake."

Remembering his name didn't have the effect she'd hoped for.

"Anyway, I'm nothing if not persistent." He continued his summation. "Helping you was my responsibility. I followed you. Watched. Learned. Planned." Tom stood. "I couldn't let such perfection go to waste. You needed a fresh start, so to speak. But I knew someone like you could never really change. So I had to come up with something a little more drastic."

"What the fuck are you talking about, you lunatic?"

"Lunatic?" Tom mused. "If trying to save you is lunacy then I will proudly wear the title." He stepped next to a shower curtain that bisected the cellar.

"Please," Franky growled. Angry. "Kill me. Get it over with."

"Kill you?" Tom gasped. "You're a riot, Franky. I told you: I'm trying to save you."

Franky turned her head away.

"C'mon now. Play the game," Tom gripped the curtain. "Don't you wanna see what's behind curtain number one?"

Franky didn't move.

Tom clenched his teeth. "Look over here or I will permanently set your neck this way." He whipped the curtain aside.

A woman laid on a ping-pong table. Obviously dead, her chest cracked open. "I want you to meet ahh ... I actually don't know her name, but she was the sweetest woman I've ever met." Tom sighed. "That's a lie too. I found her passed out under a bridge downtown and figured she'd be perfect for my purposes."

"Your purposes?"

"Yes," Tom held a large jar containing the dead woman's heart packed in ice. He held it up to the light. Spun it. "It's beautiful. Isn't it?" He set the jar down on the silver tray next to his assortment of surgical tools.

"Whatever you're thinking of doing, please don't. I'm sorry. Really. I'll be a better person, I promise."

"You know they say the true nature of man resides in the heart. His true strength. His love. His hate. All he is, is in the heart." Tom looked serious. "Someone famous said that, I think. I dunno, maybe. I flunked philosophy." Tom reached for a monitor above Franky's head and touched a box on the gray screen. A mechanical pump hummed to life.

This guy is gonzo, Frances thought. His mood swings were more sweeping than the giant pirate ship at the fair. Giddy. Angry. Happy. Just plain fucking crazy. He must be bipolar or tripolar, if there was such a thing. He was in a polar orbit for sure, banging his head on the satellites.

"This little doohickie is gonna keep your blood flowing while I take out your spoiled ticker and replace it with what's-her-name's."

"Stop, please." Frances panicked.

"You're kinda lucky," Tom went on. "I finished medical school. Of course, that was for podiatry. I don't think that's gonna help me with a heart transplant, but you never know 'til you try."

Franky squirmed.

Tom twisted a tank nozzle by Franky's head. He held a mask to his face and took a hit. "Oh, and anesthesia. I learned some of that. Lucky for you again." He placed the mask aside, not quite ready to anesthetize his patient. He whistled the same unknown tune he had whistled earlier while he prepped his hands. "This is like a first date. Don't ya think?" Tom inspected the heart again. "You know, I really should have an assistant for such a complicated procedure. I'd ask my mom but she's resting upstairs."

"Resting upstairs?" Frances questioned.

"Yes, but don't get any—."

"Help," Frances yelled, cutting off her tormentor.

"—ideas," Tom shook his head. "I mean she's resting, like in peace."

She pictured her captor's dead mother, rotting in a rocking chair like in Hitchcock's famous movie. Mummified by her cuckoo bird son.

"I do have this, however," Tom held a thick old book. "Voodoo," he wiggled his fingers like he was casting a spell. "Mum was from New Orleans originally. Her father was Haitian. A houngan. That's a Voodoo priest," he explained.

Tears dripped from Frances' eyes.

"Now, now." Tom said comfortingly. "I don't believe in this nonsense either, but I could use any help I can get." He pulled the knot of Frances' johnny and folded it down, exposing her chest. He flipped a page and pulled a chicken out of a bowl of its own blood. He held the unfortunate bird like a quill, turned another page and scrawled a series of triangles, circles and odd-looking letters above Frances' heart. "There."

Frances was still. Silent. Resigned to her fate.

"Oh, I almost forgot." Tom muttered a spell from the book, took the chicken's body and nailed it to a beam. He scooped up the mask containing the anesthetic gas and pulled it gently over his patient's head. "Ready."

Franky closed her eyes and prayed. The mask fogged and muffled her words.

"Ok, anywho. Count backward from ten to one and when you wake, you'll be a whole new person."

Tom leaned in an old chair, his feet up on the ping-pong table while he waited for his patient to recover. He was out in seconds, exhausted from the eight-hour procedure. He'd hoarded everything she'd need. IV fluids. Antibiotics. Pain meds. All procured from his residency. A small TV replayed cable news over and over.

He woke to find Franky standing over him. "Jesus ... what the..." Tom fell out of his chair. "It friggin' worked."

Tall. Naked. Train-track stitches oozed black and red from neck to ribs. Tom collected himself, reached out, and traced a finger along the angry skin. "We can work on those wounds when the stitches come out." He pulled an old bed sheet, revealing an even older mirror. He waved a hand, directing her to have a look.

"I'm beautiful," she said.

"Yes, Frances, you are. On the inside as well now, too."

"Frances?" He heard the question in her voice. "My name is Marilyn." She walked to the corpse, its rib cage wide like a Thanksgiving turkey. "That's me on the table. At least it was." She gazed approvingly at the mirror.

Tom was confused.

"This woman—Frances—I can still sense her." Marilyn concentrated. "God, she was a bitch."

Tom tilted his head from side to side. He hated to agree but... "So, your name is Marilyn?" Tom gestured to the body on the ping-pong table.

"Yes. You mean you don't know who I am?"

"No," Tom shook his head. "Should I?"

"Missing for over a week now," The television newscaster came in as if on cue. "Police are seeking the public's assistance in finding multiple murderer Marilyn Morgan. She escaped from the Adams Institute where she was serving life for a series of grisly murders. Nicknamed 'the Mangler,' her victims were all found dismembered and partly devoured.'

Tom swallowed. The dead woman on the table was the same woman in the police photo on the TV.

Marilyn snuggled up to Tom. She ran her fingers through his hair and brushed his cheek. She blew a warm breath in his ear and stretched his lobe between her teeth.

"Aaarrch," Tom pulled away. He saw blood in her mouth. His blood. He touched a hand to his ear and inspected it.

"What's the matter, baby?" A sick grin widened on her face. "Don't you like a little pain with your pleasure?" Marilyn grabbed a handful of Tom's hair and jerked his head to the side. She sank her teeth into his neck, tore out his throat, and dropped his body to the floor.

Tom twisted on the dusty cement, blood arcing from the wound with every heartbeat. He clutched his neck. A useless effort to prolong the inevitable.

The new Frances washed, found her host's clothes and dressed. "Whatcha think?" She posed.

Tom struggled.

Frances checked herself once more in the mirror and made a couple of minor adjustments. "I have a fresh start," she said. "All thanks to you." She pinched Tom's cheek, covered his face with her hand, and pushed him to the floor. She stepped on his neck. "A fresh start," she said to the now dead Tom, blowing him a kiss.

On a Scale from
One to Ten...

The Patent Trial

Rohmann Barisoff

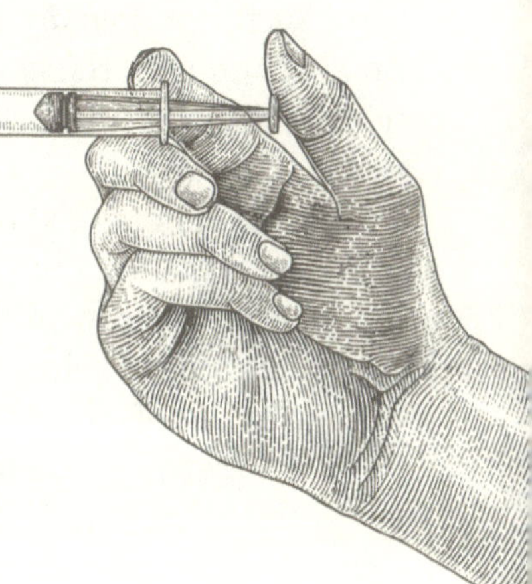

The technician led me to a lone table in a hallway deep within the underground research facility. Smiling, he read aloud an answer from my questionnaire, "'As a true man of science,' you wrote, 'I believe it is incumbent upon us all to push ever further the boundaries of what we believe is possible.'"

Yes, I responded although he hadn't asked a question.

"Well," the technician said, "as a man of science myself, I can assure you that what happens within these very walls pushes boundaries, indeed."

The technician picked a clipboard off of a hook on the wall and said, "Now before you say yes, I am contractually obligated to tell you that there have been some reports of side-effects."

Why yes, of course, I replied. Thus is the humble nature of science: a gesture made in an educated direction, followed by a few brave souls willing to be swallowed up by unforeseen (yet wholly anticipated) sinkholes scattered along the pathway of discovery and invention. Necessary evils.

The lab technician tapped a pen against his chin for several beats, and then agreed, saying, "What a profoundly agreeable outlook!"

And, I continued, who among us hasn't imbibed a cough and flu remedy bearing a label riddled with size-6 font proclamations about mood swings, seizures, and hallucinations? Or an antihistamine that bestows diarrhea, dizziness, and dry mouth upon its consumer? Not to mention erectile dysfunction.

Again, the technician tapped his chin with his pen. "You are a remarkable specimen." He clipped the pen to the breast pocket of his lab coat.

"Hm! Such a pro*foundl*y agreeable *out*look!" He yanked free the first page on his clipboard, the contractual obligations, and discarded it, letting it float down, down into a blue recycling bin tucked safely against one side of the hallway.

The technician led me into a patent trial room where we sat across from one another. On the table were three small plastic cups: one red, one blue, one yellow, all filled with a clear, odorless liquid.

I'm a man of science, so I really didn't need to be bored with any yada-yada details or procedural mumbo-jumbo.

"I feel that you are a man of science," he said, "so I'm not going to bore you with any yada-yada details or procedural mumbo-jumbo. Simply pick a cup of any color, and drink *all* of the liquid therein. After waiting exactly two minutes, I would then like you to discuss, using vivid sensory details, how the contents of the cup are making you *feel*. For example: you might say, 'Oh, my head feels simultaneously hollow and thick, and my hippo-campus is about to rupture, you'd best take cover under the table, doc.' Or you might tell me about a third eye beginning to manifest itself in the middle of your forehead, and thus, you have suddenly acquired precog-nitive abilities, and wouldn't that be miraculous? While you tell me how you are feeling in the finest of detail, I shall be writing down your every word here in my notebook."

With that, the technician settled in his chair and motioned with open hands for me to begin the trial.

I selected the blue cup.

The color of my wife's eyes, I said with a wink and drank. The liquid was flavorless, and it soaked into my tongue before it could be swal-lowed. *Concerning*, I thought. *Perhaps I have an undiagnosed tongue condi-tion wherein the pores dotting up and down its swampy length are far too large for this particular substance?* I made to remark on this troubling paranoia, but the technician went, 'shush-shush-shush,' held up two fingers, indi-cating that I was to wait the full two minutes before disclosing my expe-riences. As a man of science, I obliged.

Two minutes passed, and I was about to inform the technician of the bad news, when suddenly a thing, a growth, like an infantile plant bulb or an adventurous pimple, broke through the skin and fascia between the collarbone on my right side. The sound of its emergence was like a foot stomping on grapes. It arrived with bone-cracking pain and a gentle spurt of blood which dotted the technician's spectacles and lab coat. He looked on with disinterest and checked his watch.

"Alright, that should do it. How do you feel?"

I feel like I'm entering a second puberty, growing pains, and do you see what's begun to sprout, here, near my neck?

The technician scribbled on his bloodied clipboard, muttering, "Second puberty, that's good, very good."

The growth bit me. The meaty bulb had grown to resemble a nail-less thumb with a miniature crescent moon of a mouth full of blunt and scummy teeth. It took another bite, breaking skin. And when it bit me for a third time, it not only drew blood, but chewed off flesh two-times the size of its little mouth. A tiny tongue inside its baby-sized maw worked adeptly and efficiently in maneuvering the meat of my neck into a consumable little package, which the bulb then swallowed. I felt the food of my neck move through gurgling passages somewhere inside my chest, until it hit my stomach.

It's eating me, I said. *I'm* eating me!

"Fine, but how do you *feel*? Use vivid sensory details to describe your experience."

Physical maturity in humans typically takes quite a few years to achieve, and we require constant nourishment and physical stimulus. This little bulb however—my little neck bulb—had grown eight-fold in an instant. Hanging out of me, next to my collarbone, was the half-formed head of someone else, eyes obscured with a thin, translucent skin and the whole of it slick with primordial goo or some other far more insidious chemical derived from this unexpected ritual of second-birth.

The head twisted towards me, snapping its teeth, *clack*, but with its sudden girth it lacked the mobility to further feed off of my neck. Like any good-natured newborn that doesn't get its way with food, it started to wail. Bits of vestigial flesh strung from its top lip to the bottom snapped loose from the tension and danced in the coppery breath of its wail, like fronds in the wind.

Half-formed, relatively shrunken and with only thin patches of pre-pubescent hairs upon its head, it struggled against me in a tantrum.

"For a man of science," the technician said, "you are being a very unco-operative subject."

Hearing the voice of the technician, the head began snapping at the air, stretching as far as its thick, veiny neck would take it.

"How about a prompt?" the technician asked. He searched through the pages of his clipboard.

"Let us try prompt number … five." He cleared his throat and, careful to annunciate each word clearly, said, "Having imbibed the trial liquid, I find that my mouth tastes *blank*, and there is a *blank* sound *blanking* in my ears which is *blankly blank*."

I spoke the prompt and my second head, disorientated from two voices in the room, wailed and wailed so that I couldn't hear my own voice.

Having imbibed the trial liquid, I said, I find that my mouth tastes like alkaline, and there is an inhuman screaming sound stabbing me in my ears, which is, frankly, mortifying.

"Alkaline," the technician said with a whistle, jotting it down.

I asked the technician, What should I do about this head? It really sounds quite anguished—I think it might be hungry.

Clack, clack, went the head.

The technician tapped his pen on his chin. He conferred with his inner dialogue for minutes, then said, "Well, then I suppose you had better feed it."

The head struggled against its (my) mortal cage as if it understood and agreed with the technician. *Feed me*, its nodding head suggested, and the suggestion was madness. A man of science I was, and my previous sentiment about sinkholes along the road to great discovery was something I still stood by. *Then feed yourself to science,* a voice inside of my mind insisted. But which part of me? *Start with two fingers from your left hand—the ring and pinky fingers.*

My left hand raised into the air like an object inhabited by a spirit.

It feels like my body is being persuaded into performing some unholy ritual, I said. The marrow of my bones, my hormones—all of it, tricked and tricked and tricked again.

"For some people, science is, indeed, an unholy ritual, a violation of the sacrosanct," the technician said. "But we are not *those* people. We are pioneers at the threshold of change. Now *feed* it."

I guided my hand toward the head; it held steady with its mouth wide, its lips peeled back over the blackened gums of an upper and lower jaw. Through the skin over its eyes, I could see it watching me so that when I hesitated (I wear my wedding ring on my left ring finger, and I hadn't taken it off before I committed to the feeding), it jerked forward. And that was that. Its teeth lined up neatly against my two fingers at the knuckle and it pressed its lips closed like in a kiss, saving me from the image and leaving only the pain that came to pass when it bit through to the bone and the head sucked (Mmmm! it moaned with delight) and pulled back so that there was not a nibble of meat left. A very clean bite. Its diligent tongue went to work, synchronized with its jaws. It swallowed. I waited for the strangeness of my own meat coursing through my body into my stomach. Inside of me there felt to be a rumbling.

The technician rolled his eyes. "No one ever achieved greatness by performing half-measures. *Feed. It. More.* Do you imagine Edmund Hilary would be remembered as the man who bested Everest if he was satisfied with only ever reaching her first peak? And do you imagine Craig *Venter* is satisfied with a mere 99% of the human genome? What, the Wright brothers call it quits after the first crash and humanity never takes to the sky?" The technician thumped his fist on the table. "*Feed it more!*"

I grimaced, crying, For science! and turned away as I offered up the remaining fingers on my hand. The head took my fingers eagerly into its mouth and its dull teeth squeezed and wrenched and cracked through my finger bones, ripping free my digits.

More, I suppose? I queried the technician. However, before I could make the choice myself, a wriggling, wormy *thing* writhing around inside of my belly decidedly punched its way through my flesh like a hellish thorn. A hand arced upwards, grabbing ahold of my arm, its grip warm and damp. The rest of my hand was offered up to the head (gnashing, gnawing on my knuckles which rolled and disjointed and popped loose to be slurped up like so many wontons), soon my forearm, equally devoured, now devoid of that arm in whole.

Naturally, I began to black out in the presence of so much pain and blood loss. I recall the technician's impartial stare (a perfect pupil of science), and a sound like dumbbells striking the floor. Hands pulled at my pants, grasped at my thighs, climbed up to the hole torn out of my abdomen. Inspired by curiosity, I forcibly blinked myself to a semi-state of awareness and glanced downward—grasping at my belly and pulling it open as if it were a tent flap. Inside, knelt a horrifyingly familiar figure doused in gore like a child born of a lethal birth.

Why, I said, that's me.

"It does appear that way," the technician said, adding, "There's a word for this, isn't there? What was it..."

Autocannibalism, I said.

"I was thinking autosarcophagy."

And with a grunt I peeled my ribcage open. Hastily, I stuffed my face up into my torso, bobbing for organs. I wrenched my pelvic bone free as one might remove a tire from a car, and I clubbed the bone against the floor until it cracked just enough for me to begin sucking out the marrow.

"Why, oh why, is it that the English language has so many words that mean the same thing when just one will do? So unscientific."

I concurred through a mouthful of small intestine.

In short order, I had devoured from my feet up to my pale dead face, eyes glazed and uneven.

I saved my testicles for last, tossing the bloody little sack up into the air to catch them in my mouth; I munched and swirled the pulpy bits around in my mouth and swallowed with a triumphant, *ga-LUMPH*.

"Bravo," said the technician, rising to his feet with a hearty applause. "Bravo. Bra*vo*. Gods, it is men like yourself who keep the engine of science eternally revving."

The door to the patent trial room opened. In walked an orderly.

An eyeball I'd missed eluded my grasp, rolling away from my fingertips and rolling out into the hallway.

"This way, please," the orderly said, guiding me out of the room at such a pace that I hardly had time to bend and scoop up my eyeball and pop it into my mouth before we carried on down the hall.

The technician followed, announcing, "The road to hell is paved with *cowards* who are unwilling to pay the toll that progress demands..."

The orderly led me into a tiled room with a drain in the center.

"...to obtain knowledge, truth, or the well-guarded secrets of the universe..."

The orderly unraveled a hose laying on the floor.

"...and do they not say that great change is preceded by great violence?"

Adjusting the nozzle on the end of the hose, first to spritz and then to soak, the orderly began to spray me down, saying, "Turn, please," and "Touch your toes, if you would."

Blood, my blood, or the blood of that old dead me which bloated my belly and battled my digestive juices, washed off of me and ran down the drain like a waste of good wine.

I summoned a concussive belch; the orderly winced and the technician hummed with pride.

Once I was thoroughly wet and shivering, the orderly left the room.

The technician stood by my side, taking my face in his hands, saying, "Man," peering into my eyes with a wonder that made me weep, "*You* are one of the universe's well-guarded secrets."

The orderly returned with a towel and a change of clothes; the clothes were identical to the clothes that the orderly wore.

"However," the technician said, and his touch slipped away from my face, "there is work to be done."

And as I followed the orderly out of the room, I heard the technician say, "A wonder they always choose the blue cup."

RAINBOW ROCK

DEVIN OLDHAM

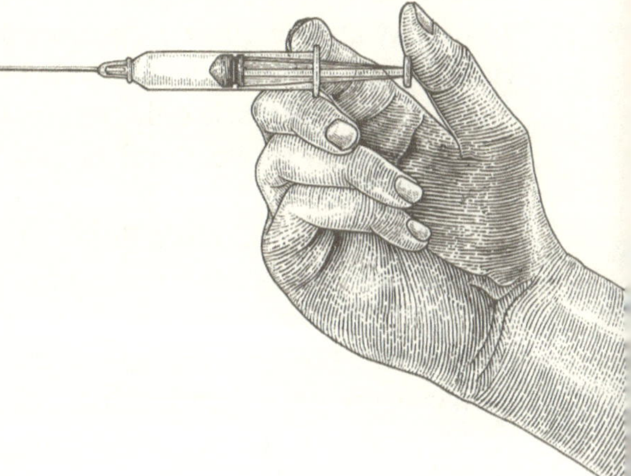

The apartment was located in what Jack's dad used to call "junkie isle," a towering block of four buildings flanking a small park called "Rainbow Rock."

Jack pulled his car into the mostly empty lot; he was greeted by a sculpture in the courtyard. The installation was a set of differently sized arches crossing over one another; they were rusty-red but Jack vaguely remembered a time when they had been painted as a rainbow. Though worn and unwelcoming, it stood in the center of the park like a bizarre monument to curved steel—an unintended reflection of the state of the buildings themselves.

Jack returned his eyes to the towers ahead and followed the hundreds of tiny windows toward the overcast sky. He produced a hastily scrawled address from his pocket and headed toward the second building next to where he had parked.

He crossed the lot and instinctively skirted around the tiny park.

The entrance to the complex was a set of double doors, one of which was covered in plywood, the other smeared with some kind of yellowish grease. He could see inside neither.

He considered pressing his cupped hands against the cloudy glass but opted to simply pull open the door. He'd be entering the building no matter what; Jack was out of options.

Inside, the entrance gave way to a musty, reeking hall. Decades of wallpaper peeled from centuries of paint, revealing the rotting wood and stained stone Jack assumed to be original to the structure. Even the brick looked decayed, like tightly packed sand, ready to crumble.

The hallway led to an elevator. Jack pressed the button to go up. It was sticky and he quickly withdrew his finger once the light turned on. He tried to wipe the residue on his thick wool sweater, but pulling his finger across the fabric only gathered an equally disgusting layer of fur.

"This better be worth it," he said to himself as the descending light stopped on the "G."

When the metal box's doors screeched open, Jack stepped inside. He was still vigorously rubbing his sticky finger on his sweater when the door chimed closed. The dissonance of the bell filled Jack with foreboding. The building, though empty, had an attitude he did not like. As if on cue, the neon light inside the cramped box flickered.

The smell inside the tight car was a mixture of human sweat and gasoline. It tingled the hairs in Jack's nose. He felt a bit dizzy and swooned briefly.

Instinctively, he covered his mouth, realizing, with horror, that he had smeared some of the sticky substance from his finger onto his upper lip. He frantically wiped at his face with his clean hand, coughing with disgust.

"You sick too?" a voice crooned from the corner.

The smell made a lot more sense to Jack when he turned and saw the hunched old woman.

Between heavy breaths, she inhaled from a plastic shopping bag; it left a green ring around the remaining skin of her protruding jaw.

"Excuse me?" Jack asked, unable to reconcile the words with the strange speaker.

The woman hobbled forward. The scent caused Jack to feel high again, like someone forcing him to sniff a dozen Sharpies.

She passed Jack, reaching for the button pad. For every floor, the corresponding button had been pried off. All except floor seven.

The button to floor seven was pristine. It glowed with a brilliant yellow shine. Maybe it was the fumes, but Jack thought it beautiful, serene even.

"Do you hear it humming?" The woman asked, as her elongated nail pushed into the plastic.

The elevator swayed, and the slight g-force of its upward movement made Jack want to hurl.

During its lumbering ascent, the woman approached Jack and placed her hand upon the left side of his stomach.

"You can feel it?" Jack asked.

"She's a big one."

The lump under Jack's skin seemed to respond positively to the lady's touch. She had a glow about her too, a serenity: her own "button-ness."

She was the first person other than Jack to ever see the lump. No doctors could find it. Anytime Jack would see a specialist, there would be nothing to show. Even a half-dozen ultrasounds revealed nothing. It was as if the lump swam through Jack's body like a creature beneath a murky lagoon; knowing when to surface, and when to hide.

The woman tickled the lump from over Jack's shirt. It bristled. She slid her nail up, and to Jack's amazement and horror, the lump moved slightly, following the gnarled finger.

"She wants to get all the way up there, to her home."

Jack stepped back. This was insane. He hadn't come to junkie isle to be felt up by some gassed-up granny.

"Mine died in '88," the lady said, staring forlornly at Jack's own protrusion. "But it brought me here too, like the rest."

Suddenly, the elevator shook to a halt and Jack was more than ready to get off. But the woman blocked his way.

She lowered her shirt collar, revealing a gnarled collarbone, and just above her left breast was a gaping hole. A pink and wet tunnel boring into delicate flesh.

"This is all that's left," she continued, now sobbing madly.

Jack tried to pass her but as he moved to one side, she matched him.

"Look at it!" the woman screamed.

The cavity of scar tissue undulated, the inner meat constricting and relaxing.

Jack reeled backward and finally threw up when he saw a white, withered slug-like thing squeeze itself from the hole.

It plopped to the grimy elevator floor and wriggled in a puddle of stringy slime.

Jack wiped his mouth of remaining vomit and barreled through the woman. He knocked her over and she hit the floor with an enormous thud.

Jack thought of her falling directly on top of the emaciated slug, splattering it, but his fear and revulsion overrode the concern. The doors closed and chime—a pathetic ding that rang tired through the musty hallway. He spit a final chunk of puke onto the carpeted floor and went on. He was alone, on floor seven.

Part 2

Jack lifted his shirt and checked on the lump. "What the fuck is inside there?"

He pushed a finger delicately into the mass, and felt it swim beneath the pressure.

It was born on his foot. He had come home from a two-day camping trip and spotted what looked like a tiny animal bite on the bottom of his sole.

After a few days, he couldn't walk; he felt like he had an acorn in the bottom of his shoe.

Eventually, it traveled upward, growing in size. For nearly a month, it lived on his left thigh. Jack refused to go to a doctor, afraid it was cancer.

Finally, one night, the thing started to pulsate, and a severe pain shot through his entire leg and into his spine, stiffening his back. He broke down and went to the emergency room. That was the first doctor to tell him that his lump simply *wasn't*.

Four doctors later, and Jack is here. In the Rainbow Rock apartments. Seeking the help of two home surgeons. "Experts" in illegal body modifications. The only people he could find that may be willing to dig around in there until they find something.

He walked to apartment seven-thirty-four and knocked. He was shaking, panicked by the already fading thought of the woman in the elevator. It was so distant, like he had watched it happen in a movie, but the adrenaline wasn't forgotten as fast.

The door creaked open, and a single eye peered beyond the chain lock.

"I'm here to see," Jack pulled out the crumpled paper upon which he had scrawled the doctor's name. "Spewn?"

The door shut, and Jack heard it unlock. When it opened the second time, he saw that the bachelor apartment had been emptied of all furniture, save for a solitary dentist's chair in the center of the room.

The man who let him in was in his sixties. He had long, sweaty gray hair that stuck to his pallid skin. He wore tiny round sunglasses despite the dimness of the space.

It took Jack a second look at the man's face to see that he had a disced bottom lip, like something from a National Geographic documentary. It was red, probably infected, and the skin there was purulent.

The guy stepped to the side and gestured for Jack to enter.

If the old woman in the elevator imparted a type of serenity to the lump, this couple did the opposite. Jack could feel his little friend retract somewhere deep inside of himself. He instinctively felt for it, and as usual, it was gone. This trip had been an especially grotesque waste of time. They would simply refuse to operate on him.

Just then, a woman came out from the bathroom area of the apartment. It had been sealed off with plastic and Jack saw that beyond the transparent sheet it actually looked relatively clean. She wore a surgical mask and Scooby-Doo scrubs.

She was remarkably normal looking. Except for what peaked out from her shoulder length black curls: tapered ears, sewn to look like those of a cat.

She spoke through the mask; her tone of voice and the way she carried herself made her out to be a doctor. Or at least, once a doctor.

"You don't look like you need your septum stretched, or ears clipped," she said on her way over to the tall hippie. She placed a hand on the guy's shoulder, and he gently closed the door, relocking the chain.

"Have a seat," she pointed to the dentist's chair.

Jack felt a vulnerability wash over him. She projected an authority that he'd attribute to any other healthcare professional.

"Are you Spewn?" Jack asked.

"That's what I am called here, and this is Brocca." She leaned against the curtained window, facing the chair. "So, if you don't need cat ears or a nose ring than why the fuck are you here?"

"I have … a lump," Jack responded.

"Then go see a real doctor."

"It … well … I." Jack was struggling. "This was a bad idea," he said as he started to rise from the seat.

"It moves?" she asked.

Jack stared at her in shock. He slowly lowered himself back into the chair.

"Where was the last place you saw it?"

Jack lifted his shirt and pointed to the left side of his stomach.

The woman placed her soft hand on Jack's bare skin. It felt nice to finally have someone believe him. And she was graceful, practiced, like a lump whisperer.

She rose from her crouch and spoke to Brocca in a language foreign to Jack. The man disappeared behind the plastic curtain and returned with a box.

He placed it on the surgical table next to Jack's chair.

Inside the box, Jack saw many objects, none of which appeared particularly medical. A leather-bound book, some rings and necklaces, all of it old, some ancient.

She dug through the bobbles for a moment and pulled out a chain, at the end of it hung a jagged symbol. It resembled a swastika, but the arms had their own set of arms. In the center of the shape, a triangle had been cut from the metal.

Spewn opened the curtains, and the entire apartment was bathed in diffused sunlight. Brocca reeled back and instinctively removed his sunglasses. The doctor crouched back down, her face intimately close to Jack's now exposed stomach. Over her head, Jack could see the courtyard beyond the window. He noticed the tops of the arches belonging to the rainbow sculpture—a constant reminder of where he was, and how he had gotten there.

The doctor, if she was one, pushed the metal sigil into where Jack had pointed. His soft, delicate skin protruded out from the triangle. "What are you doing?" he asked.

Spewn responded by pushing harder.

"Look, this is not what..." Jack began, but quickly closed his mouth.

The lump was moving. He felt it being forced out from somewhere around his spine. It almost felt like he could see what it saw. A liver or some other organ, blood, all the softness inside a person that is meant to remain within. But mostly, he felt the lump's reluctance.

It was being drawn to the surface. "That's the lump!" Jack yelled despite the intense pain. "What is it?"

Spewn signaled to Brocca. Jack couldn't see what new thing he was bringing her, but assumed it was some way to treat the infectious bump.

When she didn't answer, Jack asked again, or at least tried. But before he could speak, Brocca had, from behind, wrapped one arm around Jack's throat. The other covered his mouth.

Jack tried to scream. The lump throbbed like a second heartbeat; it was afraid.

The chaos escalated. Everything seemed frantic and Jack could not muster the strength needed to kick out. He still felt dazed from the hot-boxing in the elevator, and his peripheral vision was blackening.

When the lump made complete contact with the metal of the talisman, Spewn pressed hard enough to force it through the too small triangle. She pulled the talisman up and forced it to the center of Jack's chest. It was nothing like when the old woman had guided it. This time, the pain was unbearable. When Jack struggled too much from the pain, Brocca bore down on him and increased the pressure of his headlock.

Jack's will abated as Spewn dragged the mass up. He distantly felt the thing being carried up through his neck. Hot blood spilled from cracking skin as the triangle pulled the inflated skin up to Jack's cheek.

The sigil passed over Jack's left eye and the lump was drawn behind it. The pressure of the foreign object inside the ocular cavity caused the eyeball to pop from its socket; it hung, swaying.

Jack was awakened from his shock by a banging at the apartment door, accompanied by shrieks of terror.

"Don't let them kill her!"

Was it the old woman?

For a moment, Brocca let go. Jack felt life surging back into him. The pain, mixed with fear, sent forth a burst of adrenaline-fueled vigor.

"No! Hold him still! It's almost there." Spewn said, her tone still that of a professional.

Through his one functional eye, Jack saw that above the window was affixed a wooden poppet. Its head was the skull of a blackbird. And upon its stomach had been carved the same symbol Spewn used to guide the lump.

Jack kicked out and his boot connected with the doctor's midsection, and she flew backwards.

Brocca ran back from the door, leaving the crazed woman wailing on the other side.

Spewn held out a hand. "It's done."

Jack sprung up from his seat and screamed. He felt for his dangling eye and, as he cupped it in his palm, he saw his own hand. His forehead pounded with immeasurable agony.

Still buzzing with terror, he dashed for the door.

Brocca stopped him like a wall and gently guided him back to the seat. He pressed down on Jack's shoulders, pinning him in place.

Spewn drew a scalpel and carved a line in Jack's forehead.

The lump looked out. Seeing the world for the first time. A birth, like all births, without consent.

Jack too saw through it. And he looked upon some sister world. The serenity had returned. It now permeated his entire being. He didn't just feel serene, he had entered some fabled nirvana described only by mystics.

He dropped his left eye, letting it dangle; he no longer needed it. He saw the truth behind reality. In the sister world, the effigy of the crow was not of wood, but made of flesh and squawked with glee. He looked at Doctor Spewn; she wriggled and hissed, like a cat. Brocca looked much the same, but through the lump's lens Jack saw that he was merely flesh, stitched together by a skilled hand and given life by some glowing force beneath the skin.

Finally, Jack looked out from the window, and when he laid his eye upon the arches of Rainbow Rock, he saw they were no longer curved, but perfect rectangles. They stood tall against an ebony backdrop, radiating all colors. A testament to their name. The sky hung low enough to greet them on the black horizon. And the starless sky drooped low enough to touch.

Jack extended a hand toward the new beauty before him, laughing. The lump, the slug, fat and healthy, laughed along.

Brian the Brain

Lydia Elizabeth

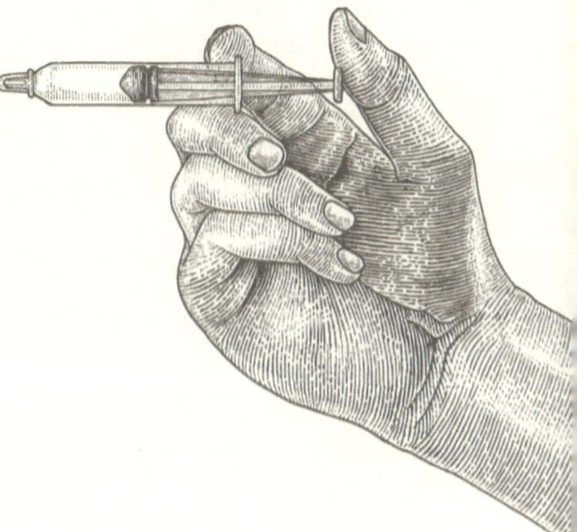

I was doing a whole lot of bumbling around, working at Smith Drug Company, when I really started hearing voices. It was sort of funny, the way I became my own puppeteer in this damn flesh prison. My alarm screeched at 5:42 a.m. every day for my shifts, waiting patiently while my body begged to slip back into rose-dusted sleep. Each morning, before my shift at Smith, I brewed greasy coffee in the big metal cup though my tired feeling never did ease. It only melted a little sometimes. I'd let the hot shower water run through my hair, too, hoping that would wake me up. I mostly did these things, you see, because my friends upstairs told me to. In my noggin, of course. They whispered to me that these little routines, these activities, rules even, would keep my threads of humanity pulsing. It all felt so delightful then.

But is *this* even living? Moldy showers and coffee grounds? At least these newfound friends—the voices—were held tight to my chest. I mean, hell, they were wrapped around my head itself! They were never sticky and artificial like this commercial hellscape I'd wound up in. Their new waxy skin melted atop my flesh, and I felt whole.

The linoleum floors and fluorescent lights of Smith Drug Company felt anything but human. If anything, it was a fuckin' alien planet in there! When I slithered through the massive sliding door, it was always the same. And I was always dead-tired there. I could tell deep down as the pit grew that I was playing the role of myself these days. It wasn't like I woke up pathetic and sickly like a little green goblin. It was a slow fire crackling the edge of a page. A knife turned inside of myself, slowly gutting me, hollowed out like a pumpkin.

I watched the whispers flume into my bitter coffee with a smug grin. It was as if their essence intertwined with my soul like an old lover. They muttered sentiments, or tidbits of information, and I embraced the chatter. More background noise at work. Friends to keep me company, and not with the fake niceties I had to play into at the Drug Company.

The voices weren't always so fuckin' friendly, though. Soon, they sucked the life out of me and placed it into a sealed-off vacuum. A whisper could be quickly accompanied by a bloodied scream or an order. Still, I found it better than listening to the buzzing of the lights above me or my coworker Sheryl's *tap tapping* acrylics on the register. The voices made me sick but everything else seemed to make me sicker.

I slipped out of the back door at work that afternoon to take a few drags from a cigarette. *For my nerves* I justified. The line of fuckin' customers was eternal that day. Sheryl and I gave each other glances between scans at the register. *Well this is going to be absolute hell, isn't it Brian?* Her eyes screamed out between sugary "*Hi, how may I help you?*"s. I could nearly feel my eyes burst out of my skull as I finished the cigarette, listening to the piercing voices above me.

I wandered off near an old bridge that reminded me of when I was younger, stupider, happier. There was a lovely river pulsing underneath where I stood. The sky was dust-colored and eternal that day, sun dipped like an egg yolk over top. I looked into the Sun's loving eyes, and I let her take me.

The most lovely crimson hue washed over my eyes. I felt safe for the first time in a long time. The beam beckoned me to step forward. It stroked my cheek and told me I would reach eternal happiness, that I would find the truth. It grew louder and *louder* and LOUDER. I couldn't get it to stop. I banged my head against a lamppost. Nothing changed. She was still there, holding my face, urging me onward to the truth. So I did what She said: gave in. I leaped from the old bridge into the cool blue, which was more like concrete on my bones. The water was truth and light away from all of this bullshit.

I awoke bruised, creaking, ogling as my veins were illuminated by stark, fluorescent lights. Sort of like the Drug Company's. *Why the fuck am I back here?* I opened up my hand to find a little bit of metal stuck inside of my wrist. The metallic smell filled my nose and mixed with an odd vinegary fluid. I realized this was not Smith Drug Company at all.

I tried jolting around my post at the hospital bed, but they strapped me down entirely, with mystery fluid dripping into my veins. My innards were stretched further by so many wires and tubes and trinkets. The suffocating wires wrapped around me like a python.

A creaking, old surgeon stepped into the sterile room to speak with me.

"Sir, can you explain why we found you at the bottom of the river?" he asked, his unblinking eyes ogling me.

I was already stuck here, so I figured, fuck it, why not give him a little story? I had better just explain the whole thing. I droned on and on about my voices and their bizarre, yet precious, nature. *Maybe someone will finally understand...* Before I could finish articulating, I heard a sour whisper.

"We had better bring in the psychiatrist," he said to another white lab coat.

I felt life draining out of my face. I was a puppet hopped up on drugs and wires. I could hardly keep track of the various figures in masks and long coats and stethoscopes. The psychiatrist looked slightly more human with a funny little tweed suit. He looked like a small British man to me in that outfit. I guffawed at the sight of him. He looked puzzled, then sat down next to me, trying to make me feel at ease, I suppose. *Fuck you fuck you fuck—*—the voices started up again. His presence and false niceties made me want to vomit up all the pink candy-medicine they had dripped into my body. Despite my initial lack of regard for the psychiatrist, he had these piercing cyan eyes that sent chills down my spine. I had never seen eyes so blue, so convicted. When I told him my story, those same eyes squealed with delight.

"We have never had the opportunity to study a patient quite like this. This may be groundbreaking for our work," he divulged to his lab assistant, but his sheer trepidation made their muttered sentences quite clear to me. This was the last I remember before a wash of gas poured over me and I was dipped into a dark cavity of time and space.

I regained consciousness slowly, woke up groggy and sour. *Where the hell am I now?* I could see it was the same lab, but—*holy fuck, am I seeing that right? What the actual fuck? How am I conscious? Did they mean to do this? These sick fucks, these monsters!*

I realized there was a strange wash over my eyes. I seemed to be placed on a metal shelf and I could see where the shell of my human body used to lie. He who lies there was me, Brian. Now, I am The Brain. If I had a mouth to laugh with, trust me, I would have cackled.

Just when you think your low-life job is the shittiest thing about your life...
Well now they've got me floundering in this terrible germicidal marinate,
some enigmatic aquamarine brine. All I know is that it smells absolutely
foul. I can only assume this was an experimental surgery, to say the least.
After all, my nerves and eyeballs were placed in the pickling fluid, too.
God only knows how they accomplished that one.

I slowly pieced together what they were trying to do, or if it was, they
succeeded. My brain had been stripped of the voices. Now, I'm not only
just The Brain, I am *my* Brain. All of the thoughts that the whispers had
muddled are clear as day as I float around in here, a stupid sea sponge
with only my own conscious for comfort. Which is *not* comforting, at all.
I hate those fucking lab coats for that. I despise the looming, bald psychiatrist who pretended to be my friend. In this jar, you see, no part of
me touches the outside world. I'm sealed off. My only associate is this
desolate, antiseptic land. There is nothing humanoid about my current
experience. I am sterile and sealed away and *hidden.* I imagine the masses
ogling at me, including my coworker Sheryl, their stomachs churning with
disgust, for I am a reflection of their truest, cerebral selves.

The doctor slid open the bitter, infertile door to the room which con-
tains my entrails. I watched in agony as he dug into my body with scal-
pels and iris scissors. It was absolutely vile, watching him carve into what
remained of Brian like he was only a juicy Thanksgiving turkey.

I could tolerate it no longer. I gathered every ounce of rage I have
felt throughout my life and flung myself, brine and all, toward the doctor.
The glass bounced across the room, landing on the doctor's cheek. He
was knocked down hard against the cold linoleum beneath his feet.

With the doctor unconscious, I figured this was my real chance. My
brain squealed with delight. I slithered over to my shell of a body, cold
and propped up on a metal table. I could move this brain apparatus more
easily than I expected, even more easily than my human body, perhaps.

I made my way up, slowly creeping up the table to my own body. It
was the most bizarre sensation I have ever experienced. I could watch
it all from afar, as my eyes were trapped in the jar. It was perfect though,
as I could double-check that the doctor was still knocked out on the
floor every so often.

Once I made it up to my body, I groveled through the opening in
my skull back into my brain. It was dark and clammy there. I waited in
anticipation.

Fuck, is anything going to happen? Is my idea completely fruitless?

I panicked inside the shell of my former self, until I felt a visceral *zap!*

The doctor loomed over me and hooked my body up to wires and trinkets.

What the actual fuck is he doing to me?

Before I knew it, I was back to being Brian. Or, at least, some version of him. They must have given me some more of the disgusting, dripping medicine because I blacked out during the entire operation. Maybe it was better that way, I suppose. I woke up outside of the office, where they dumped me. Their secret operation couldn't be foiled. If I knew where I was, it would be a liability, sure. I felt such immense rage at the lack of explanation, the lack of regard for my body, the utter pain that I felt from the surgery.

What was I now? A monster? A brain? A person?

They had successfully ridded me of the voices, but what now? Am I doomed to live an eternal life of my *own thoughts?* I shuddered at the idea and vomited bile by the side of the road. For some reason, though, all I could worry about after that was work. I lifted my thumb up and waited, alone and pathetic on the edge of the land, waiting for a kind stranger.

An older trucker sipping on a Bud Light stopped when he saw my thumb.

"You don't look so good, buddy ... need a lift?"

"Christ, you wouldn't believe it..."

So off we went, back into town. It all felt like a bizarre dream. In my gut, I felt that's what those grimy white lab coats wanted it to feel like and I became enraged once more. I sat in the hot truck stewing in my own misery.

The trucker told me about his life on the road, how this was just a passing stop for him, not his home. He came from the big state of Texas where everything was bigger and better. God, how I grew jealous of his freedom, his nonchalance, and his non-surgical brain.

"Thanks for the lift, really, you don't know how much it means," I told him as I shut the door. He gave me a gentle smile and geared up again.

So there I was, back at Smith Drug Company. I started sweating, thinking of what my boss would do. *How long was I gone? Was I acting differently?*

I started into the biting fluorescence, listening to the clock *tick, tick tick* at me.

"Well, well, well, look who it is..." my boss chuckled at me. "You don't look so hot."

"Yeah, I know. Sorry," was all I could think of to say.

"Brian, you can't just leave for a smoke break and never come back, you know. Do you know how busy Sheryl was at the register? You can't be doing that shit."

I sighed and apologized. He was always a hard ass. No use in explanations, I figured.

"You're fired," he told me solemnly.

I stuttered for a minute, fumbling with my words. I debated explaining the whole thing to him until I figured, not only am I a monster now, but I seem like a liar. *Fuck.* I grabbed my things from my locker and walked over to my favorite bridge from my childhood home.

I stood there, letting the breeze slap my face until I felt the slightest bit alive again. I pulled out another cigarette. *The rat race begins again...*

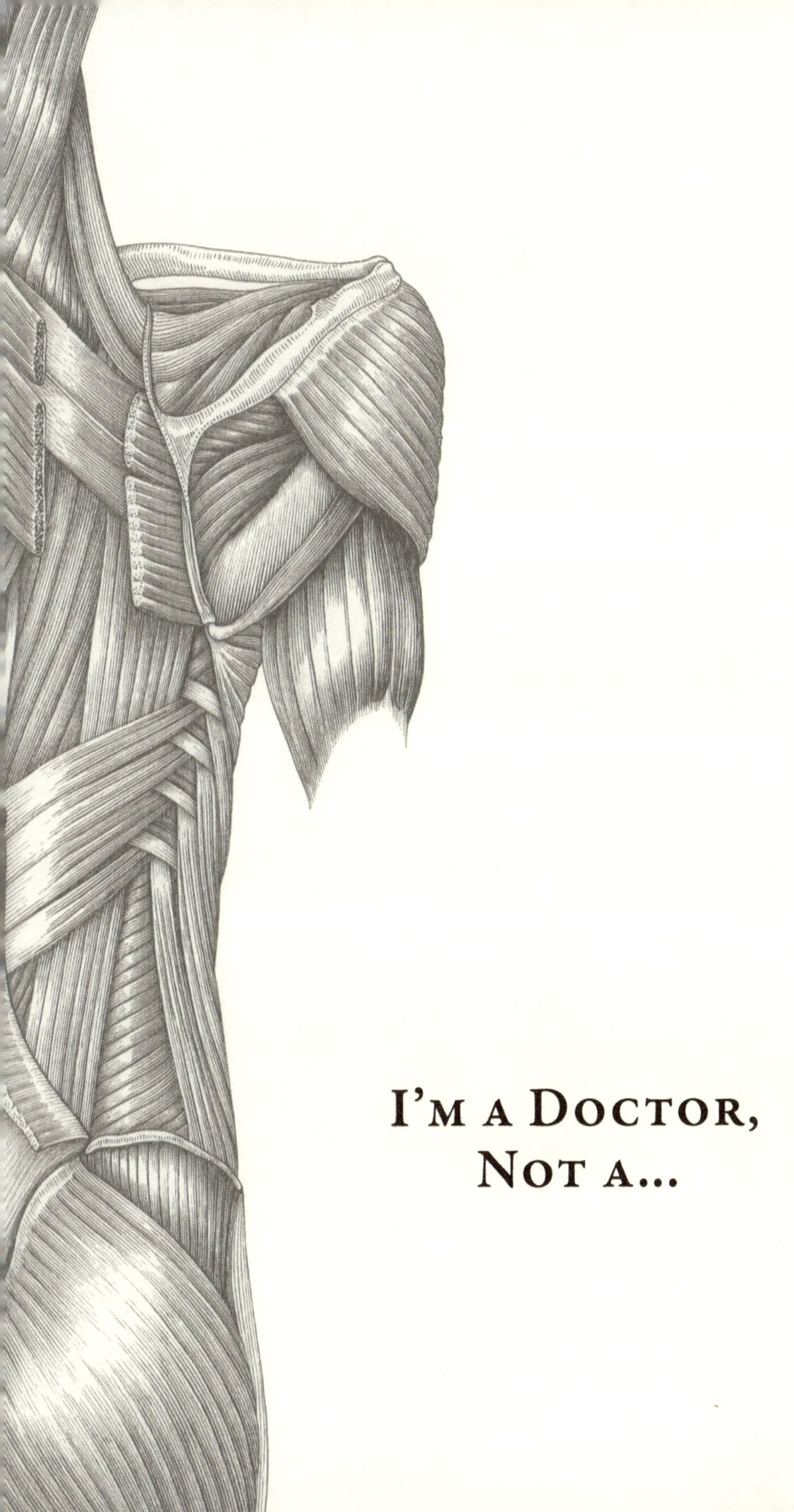

I'm a Doctor,
Not a...

MY BROTHER'S KEEPER

ALEXIS AUROL

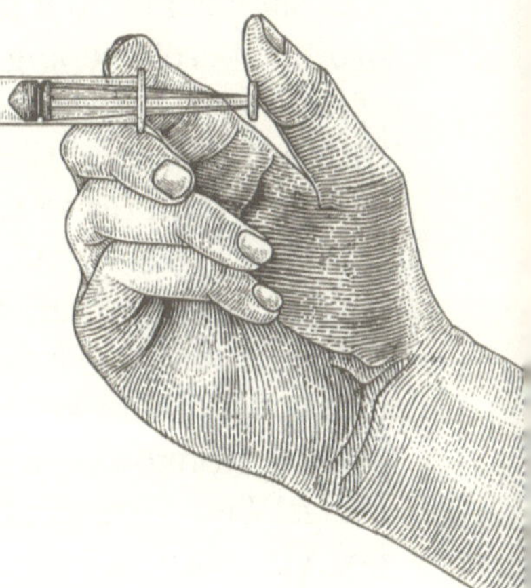

My older brother is a doctor, and for my entire adult life, I have consulted him about any illness. He has always said I am just cheap, but it really is about trust. My mother died when I was quite young from an incorrect dose on a prescription written by her doctor. I have long thought that her death was the impetus for Samael's choice of medicine.

Now that he has died and become a demon, I am in a quandary. It is not the undead part, but the demon part that concerns me. I mean, he may have lost his license when he died but he didn't lose his memory. He should be current with medicine for at least another twenty-five years, longer if he keeps reading his journals. Long enough to last my lifetime.

But aren't demons supposed to be evil? It sort of goes against the Hippocratic Oath. Did his oath die with him or does his current oath to the devil supersede it? Is there a family exemption? Too many questions.

He only drops in for brief visits. Just enough time to get a quick medical question answered, not enough time to delve into a philosophical discussion of what it means to be a demon.

I don't really understand his choices. I mean, he is ten years older, so we didn't spend a lot of time under the same roof, but in the forty-six years I have known him, nothing suggested an aspiration to live down below.

Samael has always leaned towards herbal and homeopathic remedies, so I thought nothing of it when he prescribed monkshood for a rash on my leg that turned into an infection. Then I found out that the plant's alternate name is wolf's bane, and it might have been used—rather than hemlock—to poison Socrates. I changed to a topical corticosteroid and told Samael I ran out of his cream. The first seeds of doubt in my demon brother were creeping in.

My next ailment was lower back pain. The diagnosis was osteoarthritis and he prescribed grapple plant. This was a much-diluted remedy, so I took comfort in the fact it wasn't as toxic. Then I found out it was called devil's claw. What on earth was Samael playing at?

Over the next few months, I had a stomach upset and he prescribed a medicine based on henbane, unfortunately also called devil's eye. Sciatica was treated with belladonna—devil's cherries. Kidney stones led to a prescription for a spice called food of the gods, but also known as devil's dung. When he treated the flu with yarrow, I thought things were looking up. A cursory investigation showed it was also called nosebleed which I felt wasn't too bad. Then I found out that it was otherwise known as devil's nettle or devil's plaything.

I finally confronted him. At first, he brushed me off.

"Many common plants have unusual names. Fenugreek is known as bird's foot, St John's wort as goat's ears, foxglove as bloody fingers, snapdragon as dog's mouth, valerian as capon's tail, and so on."

"Yes, but Samael, none of those names sound as bad as all the medicines you prescribed me. Most have the word 'devil' in them. I know wolf's bane doesn't sound as bad, but it was used to protect against werewolves. I am almost surprised you didn't prescribe garlic to ward off vampires or rue to ward off an evil magic. I don't know what you might prescribe to ward off faeries."

He said absently, "it is much better to appease faeries by leaving gifts—maybe butter or milk—than to try to ward them off."

"So, there is a purpose to your prescriptions."

"Yes, getting you better. Other plants have more sinister names such as horehound a.k.a bulls' blood, or plantain, known as adder's tongue. Several traditional plant names are oddly disturbing. It doesn't detract from their useful properties."

"Still not named after the devil."

"If I wanted to ward off evil, basil is much more effective than rue."

"Still avoiding my questions."

"This is ridiculous."

With that he dissipated.

I knew when I had been blown off. I would have to dig deeper. My dispute with Samael distracted me from the purpose of his visit: my upset stomach. I had to pick up some Pepto-Bismol.

Maybe the problem with my relationship with Samael wasn't merely the age difference. I only called him when I was ill. That would have to change. I also needed to understand him better. I mean, why would a doctor, if he wasn't Josef Mengele, become a demon? Why did he die so young anyway?

The thing about Samael was that he was always so disgustingly healthy. He never even had a cold or an allergy. I suppose it is a good quality for a doctor to have, being around contagious diseases all day, but it isn't a family trait. Most of us have more than our share of medical complaints. That was why it was so darn useful having a doctor in the family.

But Samael is different in so many ways. He is an Adonis of a man—exceptionally tall with an eight pack; longish, curly, blond hair; a chiseled jaw; and blue eyes the color of a crystal mountain lake. This wasn't my description. My wife, but then girlfriend, had described him thus upon first sight. She wasn't the only woman to swoon over him. He had that effect on most women and a good number of men. It made for an amazing bedside manner.

By contrast, I take after most of my family. I am average—average height, average weight, average looks. I have dark hair and a steadily receding hairline. I expect to be entirely bald by age seventy. No one is going to write poems about my brown eyes. I have also never been a ladies' man.

Another contrast between Samael and me is our intelligence and interests. Samael loved school and became a doctor. I never did well in my classes and considered a job indoors to be a penance rather than a career. I started a business as a home contractor because I liked to work with my hands. I concentrated on family and raising my two kids. Samael was off saving the world. When he was alive, he was not only a healer, he was a humanitarian. He volunteered for Doctors Without Borders and traveled around the world providing medical care. His quest for sainthood had probably added to our disconnection.

I decided I needed another perspective and went to talk to Aunt Ellen. She had virtually raised us after my mother's death. My father had thrown himself into work. Aunt Ellen had ensured there were meals on the table, listened to our woes, checked our homework, and, in my case, kissed any injuries better.

"I think you can guarantee that your brother's choice to become a demon serves a higher purpose."

"What do you mean?"

"He had to choose to bind his soul, correct?"

"I suppose he could be tricked into it."

"Does that seem likely? He is a very intelligent man."

"Okay, he chose."

"When he was fifteen, he was suspended from school for fighting. He was defending a younger boy. He had to change colleges because he took the blame for a stupid party thrown by his fraternity brothers."

"It is one thing to start a fight, it is another to serve an evil master."

"It is only a matter of degree. He has the soul of a martyr."

I sat back in the chair and Aunt Ellen poured me more tea. "I always thought he was aiming for sainthood."

"No, Seth. Sainthood implies an innate goodness but also a desire for recognition. Martyrdom, in my books at least, comes from a need for suffering to feel validated."

"Why would he need to suffer?"

"I can't tell you."

"Could he just be a masochist and want to feel the fire?"

"I think he needs a purpose to his suffering, even if it is not a reason we would consider valid. When he was about six, he attached his tongue to the gate by licking the metal during the winter. It wasn't unusual amongst the children. At that age they seem to need to test things out for themselves. The boys are particularly susceptible to dares. Samael was advanced for his age, so I was surprised he still needed to experiment for himself. I thought he must have done it on a dare. He did in a way. His best friend was dared. Samael knew what the result would be and that it would be painful. He took up the challenge on his friend's behalf."

Aunt Ellen had given me a lot to think about. When I left her house, I chose to walk home and think. I passed a soup kitchen, then stopped and backed up. I looked through the window to see Samael serving up the food. What demon would do that?

I went in to confront Samael.

"You might be the first demon to be canonized."

He paused in dishing up the plates and looked around. No one appeared to pick up on my demon comment.

"We'll talk later when we have some privacy. I'll come to your office."

It was past office hours, so I was able to catch up on some paperwork while I waited. Samael arrived about two hours after me. "That was a long dinner hour. I was afraid you stood me up."

"We were short-handed today, so I had to help with the clean-up."

He didn't seem inclined to volunteer any information, so I asked, "What were you doing at the soup kitchen? It seems like a strange place to find a demon."

"It's a secular operation. I don't need to interact with any clergy."

"Samael, I want answers. If I don't get them, I plan to haunt every place where you are doing good works until I get them."

"I am there undercover recruiting souls."

"Have you found any?"

"One, maybe two."

"That doesn't seem to fit with your character. I had to stretch my imagination to think of you giving up your own soul. It is beyond belief that you are recruiting others."

"I suppose I should be flattered."

"Don't be. Just tell me the truth."

"There are always a few people who choose a dark path. Nothing will save them. Offer them something that appeals to their greed, and they will willingly sign over their soul. They know they will be heading to hell in any case. Why not profit in the short-term?"

"So why recruit at all?"

"I have to work at something to fulfill my contract. At the soup kitchen, I can do some good while I recruit."

"Why not provide medical care?"

"I no longer have a license."

"I bet there are some parts of the world where only your skill would matter, not a piece of paper."

"As part of my demon contract, I had to give up medicine. There is a loophole that doesn't consider herbal remedies to be 'medicine.' But I am still restricted in what I can use. I was told wolf's bane wasn't adequately evil. Since then, I have only used remedies with demon or devil in the name. Some are less toxic than wolf's bane, but it seems that it is the name not the potency which is of concern."

"So, if I need an operation I am on my own?"

"You always were. I provide family medicine. I can give you a referral to a good surgeon though."

"What did you gain through selling your soul? It certainly wasn't a long life."

"There was a chlorine gas leak in the poor part of town. We all were doomed. It might have eventually covered the whole city. Many of the people would not have died in a state of grace. I bargained for the entire natural lifespan for all those affected by the leak. It not only saved thousands of lives, it allowed people to turn their lives around and save their souls. I had to die immediately. What is one man's life and soul compared to the lives of thousands?"

I didn't want to debate philosophy. But I doubted if many others would have made the same bargain.

"So, this is it. You spend eternity trying to fit good works in amongst a few evil deeds."

"Pretty much."

"I don't believe you. I know you. You are incredibly intelligent. I think you have an angle."

"No angle. I merely adhere to the letter of the contract. The devil obviously hasn't had a good lawyer look it over for several centuries. There are hundreds of loopholes. I intend to exploit every single one."

"That sounds more like you. What can I do to help? I am your brother, after all."

Samael smiled. We got down to considering the contract, clause by clause.

The first thing we found was that although Samael had been told that wolf's bane was not allowed, it was not explicitly written in the contract. If the whole range of herbal and homeopathic remedies were opened up to him, he would have an extensive list of treatments. Acupressure, acupuncture, and an array of non-western treatments were also possible. The contract only said that he could not continue to practice medicine in the manner he had before.

We consulted the internet to peruse legislation and legal cases. Chiropractors, midwives, emergency medical technicians, and nurse practitioners were also not considered to be doctors. PhDs were often not doctors although they participated in clinical trials.

I argued that since the phrase was "not continue to practice medicine as before" if he could get new accreditation, he might be able to become a surgeon or oncologist. Samael wasn't as certain of that interpretation as I was. Since he would be the one to take any punishment if he broke the contract, I deferred to him.

The contract also didn't specify that he needed to be evil one hundred percent of the time. That was obvious since he was working for charities. He only had to complete a quota of evil acts. Since it was difficult to recruit people to sell their souls, his quota for this work was much lower. There were a lot of blackhearted people on the lower east side where Samael was plying his trade —drug pushers, pimps, pedophiles, crime bosses, and the like—so meeting his quota didn't seem to be a problem.

We worked through most of the night and still had hundreds of pages of the contract to work through. Samael no longer needed to sleep but I did. We broke up our meeting and agreed to get together again the following week. This was going to be a marathon, not a sprint.

We carried on for several months. Some nights, we only got through one or two clauses. Samael implemented what we discovered as we went along. He was pretty much practicing a modified form of medicine full time. He had even decided it was worth the punishment to attempt to get accreditation as a surgeon. It took some sidestepping, but he was allowed to attend college in a far-flung country based on the endorsement of a colleague from Doctors Without Borders. Being able to dissipate and reappear anywhere in the world at will, aided in time management.

We were having one of our meetings when the devil appeared. He was a very handsome man. I shouldn't have been surprised. It would take an attractive personality and great charm to convince so many people to sell their souls. A good-looking facade wouldn't hurt. At the moment, however, he was choked with anger. His face was red, and his eyes bulged. Aunt Ellen used to tell me not to make a face or my features might stay like that. I wondered whether anyone had mentioned that to the devil.

After a few incoherent noises, he was finally able to produce a sentence. He pointed at Samael. "*You.* You have managed to do more good works than an entire monastery. You are ruining my reputation."

Samael answered, "I meet my quotas. I do everything by the contract."

"But not in the spirit of evil."

"What attitude I should take is not in the terms. Besides, how could I convince anyone if they didn't like me first? I am certain you use the same technique."

I thought the devil might have a seizure. But it was only a tantrum. He let loose a torrent of abuse and curses.

"How I approach a target is not relevant. It is your behavior that is in question. You work at charities. You minister to the poor and sick. What are you doing?"

"Completing my contract."

"Blast the contract. I'll void the contract."

"No."

What was Samael playing at? I would have taken the offer and ran. It showed what I knew.

"What do you mean no? You can't say no to me."

The devil was in full tantrum mode, dancing around and waving his arms.

Samael said, "If you merely void the contract, all those people will die, including me. I want more."

"What?"

"All the benefits I bargained for remain, including but not limited to, the lives that would have been lost in the chlorine leak. I get my soul back and at least twenty-five more years of a healthy life. You don't interfere with me or mine again in perpetuity."

"I can't," the devil bit out. "It might set a precedent."

"Fine. I can continue as is. But perhaps I'll talk to my peers about our contracts. We could review each contract in detail. Maybe it's time the demons unionized."

"You wouldn't."

"I don't think I give you enough credit for my actions. I should probably talk up your contribution to my charitable work."

"I'll have a new contract drawn up."

"No need. I have one right here—plain language, no legalese, only two pages."

The devil and Samael signed the contract in triplicate, and I witnessed it. I was certain the devil would get his mojo back. It might take a while though. He looked inconsolable when he left.

I turned to Samael. "You had a contract already drafted."

"You know I believe in being prepared. It wasn't hard to predict that the devil would be angry with my behavior. The only question was how he would react. I trusted in the contract. I have to say, the one year of law school I took before switching to medicine has been very useful."

I just shook my head.

I thought Samael would return to family medicine. However, it seemed that in bargaining to retain all of the benefits he received under the initial contract, he kept his ability to dissipate and the lack of need for sleep. It gives him incredible time management skills. He is continuing his surgical residency and his good works. I insisted that he see a psychiatrist. I want him to curb his martyr tendencies. If things work out, Samael may become the first saint who was once a demon. The beatified Bartolo Longo was once a satanic priest, so the path to open.

Malpractice

Julie Kathleen McNeely-Kirwan

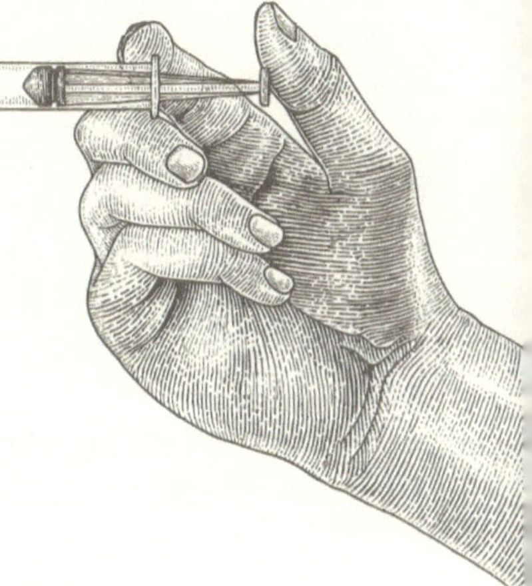

"You will not like this."

There was satisfaction in my doctor's voice, but what did I expect? Most inhuman healers were part daemon. "Kindly" would not be the word to describe them.

"I did not think I would," I responded, keeping my tone carefully neutral.

We sat in a room that vaguely resembled a Victorian doctor's office, somewhere in Phoenix. The room looked conventional at first glance, but every detail veered wrong. The flowers on the wallpaper were distorted and looked as if they might bite. The glass display cases contained biological specimens, but these were the stuff of nightmares. The furniture was overstuffed, over-sized, and brothel-red. The soft background music featured singing in a language unknown to living humans and was occasionally punctuated by choruses of low purgatorial screaming.

Daemons. They never quite get the human stuff right.

In this room there were no disinfectant odors, no needles or swabs, and nobody was going to check my reflexes with one of those little rubber mallets. Daemon healers did not examine. They Saw.

That is what my white-coated and otherworldly doctor had done. With her gemstone eyes she had Seen into my core, past an assumed surface and flesh.

"Tell me," I urged her.

My doctor was some kind of hybrid. Had to be. Because there were not only claws on display, but leaves, feathers, and some really good designer shoes. What her daemon lineage was mixed with was hard to say. Possibly a forest spirit. It was hard to be sure. My inhuman brethren can't keep their tentacles off each other. Nor did they try. Give one pack of shape-changing psychopath hunters a week of vacation and, nine months later, there will be a whole new breed of beasts warring to take over some corner of the cosmos. Or Scottsdale. Usually it's just Scottsdale they're fighting over.

Why Scottsdale? Maybe because, as cities go, it's materialistic and hot. Probably makes some of them feel more at home. Or it could be just a place where more of the populace is selling what some of my brethren are trying to buy.

There's nothing like a marketplace to bring sentients together.

"Please just tell me what the problem is and what I need to do about it." I tried to keep the pleading out of Clara's voice.

The doctor continued to sit there with her claws clasped together primly on her gigantic library desk. I realized she was waiting for payment. As if anyone of my piddling magical stature would even try to stiff a daemon physician.

Sighing, I handed over a small canvas bag, remarkably heavy for its size. I also gave the doctor an envelope. The finest linen paper, black, with opalescent white ink. (Never give anyone with a fraction of daemon DNA anything signed in blood, or red ink that can be mistaken for blood. It leads to all kinds of misunderstandings.)

Dr. Shoal carefully opened the bag and counted out the standard twelve pieces of gold, gently nipping a couple along the edges to be sure they were real. (Her canines could intimidate a werewolf. And probably had.) She then opened the envelope, slicing it with a long, chitinous claw sharper than any letter opener. In it was the name and address of a profoundly beautiful human being with an unusual outlook. Put briefly, this human being viewed other human beings in the same way a mountain lion views bunnies.

The doctor blew upon the note and my handwriting began to glow deeply. I could sense the doctor's satisfaction over the quality of my find, as confirmed by the glow. What Dr. Shoal wanted with this person, I didn't know. Or care. This human was breathtaking to look at, but the fact that she was an intra-species predator made this particular Beauty fair game for the Beasts.

Having made sure of payment, Dr. Shoal sat back and did her best to eye me with something like professional medical concern.

The truth was, she looked kind of amused. It annoyed me.

"You are possessed." She had the kind of fake British accent any American celebrity would envy.

I sat in an enormous Victorian chair, puzzled, waiting for the joke to be explained. No explanation was forthcoming.

"To be possessed requires a physical body," I said, trying to sound respectful instead of impatient. "I have no physical body. I am the spirit who possessed this body."

I gestured downward at my respectably clean, reasonably attractive, female body. Really, I took rather better care of my current vessel—a martyred and perpetual family caregiver—than the actual owner ever had been. Who came up with the auburn dye job and good haircut? Who ordered yoga pants in the correct size and flattering colors? Who scheduled the spa days?

Me, that's who. And did my host complain? Never.

Which turned out to be the problem.

Dr. Shoal looked at me and shook her head. "Why do we not possess those whose minds are mostly gone? Why do we avoid the very young? Because the takeover of a human body must be non-consensual. Proper possession requires resistance. Your human subject is actively cooperating."

I stared stupidly at Dr. Shoal in hopes that I misunderstood. She stared back, apparently disgusted by my determined lack of understanding. She tried again.

"The original owner of the body not only ceased to resist—she voluntarily ceded the body to you, making you the owner—but she never left and now she has started to interfere. This makes you the one who is possessed."

"And now that I want to leave?" I asked in growing horror.

Shoal went on in her oh-so-upper-class accent. "She's fighting you, clutching on with everything she's got. Apparently, it has something to do with a—what do humans call it—a genetically-based orgy of mutual pain infliction?"

"A family reunion. Yeah. She answered the phone one day while I was napping and there was her ghastly old mother in Florida. Declared it was Clara's turn to host the family get-together. Clara's already being bombarded with phone calls from relatives asking her when she's going to have their flights scheduled."

"Yes. A family reunion. Like weddings, but without the human sacrifices?"

"Um ... yeah."

I did not bother to correct her. Metaphorically-speaking, Dr. Shoal had been correct.

Sounding obscenely cheerful, Dr. Shoal added one last spoonful of poison to my stew of misery. "But it's worse than that. There is a good chance this Clara creature will never let you go. Or, anyway, not as long as she lives. Her will is considerable and she ... likes you."

The not-so-good doctor shuddered with distaste at the mere concept of human attachment. I shuddered, too, but my shuddering related more to the specifics. After decades trapped in a body with Clara who knows what bad habits I might pick up? I'd probably start knitting or worrying about how other people felt. Yech.

Dr. Shoal sat back comfortably and clasped her clawed hands, smiling in satisfaction. "Well, that's all the time I have for."

"Wait!" I yelled. "You're supposed to tell me what to do to get out of Clara! That's what I paid you for!"

"Yes, and normally I would help you resolve this problem. But watching it play out would be so much more fun."

And then Dr. Shoal smirked. But her self- satisfaction didn't last long.

As my anger rose, something began happening on the huge desk, near Dr. Shoal's elbow. The black note where I'd written the Beauty's information started to smoke, then caught fire and rapidly turned to ash. Dr. Shoal shot up from her seat and stared at me angrily, flushing blood red.

I did my best to look bored.

Furious now, she leapt out from behind the huge desk, waving her hideously clawed appendages, her demonic face fixed in a snarl.

I stared at her, unmoved. I was no major magical power, but that made no difference when it came to transactions among our kind. We do have our rules.

My voice was ice cold. "You know as well as I do. Under Daemonic Law, a deal is a deal. I just burned the name and address you wanted so badly. But it is also probably peeling away from your perfect daemon memory—because you don't get to keep what you didn't pay for. You didn't give me a way to fix this. No cure, no Beauty. You could have tricked me into giving you what you wanted—Heaven knows your kind loves trickery—but you didn't even do that successfully."

Dr. Shoal growled and lunged toward my face, curling her knife-like fingers as if to rake them across my borrowed flesh.

I chuckled and Dr. Shoal went silent, startled by my cavalier attitude. "Go ahead. I have always gravitated toward risk takers. Violent death is nothing new to me. My bodies have died in a hundred wars. I've died in car accidents, plane crashes, and ship sinkings. I've been burned at the stake and shot; not to mention stabbed, throttled, and defenestrated. I died from both major forms of the plague and the sweating sickness. Bears ate me, bricks fell on me. I once suffocated and baked in a tsunami of molasses. Can you top that?"

Never ask stupid questions. The daemonic doctor leaned forward and cut my throat from ear to ear. But quite shallowly, so that a single drop gathered and ran from the scratch. The scratch stung like it was packed with salt, but it was nothing compared to pain I had known before.

Besides, I never did know when to shut up. "Go ahead. Slice and dice me. I'll resist. It is, after all, required. As you well know, I cannot kill or permit to die, any human body that I occupy, not on purpose. The human being I share a body with can make those decisions, but not me. But you have ten times my strength and twice my speed. We both know how it ends.

"So you kill this body and what happens? You send a troubled soul to Heaven—your Boss is gonna love that—and I get to go on my merry way. You will have solved my problem and done so without getting the name you wanted. Wouldn't look good, would it?"

I leaned back, eyebrows raised. Dr. Shoal was looking less furious and more worried. She backed off, then slunk to her chair behind the library desk.

In a moment or two she was calm again, if a touch sulky. Daemons were like that.

"Twice? I have five times your speed. And I want that name and address back. My healing class reunion is having a Competitive Seduction with the usual finale, and we need several humans the Other Side won't quibble about. I want mine to be the best."

I grimaced. If you want to know what a daemon means by the "usual finale" for a seduction, don't think cigarettes or snuggling, think "praying mantis."

"Oh, there won't be any quibbling. The Other Side has little claim to this particular human. As for the best, who can say? But it is rare to find anyone so beautiful on the outside and so very dangerous on the inside," I said, trying to be my most persuasive.

Dr. Shoal huffed again, but I foolishly hoped she was done trying to welsh on her end of the bargain. I waved my hand, taking a chance.

The note reappeared on the desk, unburning, the smoke sucking away and the ashes turning back into paper. It was all deception, of course. I could easily create illusions, but truly restoring a destroyed object takes enormous effort.

After one more dirty look, the doctor snatched up the note and tucked it into a pocket of her white coat. Then she looked at me and held a clawed finger up to her sharp-toothed mouth. This was the universal gesture of secret-keeping.

She wanted to make sure Clara wasn't in on our next conversation.

I closed my eyes and used my rapidly depleting energies to check that Clara was still in a deep sleep and would not rouse soon. Clara slept from 10 until 6, like clockwork, so I had crept out in the middle of the night for my appointment, first deepening her natural rest with the kind of dream humans have trouble tearing themselves away from.

In my enhanced dreamland, Clara was currently in the middle of a never-ending buffet of chocolate. Thanks to me, she could actually taste it. She had also somehow managed to invite her recently-deceased grandmother—Dina certainly wasn't in my script—and the two were giggling around the buffet table tossing bits of fudge at each other. Odd, for two such serious women. I began to enjoy watching them.

"Excuse me," said Dr. Shoal, her fake British accent maxed out. She apparently had one more snarky remark to make and wanted to be sure of my full attention. Daemons always did want the last word. "Your human has some truly astonishing anger, by the way. Almost inhuman. I, of course, can pick up on such things. A more accomplished spirit of darkness could have gotten a nice murder or two out of her. You are no daemon."

Instead of gnashing my teeth or shooting flames from my eyes, I shrugged. Certainly, possessing Clara hadn't worked out to plan. The doctor looked disappointed.

After our little anti-climax we finally got down to business. The doctor told me what to do. Spells, rituals, supportive herbs. It was a blur, but she prepared a prescription of sorts, too. It looked unfamiliar, but I hadn't been to the doctor in two or three hundred years. Frankly, it usually wasn't worth the cost or the risk, daemons being daemons. Besides, usually when there was trouble, I just moved on to the next body. But the inability to move on had been precisely the problem this time.

The spells and rituals were designed to allow more control over Clara's body. I hoped the herbs would give me enough energy to keep the Lee family reunion from destabilizing the Universe. Or destroying Clara's house.

As it was, half Clara's relatives would spend all their time complaining because the food was or wasn't vegetarian/vegan/low fat/low salt or pescatarian. Meanwhile, the other half would take advantage of the distraction by quietly sneaking down the hall and going through Clara's jewelry box. Or her underwear drawer.

The above excepted the multiple cousins in their fifties who would get drunk and fight each other over boys they knew in high school. Then they'd get even drunker and fall into one another's arms crooning about how much they loooooved each other. The climax was them throwing up on everyone's shoes.

The Borgias were better guests.

As I mulled, Dr. Shoal handed me the prescription, smiling slightly. It made me uneasy.

"Of course, I also have to send you to our Possession Specialist for the herbs."

Worrying, I gathered up my purse and went next door, the doctor following. My scratch still stung.

Angelica, in an adjoining office, was only slightly less irritating than her boss. Angelica was some kind of fae and very officious. Before the doctor left, she and Shoal shared a look or two and quietly chatted in a dialect I didn't know.

Bustling around with some stinky herbs, sniffing and stirring along the way, Angelica made small talk, or tried. "Why didn't you possess a nun? They always put up a good fight. Or one of those preachers on television? You can't play cards without that bunch getting their knickers in a twist."

"Everyone possesses nuns," I pouted. "Aside from being cliche, it's expected. They're ready for it. Let Sister Imogene, who's not a morning person, spend ten minutes looking cheerful over her English muffin and, next thing you know, an exorcist shows up screaming in Latin and ready to drown the nearest evil spirit in holy water. And it's always so cold.

"As for televangelists, when was the last time anyone could tell the difference between one who was possessed and one who wasn't? Don't even get me started on them and lust and fornication. I wouldn't trust one of those maniacs with my houseplants."

Angelica looked thoughtfully at the Venus Flytrap on her desk.

"So, I tried something a little different," I said, beginning to ramble.

Before I could expound any further, Angelica decided she was bored and shook the bag of herbs at me, smiling brightly. "You know this is going to make you puke, right?"

By the time I was done, it was so late it was early. I trudged over the small parking lot to Clara's modest Nissan Versa, holding onto my bag of herbs. When I opened the door and flung myself down behind the wheel, there was a voice.

"My God, that stinks. I've been dead for months and that smell is about to gag me."

Almost jumping out of what was not my skin, I turned to see an otherwise well-groomed old woman covered in chocolate and sitting in the passenger's seat. It was Dina, Clara's grandmother.

I found myself worrying about what the dream chocolate might do to the upholstery. A sad state of affairs for someone who'd found the bubonic plague pretty hilarious.

"Those herbs aren't going to do anything but make Clara deathly ill. Won't kill her, but she'll wish they would. The spells and rituals are crap, too." The old woman spoke matter-of-factly and licked the chocolate off her fingers.

I read over my instructions carefully and my heart sank, or it would have, if I'd had one to call my own. Reviewed carefully, the herb mixture was the same one I used for bed bugs, but with herbs added to cause intestinal symptoms. The spell itself was a self-help affirmation translated into Latin using a third-rate app. Translated back it said something along the lines of "I am good enough and strong enough to double cross stupid people. Ha."

The ritual dance looked like it was based on the Hokey-Pokey.

So, yeah. This had been a waste of time.

First things first. I made a phone call on one of my little burner phones. Somewhere in Scottsdale, a gorgeous human being answered the phone in a husky voice. Beauty. Always ready for the next adventure, that was Beauty.

I wasted no more time.

"You don't know me. But you could say that I appreciate your value. Someone is coming for you. Tonight. To seduce you. She will probably pretend to be a doctor. She'll be pretending a lot more than that. Do not let her touch you."

I could feel the beautiful predator listening intently on the other end of the line. Suddenly, it seemed like she deserved a better shot at survival than she was getting. Beauty couldn't help being what she was, but at least she worked toward a kind of perfection. Dr. Shoal, on the other hand, just seemed sloppy and spoiled.

It seemed only right to even the playing field a bit.

"Oh, and one more thing. It would be wiser to run than to fight, but if you must stay and fight, use salt. Lure her in and close the circle around her. Then you can negotiate. Or leave her there."

I turned off the phone.

"Salt? " The old woman was by now completely clean, and the uphol-stery seemed unstained.

"Silver works on fae, salt is better on daemons."

"Good to know. Think I will root for your pretty predator. At least she's human." The old woman seemed serious.

"Barely. Now, you tell me what's going on."

"I am a guardian from beyond. Big whoop. I've gone from being a live person who gives advice that other people ignore to being a dead person who gives advice that other people ignore. Anyway, Someone from the Other Side has taken an interest in Clara. Largely because you have. So I was fast tracked through Purgatory and sent to keep an eye on her."

This struck me as very odd. "Newsflash. It's not me who won't leave her alone. Not anymore. Maybe once I deal with the family reunion Clara will see reason on letting me go. Any ideas on that?"

"On her seeing reason, no. Clara is a world class martyr. On dealing with the family reunion, yes. Just don't let it happen."

"And we stop that by...?"

"Asking for money. Making people pay for their own plane tickets. Up front. One email, one text. You'll see."

At home, Dina dictated a communication which I sent out to Clara's array of relatives. In it, I clearly stated that each family was responsible for its own travel. Up front.

By the time Clara woke up the family reunion was a dream lost to the family's universally maxed-out credit cards. At first, they were mad at Clara, but then they started yelling at each other, because everyone knew that *everyone else* expected her to front the money. It was divine. Clara was so happy not to be facing a reunion she let me out to play.

But I came back. Hey, how often have I been wanted anywhere?

Meanwhile, in North Scottsdale, the cops were still trying to explain the hotel room where they found an enormous pile of salt covering the burned remains of ... something.

Later, I was in the car, in Clara's body. She usually let me drive. We were going to the movies. Dina was staying home to do ghosty things, maybe haunt the noisy next-door neighbors. A phone rang and I realized I had forgotten the burner.

Cautiously, I picked it up off the passenger's seat. "Hello?"

"Thanks for the warning. And the advice." The husky voice was almost purring. "Be seeing you. Oh, and I do hope you and Clara are both well."

MIDNIGHT AT THE OPAL PUBLIC LIBRARY

AMY COLES

Poppy Noxwell crammed the loose papers into her saddlebag and shoved her head into her helmet. Two thousand dollars was a ridiculous amount to pay for a consultation—not even for the full treatment, just a consultation—with a specialist. There's no way that's going to happen, even if she could afford it. It was the premise of the matter. Two thousand dollars to speak with a spectral malady specialist for thirty minutes was like, sixty-something dollars a minute. It doesn't matter how big your brain is or how specialized you are, nobody's time is worth sixty-something dollars a minute. At that point, you're just taking advantage of the vulnerable.

Poppy flashed her turn signal. There was something therapeutically relaxing about the gentle rumble of her bike beneath her. She checked her side mirror and, confirming the way was clear, started to pull away from the curb. Only when she looked back ahead, there was a person right in front of her. Poppy violently jerked the handlebars, sending her and the bike swerving into a parked minivan. There was a loud crunch and the bike tipped, tossing Poppy into the middle of the road. Car horns immediately started blaring around her. *Gods forbid anyone show an ounce of sympathy in the big city*, she thought. She shook her head and scanned the spot where the person had been, but there was no one there now. "God damnit," she grumbled, punching the air. She pulled out her phone which had thankfully come out of this unscathed, while one good soul guided her out of traffic by the elbow. But she paid them no mind, focusing solely on the device in her hands.

The phone rang a few times before a cheery voice picked up, "Hey Poppy, give me a sec, the sweet mushroom pies are done."

Poppy waited impatiently, batting away the concerned civilian as she heard her best friend pulling baked goods out of the oven. A second later, her voice reappeared, and Poppy wasted no time: "The ghosts of Christmases past, present, future, birthdays, Kwanzaas, and leap years are literally driving me into minivans, and I am *this* close to losing it." She held up her fingers indicating a quarter of an inch, even though Sybil had no way of seeing the gesture through the phone. The concerned civilian backed away at that.

"Sweetheart, I hear you, I really do. But I need you to get someplace a little quieter because I almost *can't* hear you."

Poppy's vision refocused on the world around her. There was a sweaty man with a baby on his hip shouting something and pointing angrily between Poppy's seriously scuffed motorcycle and his now gently dented minivan. The baby started crying.

Grumbling at the exponentially increasing stack of inconveniences that were making up her day, Poppy shoved past the man and hustled into the nearest hipstery-looking café. It was fairly empty, it being mid-afternoon and all, so she flopped into the nearest booth and raised her phone again.

"I'm ready to try anything, just tell me what to do. I'm fucking desperate here."

"Watch your language in a public place," Sybil tsked. "Are you actually ready to listen to me, or are you going to resort to name-calling again?"

"Your other friends *are* complete nutjobs. I'm not being malicious and name-calling, that's just a fact. Like Periwinkle with her collection of cat whiskers."

"They're just keepsakes from her departed pets," Sybil argued.

"Or what's-his-face whose entire career is being living furniture."

"That's Alistair and he makes good money letting rich warlocks kick up their feet on him as a footstool."

"It's not normal, Sybil. Nutcases. All of them. But if you think any of them even have even a one percent chance of helping me, I'm in. Whoever—whatever they are, I'm game."

Someone cleared their throat and Poppy looked up at a frowning barista. "Excuse me ma'am, but you're bleeding all over the booth and we have a strict no outside blood policy." He gestured his head towards the sign in the window and crossed his arms.

Poppy looked down to see the sleeve of her leather jacket shredded, and her forearm torn from road rash. She clenched her teeth at that and gave the barista her best fuck-you smile. Without breaking eye contact, she waved her hand over the injury, closing up the wound with a minor healing spell. "Better, asshole?"

The barista slow-blinked, "You need to buy something, too."

Feeling like she was about to blow, Poppy sent him off for a gluten-free cake pop—the cheapest thing on their menu.

"I know someone who can probably help," Sybil's singsong voice came through the phone. "They're a bit unconventional, and if I told you too much more you'd probably back out. But they work locally and take drop-ins so we can probably go tonight."

"Yes, anything. I'm in!" Poppy accepted the pastel blue cake pop from the barista and nearly jumped out of her seat at the man now sitting across from her in the booth. He was in cycling gear, probably mid-thirties. But his helmet was askew, revealing a slush of grayish pink brain where his upper forehead should have been.

Poppy threw her cake pop at him, but it passed right through his right pectoral as he flickered out of this plane of existence.

"Just tell me where and when."

The thought of two bottles of cheap wine when Poppy got back to her apartment had been mind-tinglingly tempting, but she knew she needed to be sober for her appointment with Sybil's ominous acquaintance. Which is how Poppy found herself waiting, completely sober, in the shadows outside the Opal Public Library. She glanced at her watch, and just as the hand struck midnight, Sybil appeared in a poof of peach-scented smoke. Teleportation charms were temperamental at best, but Sybil always seemed to make them work, arriving exactly where she intended. As the smoke cleared, Sybil enveloped her friend in a big hug, her bush of lavender curls tickling Poppy's nose.

Poppy gave her a quick squeeze in return. She wasn't much of a hugger.

"I know you've had a rough day, so I brought you some fresh-baked speckled mushroom mini pies. They're a natural remedy that will clear up headaches, give you energy, and will promote solid healthy poops," Sybil listed the benefits off her fingers and smiled hopefully.

"Thanks Sybil," she said, placing the container in her pocket. "You know I always appreciate your baking, and while curing headaches sounds amazing, curing these ghost flickers is at the top of my priority list. So—" she gestured to the gothic-style cathedral of a building behind them. "—why are we at the library and not, oh I don't know, at a clinic or specialist's office?"

Sybil grabbed hold of her hand. "If I tell you, you might still back out. Come, I want to introduce you to someone!"

Poppy did not like surprises, but she figured the quicker they got inside, the quicker she'd get her answers. So Poppy let her friend lead her up the stone steps to the library, realizing how odd they would look to anyone out for a midnight stroll: a little witch with lavender hair and strawberry-print overalls, accompanied by a witch with a black pixie cut, pleather pants, and a sexy—if she does say so herself—biker jacket, jogging up the steps of the public library at midnight. But weird was how Sybil operated and Poppy learned to just go with it.

The inside of the library was exactly what she expected: rows upon rows of old tomes, with a smattering of old oak study tables throughout. Sybil led them through a maze of shelves, seeming to know the way, until they halted at an ancient reference desk at the top of an ornate staircase.

"Now please, please, *please* keep an open mind," Sybil said, flashing Poppy her best puppy dog eyes. Then she dinged a bell on top of the desk.

"Can I help you?"

Poppy nearly jumped out of her platform boots. If she had a dollar for every jump-scare she'd encountered today, she'd have like twenty dollars.

The person now sitting behind the reference desk seemed to appear from out of nowhere. They wore long red robes and had a red swatch of cloth wrapped around their head, hiding their eyes.

They're blind, Poppy realized.

"Hi, The Librarian, I brought you crescent macaroons," Sybil said, retrieving yet another tin of baked goods from her tiny satchel purse, handing them to the person—The Librarian—who accepted them with a bowed head. "I have the friend I told you about here: Poppy Noxwell, age twenty-seven, five foot seven, one hundred and eighty pounds—"

"Sybil!" Poppy interrupted, stepping on her friend's foot. That elicited a small yelp, but Sybil stopped talking. In what world was it okay to announce your friend's weight to a strange person in a dark library? "It's great to meet you," Poppy offered, turning to The Librarian. "Are you the one who can help me with a ghost flicker problem?"

Sybil and The Librarian bobbed their heads at the same time as if to say, *not quite*. "Follow me," was all The Librarian said.

A person of few words then, Poppy thought.

They trailed behind the flowing red robes as The Librarian led them through the barely lit library, which was surely an impossible labyrinth. To Poppy's surprise, they passed right by a copper caged-off section.

She quickened her pace to walk beside The Librarian, "Um, I thought we'd be finding answers in a powerful restricted Grimoire or something."

The corner of The Librarian's mouth twitched, the most emotion Poppy expected she'd see out of them. "Come," was all they said in reply.

Sybil smiled encouragingly and Poppy had to roll her eyes. It was like her friend expected her to snap and quit this at any moment.

The Librarian led them into the children's section where a collection of short shelves and colorful floor mats looked eerie in the dim lighting of the closed library. They came to a stop at the beginning of the nonfiction section. The Librarian plucked a thick book from the shelf: *Encyclopédie Pour Enfants: Q-S*.

The book shuddered at The Librarian's touch and started purring.

Poppy's mouth dropped open. "Are you insane? You can't keep your Grimoire out in the open like that, anyone can just up and steal it—any child could accidentally open it. Then guess what? It's bye-bye little Timmy! What the actual fuck, librarian?"

Sybil let out a little squeak as The Librarian turned to Poppy, growing to twice their height to tower over her. Poppy stood her ground, not inclined in the slightest to bow to such a blatant show of intimidation.

"I am *The* Librarian," The Librarian corrected her in a now booming voice. Then a magical icy downpour of water dropped on Poppy's head, eliciting a yelp of surprise. "If you must know, my Grimoire is disguised as one of the few books that doesn't get used." They showed Poppy, who was now shivering, the Grimoire's cover. "Nobody uses physical encyclopedias anymore. Children are not instructed on how to use them. And" The Librarian added, pointing to the title, "the French population in Opal City is so miniscule. It barely exists. The restricted section is the first place any thieves would go looking for valuables. This is the safest place for a Grimoire in the entire library." Then, without warning, The

Librarian opened the Grimoire and a blinding flash of purple light had Poppy squeezing her eyes shut and ducking.

The scent of disinfectant filled Poppy's nostrils and she opened her eyes. She was dry now and was standing alone in the middle of what looked to be a makeshift doctor's office. The unmistakable stone walls of the library told her she was still in the building, but the shelves of ointments and bottles, the counters and cabinets lining the walls, the examination table, and the general smell of cleaning products told her this wasn't a place library patrons frequented.

"Good golly, you've made it! Have a seat on the table ma'am and I'll be with you in a jiffy."

Poppy startled for the umpteenth time that day, realizing she wasn't alone. A little girl wearing a doctor's Halloween costume and a play stethoscope around her neck closed the cabinet she'd been rummaging in and skipped over to a counter, pouring something into a large mixing bowl. Poppy squinted at the girl and confirmed that she wasn't the least bit transparent. *Good.*

Her body relaxed at that, and she dutifully hopped onto the examination table, amused. If she had to entertain this kid while she waited for the doctor, that was fine by her. She wasn't much of a kid person, but she could handle just a few minutes with one.

Once the girl was done mixing her concoction, she skipped over to Poppy and lifted her chin, "Good evening, ma'am, my name is Dr. Pumpkinshine, I am nine and a half years old, and my favorite organ is the liver. What seems to be the problem today?" She procured a clipboard, holding a purple-coloured pencil to the page.

"It's a pleasure, Dr. Pumpkinshine," Poppy grinned in what she hoped was an amiable gesture. "You see, I have a strange cough I just can't seem to kick. I've heard you are the best doctor in town and I'm sure you can help me."

The girl frowned and flipped to a typed-up page on her clipboard, "My handy patient chart says here you have been seeing ghost flickerings for the past week, but I don't see a gosh darn thing about a cough. Can you pretty please elaborate on what type of cough you have?"

Poppy blinked once. *Where the hell was the doctor and how did this child even get in here?*

"Listen sweetie, I think we should wait for the real doctor before we begin. Are your parents around here somewhere?"

Poppy made to hop off the table and look into the hallway, but the girl moved in front of her with great speed. Her eyes had gone completely black, and she slowly smiled, revealing rows of little razor-sharp teeth. Her tongue flicked out of her mouth like a snake's. "You must be mistaken, *sweetie*," she spat that last word, which sounded ridiculous coming from the voice of a little girl. "As I said before, *I* am Dr. Pumpkinshine. You will show me respect, or I will make sure these ghosties follow you around for the rest of your miserable life."

Poppy recoiled at the demon child before her. *Where the fuck was the doctor*, she thought shooting a glance at the door on the other side of the room.

Then Dr. Pumpkinshine raised her hand and a wave of ice water crashed over Poppy's head, drenching her once again. Poppy yelped and instantly started shivering.

The Librarian chose that moment to stroll into the makeshift office, "Ah, I see you've met my niece, good." They bowed their head as if everything were going swimmingly and glided closer, placing a hand on Dr. Pumpkinshine's shoulder. Her eyes instantly reverted back to an innocent hazel hue and her teeth dulled to look human. "Freya here is apprenticing with me this summer, specializing in spectral anomalies and maladies. She is a bright young study, and I am sure she can help you."

She was The Librarian's niece then—that explains the downpour spell. Must be a family favorite.

Poppy fiddled uncomfortably with a clasp on her drenched biker jacket while The Librarian bent down and straightened the stethoscope around Dr. Pumpkinshine's neck. Then, with a wave of his hand, The Librarian disappeared, leaving Poppy with the child doctor alone.

Yes, she had told Sybil she was desperate for anyone who could help her. But a demon child? Was she really that desperate?

Dr. Pumpkinshine waved her hand and the water instantly evaporated off Poppy. "I'm sorry about that," she said, pulling up a rolling chair and climbing onto it. "I get angry sometimes and I know I have to work on controlling my emotions better. I hope I didn't scare you."

She looked so innocent now, but Poppy knew demons ran hot and cold like that. In any case, she *was* that desperate. "It's alright, let's just get on with this." She tried to smile but suspected it came off as a grimace.

"Okay! Why don't you tell me how this all started?" It was a reasonably professional thing for a doctor to ask, but Poppy had a hard time taking Dr. Pumpkinshine seriously as she watched her kick her dangling legs through the air, trying to get her chair to spin.

Poppy sighed, thinking of her damaged motorcycle and the man with brains oozing out of his skull. Looks like she's going to talk about her sex life with a nine-and-a-half-year-old.

"It started about a week ago when I was out clubbing at The Poisoned Cauldron—a grown up place," she clarified. "It was my first time there because I was meeting some friends I hadn't seen in years, and they insisted it was the place to be. And they weren't wrong, the place had a killer dance floor with smoke and dancers and hellfire. There were lots of fae around—and they're always a good time. Well, maybe too good a time because I got hammered pretty fast. I remember just vibing on the dancefloor when an absolute goddess started dancing with me. She looked like a fairy, but I was honestly too out of it to know for sure. She had these piercing white eyes and glowing golden skin. Her cheeks were dotted with white freckles, and she wore this body harness. Oh my god, that body harness."

Dr. Pumpkinshine cleared her throat, pulling Poppy out of her reverie.

"Sorry," Poppy offered weekly. "Anyway, I went home with the fairy goddess and we, um, played around?" *How was she supposed to explain this?*

Dr. Pumpkinshine sighed, lowering her clipboard, "Oh good gracious, I know what sex is, Miss Noxwell. Please, I need to know exactly what happened, down to the last doorknob, so I can try and figure out what caused your ghost flickers. Understanding the cause will help me figure out how to cure you."

"But it's ... inappropriate," Poppy argued.

"Okay," Dr. Pumpkinshine hopped out of her chair and made for the door, "Have fun with our new ghostie friends then— "

"Wait, okay, fine. Please come back, I'll talk." Poppy buried her face in her hands as she continued. "The fairy goddess took me to this beautiful rooftop garden on the building where she lived. It was totally unexpected. Like, usually you just go home with a person to their crappy bachelor apartment, fool around, and part ways. But no, she had tealight candles lit everywhere, and a nest of fluffy pillows and blankets, it was perfect. I felt like I was in a movie. Anyway, we ended up having sex..."

"What kind?" Doctor Pumpkinshine asked without missing a beat.

Poppy raked a hand through her hair, "Um, oral? And some hand action." Gods, this was so awkward. This is definitely the last time she takes medical referrals from Sybil. "Um ya so, the sex was ... amazing. And we fell asleep together, but when I woke up the next morning—okay, afternoon—she was gone. I didn't get her name or number and haven't been able to find her since. It was that morning that the ghost flickers started."

Was it ridiculously hot in here? "I need some fresh air." Poppy went to get up, but a metal arm snapped out of the table and secured Poppy to the surface like a nightmarish seatbelt. "What the fuck?" Poppy shot the doctor a glare.

"I suspect I know what the problem is, and I can't have you running off now," Dr. Pumpkinshine said.

Poppy really was just going to get some fresh air to cool off her beet-red face, but now the idea of making a break for it sounded like the right thing to do. "Get this shit off me," she growled. Poppy waved her hands over the metal bracket, trying to work a simple unlocking charm, but nothing happened.

"This nifty room is warded against outsider magic," Dr. Pumpkinshine explained as she snapped on flower-print latex gloves and assembled a strange assortment of items including a scalpel onto a tray, which she brought over to Poppy.

"Hell. No." Poppy could feel herself starting to panic and reminded herself to control her breathing.

Dr. Pumpkinshine raised her hands and shot a gust of wind so strong it knocked Poppy's upper body flat on the table, from which metal wrist clasps snapped into place around her arms.

Poppy pulled and thrashed, but she wasn't budging.

"Please don't be a scaredy-cat, Miss Noxwell, this is actually a very simple procedure." She spun a scalpel expertly between her fingers. "It was all really quite easy to figure out—your condition, that is. You met this fairy goddess on the summer solstice, didn't you?"

Poppy stopped thrashing at that. "Yes, how did you know?"

"Because the longest day of the year is the only time the most powerful of the spectral community can interact with our living plane of existence. It's super-duper likely that your fairy goddess was a ghostie come to play in the real world for a night. That would explain why you haven't been able to find her since, and it would explain your ghost flickers!" Doctor Pumpkinshine proclaimed proudly.

"Wait, how did I get ghost flickers? It was an STD, wasn't it?"

"Yes and no. When you were canoodling with your fairy goddess, she must have left an itty-bitty shred of ghostly essence inside you, which is why you can now catch glimpses of the spectral plane of existence. So it's not quite a sexually transmitted disease, but you did most likely pick it up during sexy time." Dr. Pumpkinshine pushed a button on the side of the table, and it mechanically titled so that Poppy was nearly vertical. Then, Dr. Pumpkinshine plucked a cup of a sparkly black liquid off the tray and held it to Poppy's lips.

"Drink up!" she ordered "we'll need this to circulate in your bloodstream so we can locate the ghostly essence inside you."

That sounded somewhat sound, so Poppy squeezed her eyes shut and gulped down the syrupy substance. She gagged as it slid down her throat, but she forced her stomach to settle. "Bleh, what was that?"

Dr. Pumpkinshine shot her a mischievous look, "It's so totally icky, you don't want to know." She giggled.

Poppy shuddered, no she probably didn't want to know.

Then Dr. Pumpkinshine shifted into her demon form. She took a pair of star-shaped glasses from the tray and placed them over her black eyes. She took in every inch of Poppy, which made Poppy want to squirm. She really didn't want to be demon dinner.

But Dr. Pumpkinshine paused over Poppy's stomach and moved in close. What she was seeing, Poppy had no idea. "Do you have both your kidneys?"

"Yes ... why do you ask?"

Dr. Pumpkinshine ignored the question and took up humming a ridiculously upbeat tune. She took off the glasses and used a butterfly clip to hold up Poppy's shirt, exposing the skin where her left kidney was. "The pesky ghostly essence has migrated to your kidney, so the easiest thing to do would be to remove the whole thing. It's a super simple procedure."

Poppy's eyes widened and she started thrashing and spitting curses that did nothing.

Dr. Pumpkinshine, unfazed, took hold of the scalpel and smiled up at Poppy, showing off her razor teeth. "This is going to hurt a lot, but don't worry, you'll probably pass out from the pain pretty quick.

"What about anesthesia?!" Poppy shrieked.

Dr. Pumpkinshine fell to the floor in a fit of giggles at that. When she was able to catch her breath, she wiped away a tear and grinned at Poppy, "You're so silly! This is a library; we don't have the funding for something as extravagant as anesthesia! We barely have enough funding to keep the freaking air conditioning on!"

Poppy paled as she realized what was about to happen, but Dr. Pumpkinshine didn't give her another chance to protest as she hopped up and drove the scalpel's blade into the side of Poppy's torso.

At first, there was just a vaguely cold sensation, and then the pain shot through her body like hellfire. She screamed as Doctor Pumpkinshine cut through layers and layers of skin. Her voice quickly extinguished itself as her vocal cords went raw with the panicked exertion of her cries. Dr. Pumpkinshine squeezed her little hand inside Poppy's torso, and the shock of the pain was so intense that, mercifully, Poppy finally passed out.

The sound of a TV dragged Poppy back to consciousness. She didn't understand where she was at first as her bleary eyes focused on a TV playing the popular Ice Queen movie. A blur of movement led Poppy's focus to a little girl in an Ice Queen costume, dancing along to a song about letting her worries go. They appeared to be in some sort of playroom.

"You're awake!" A peachy scent wafted over Poppy as Sybil brushed a gentle hand over her forehead.

That's right, I'm at the library with a psychotic demon child. Poppy shot up at this realization and winced in pain. There was a gauzy bandage covered in kawaii ghost stickers over her side where her kidney was removed.

"You cut me open," Poppy said.

"Eek! My patient's awake," Dr. Pumpkinshine squealed excitedly. "How do you feel? Do you see any ghosties?"

Nope there were no ghosts. But she really couldn't be sure until she'd walked around more and visited different places. "I feel a little sore and my throat hurts," Poppy admitted.

"Understandable," Dr. Pumpkinshine nodded, "You were screaming like a banshee! My throat hurts too when I sing a lot. But those are enchanted to speed up the healing process," she said, pointing to the ghost stickers. "You should be right as rain by tomorrow!"

"I am very proud of you, Freya" came a deep voice. The Librarian stood in the open doorway, looking as emotionless as usual. "You are progressing nicely with your training. However, next time I would implore you to sell the kidney on the black market instead of eating it. We all know the library could use the extra money."

Poppy winced, having forgotten about the disgusting dietary habits of demons until now.

Dr. Pumpkinshine licked her lips shyly. "Sorry The Librarian, I'll remember that for next time."

"Speaking of painful and uncomfortable things," Poppy jumped in, "how much do I owe you?" She directed this question to Dr. Pumpkinshine.

"Oh, Miss Noxwell, it's a freebie! But if you could leave me a five-star review on *Rate My Demon MD*, I would be so super happy."

Poppy shook her hand, "It hasn't been a pleasure exactly, but I'm grateful for your help. So thank you Dr. Pumpkinshine."

"Dr. Pumpkinshine professionally and swiftly diagnosed and cured my ghost flickers in less time than it would take me to cook a kidney bean dinner. I highly recommend her services, especially with spectral maladies.

5/5 Stars."

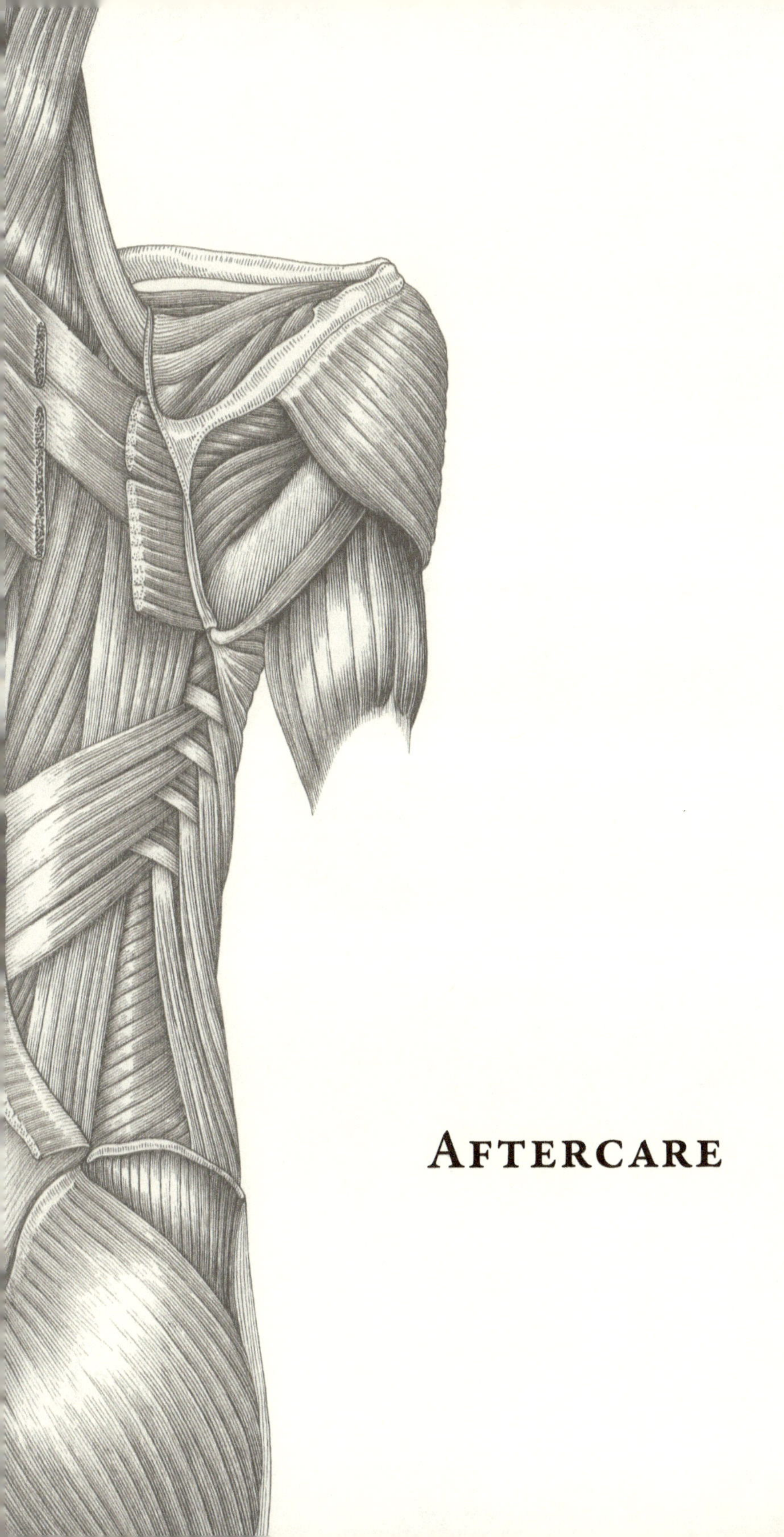

AFTERCARE

NOSEBLIND

N.M. BROWN

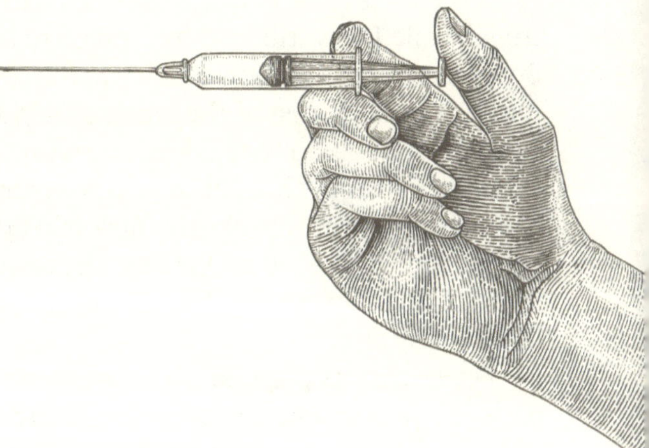

I've been walking around for the past five and a half weeks without feeling like I'm truly alive. The positive test showed up first, and the symptoms came to plague me shortly after. Our son was kind enough to agree to stay with us until we got back on our feet. We were able to find an eldercare nurse willing to expose herself to the sickness to come and help out.

"Martin, where's your mother?" I wheezed through burning lips.

His eyes shot skyward in annoyance. It literally looked like he was counting internally to keep from snapping, just as he did as a child. Some things never change... "Dad, I told you. Mom's sleeping upstairs in the guest room. You two HAVE to keep apart so you both can get better. Rosemary even said so."

"B-but we both have the same damn thing!" I insisted. "And yeah, that's easy for her to say, exposing herself to hell all. What the hell does it matter if we quarantine or not? And in our own house no less."

"What if you start to get better, and then she reinfects you again, or vice versa? I dunno how that shit kinda shit works, Dad." My son was clearly agitated. "Let me warm you up some dinner. I made pot roast and vegetables." He replied in a softer, practiced, and more patient tone.

Pot roast. Of all the things I'd grown to hate over this sickness, it's those goddamned roasts. That grey-marbled meat glistening in a puddle of grease next to smushed vegetables. It seemed to be all that idiot son of ours knew how to make apparently. Thank God I can't taste or smell. That seems to be the only positive I can find about that situation.

It seems callous, maybe even selfish, to complain about something so trivial while I was still healthy enough to be in the comforts of my home. But you never realize how much you rely on your sense of taste and smell until it's gone. I missed the smell of my wife as she slept, a mix of perfume and shampoo with a hint of sweat. I missed the taste of caramel corn. Amy had just bought me a large container of it before this shit hit. The loss of senses was like the flick of a light switch. I was driving in my car, smoking a cigarette. One puff, the taste was there. The next, nothing. Which I guess wasn't a bad thing, right? Satisfying or not, cigarettes taste like flaming shit.

Fever dreams plagued me throughout the entire night. I alternated between feeling like I was on fire to freezing from my own bursts of sweat. My body was exhausted by the constant failed attempts to regulate its own temperature. So many visions of my wife sunken into the middle of our bed gasping for breath. She became more withered and sallower in each one. I dreamt of piles upon piles of grayed, salted meat. And the fucking meat.

I saw Amy and I sitting at a lavish banquet table in one of them. The glow of our recovery was still fresh on our faces as we sat in anticipation of food we could actually taste. Rowland came into the room with two shining silver trays with matching domes over the food. His teeth were unnaturally elongated and sharpened as he smiled and set our trays down. Despite his alarming appearance, our eyes still danced with excitement at what the covered plates would contain.

My lips curled in a sneer of horror as an ungarnished slab of gray meat was revealed, but Amy didn't seem to mind. I was surprised to see her pick the food up with her hands, completely abandoning the corresponding flatware beside it. Her teeth morphed to resemble our son's as she tore into the meat and began chewing ravenously. I normally loved it when she ate; a gal needs some meat on her bones. But seeing her then, I was almost to the point of gratuitous disgust.

I awoke with a mortified start, my throat aching with thirst. I called out to the nurse multiple times and was relieved to hear footsteps coming down the hall. However, when the door opened, Martin was on the other side.

"Did Rosemary leave?" I asked breathlessly.

"Oh yeah, Dad," he remarked flippantly. "She left ages ago."

"Damnit, I didn't get to thank her or even say goodbye," I grumbled. My train of thought was interrupted as something nagged at my periphery, a flash of key-lime green. The gold chain attached to the handle confirmed my suspicions. "B-but she forgot her purse," My throat grew tight as I felt an oncoming fit of coughs flirt with my lungs. "You need to go give it—" My sentence was cut off by hacking sputters, but I managed to gesticulate the rest of the sentence.

"Shit," Martin muttered. "Yeah, sure, Dad. I'll get that over to her right now. If I hurry, I may catch her around the same time she gets home. I'd hate for her to worry."

He turned out to be such a damn decent kid, not that I can let him know that too often, of course. The sweetest dish can be ruined by the slightest bit of salt, and I wanted my boys to keep grounded with their hearts protected. It was sure as shit too late to help Clark.

Tears pricked the corners of my eyes the moment the name popped into my head. Clark was our eldest son and the polar opposite of Martin. No, see, Martin was born with a heavy sense of entitlement, something I've heard is common among youngest children. However, he never grew out of it. My son always thought life owed him more. And he wasn't willing to work for it either. His mother always claimed that it was the one trait a human could possess that would destine them to a lifetime of disappointment. But I, for one, feared much worse.

You see, people like Martin don't hesitate as much during decision-making. They don't feel like they're stealing anything that should already be theirs, whether it be a human being or otherwise. Life's game of being in the wrong place at the wrong time can kill even the most innocent of people, let alone someone who's constantly making shit decisions. I'll admit that Amy and I spent more than a few nights teary-eyed in fear for his future. We worried about both of our boys, just in different ways. Amy always joked that we would need a college fund for Clark and a bail fund for Martin. I know, I know ... those types of statements are now recognized as psychologically damaging, but this was the 80s. Everything was different then.

Clark oozed confidence. After 12 hours of labor, he came into this world as a little man. He was always the happiest child. I'd never met anyone with a bigger heart, which is why I think the depression hit him so hard. My firstborn took his life with a knotted rope, leaving his mother and me with a hole in our hearts that never healed. Martin wasn't the same after that. It seemed to be a wake-up call of sorts to him. He'd blossomed into the attentive son that Clark used to be.

Of course, these thoughts flew from my mind as soon as I saw what was for dinner that evening. "Grey meat, always this grey fucking meat!" I spat. You can either blame the fever or think that I'm a cranky old man, the hell if I care. Just because I couldn't taste anything didn't mean I had to eat the same thing every damned day, did it? I was so fed up at that moment that I was sure prisoners in jail ate better than I had in the past week.

Martin's voice interrupted my thoughts. "I'm sure that was rhetorical," he commented smoothly. "However, what you fail to realize is that ALL of your senses are weakened because of this thing. What color is my shirt, Dad?"

"Blue?" I answered though it came out resembling more of a question than a statement. I looked him over, flabbergasted at his calm demeanor.

He shook his head in stern satisfaction. "My shirt is green, Dad, green. See? What'd I tell ya?" He plucked a piece of meat off of my plate before shoving it into his mouth contently. "You have no idea how much the senses are all tied into each other. But you live and learn, right?" He rose to his feet, ruffling my hair condescendingly before entering his bedroom and closing the door. *He hadn't even wiped his fuckin hands*, I thought bitterly. I pictured a sheen of multicolored oils left behind from his touch across my scalp and hairline. I instantly wanted a shower.

Sadly, my balance was less than perfect even on the best of days, let alone with my equilibrium being disturbed from the virus. The last thing anyone needed was for me to slip and fall in the tub. One wrong step is all it takes. And I sure as shit didn't feel like having Martin watch over my naked body after the conversation we just had. I remembered that Amy had Rosemary bring her over some dry shampoo since she was too weak to bathe herself.

The wheels in my head began to turn, and I decided to take action while I still had the wherewithal to do so. I couldn't help but form an impish smile as I imagined the thrill of sneaking into Amy's room for a kiss. She was my wife, after all. I'm sure she missed me. Sometimes, one little act of love can be the best medicine that there is. With love in my heart, I made my way toward her side of the house.

One foot trudged in front of the other until I'd reached most of the way there. I took one final look around, summoning the spirit of forbidden love we'd retained in our youths and grabbed the doorknob. Martin's face popped through the other side of the door before I had a chance to turn the knob. "Dad," he chided. "You know you aren't supposed to be in here. I was just coming to get you."

"How did you get in here? I just saw you enter your room. Never mind me, I just want to see your mother. I need some of that dry shampoo she has for my marinated scalp. I probably smell like a rotten rib roast out for trash day." He guided me backward gently until we were both clear of the door and shut it behind him.

"Hey, everything's fine. The other day when I returned Rosemary's purse, she gave me some warning signs to watch out for with Mom. She said if I noticed any tucking around her lungs, it indicated struggling for breath. She said any respiratory damage at your age could be catastrophic and to take her to the hospital right away."

"Okay, and?" I waved my hands impatiently, urging him to get to the point.

"And ... I took her in yesterday."

The adrenaline of anger rushed my veins for a brief moment before leaving me exhausted in its wake. "You should..." *COUGH* "You should have come and gotten me, damnit!" I wheezed. "What the hell were you thinking?!?"

Martin raised his hands in mock innocence. "Well, I tried to wake you up before we left, Dad. You wouldn't rouse. I was scared you were dead for a second, but then you coughed, and I knew you were alright. Mom said she wanted you to get your rest. She said you can't go kicking ass with one foot in the grave."

The comfort of recognition soothed my hammering heart instantly. Amy had said those exact words to me every single time I'd been sick. I used to scold her for being morbid. But right then, I'd never heard anything that made me happier in all my life. "Well..." I murmured apologetically, rubbing the back of my neck. I winced from the pain of my stiffened joints, and the sharp, unexpected intake of breath induced a fresh round of rib-wracking coughs.

"Now, let's get you back to bed. I don't want to take two trips to the hospital in a forty-eight-hour span," he joked dryly. He gingerly guided me by the shoulders, and I couldn't help but recall the times when I had once helped him walk. It seemed like at least two lifetimes ago.

"You really should see your mother, Marty. She shouldn't be in that hospital alone." I protested.

"Regulations, Dad," he reminded me. "You know everything's different now."

We didn't speak as he brought me my supper, not one word. Trust me, I had plenty in reserves, though. All I needed was one opportunity, one time of him mouthing off to lay into him. But he didn't so much as flinch. I kept ruminating on Amy being alone in that hospital room, cold and terrified. Those thoughts eventually haunted me into a fitful sleep.

A kaleidoscope of blue and red lights smattered across the blank wall of my bedroom, waking me from an already fitful sleep. My fever had once again broken, drenching my bedsheets in a sickly sweat. The slippers weren't even on my feet all the way before I heard them break down the front door.

Officers swarmed the perimeter of my yard and were now making their way into my home. They came in twos, a mass of head-to-toe black clothing and shiny black boots. I heard one rattle fellow officer's names off in alarm outside of my wife's bedroom. *Goddammit*, I thought bitterly. *The woman is SICK in the hospital, for Christ's sake. Now they want to rifle through her things?! Haven't we been through enough?*

It had been hard for me to get out of bed even before the sickness crept its way into our home. But now, between the fevers and inner ear imbalances, as aforementioned, the task seemed momentous. However, the last thing anyone needed was for me to fall in haste. That's all it takes is a fall, just one damn fall for authorities to deem you unfit to care for yourself. I sure as fuck couldn't care for Amelia right now. What if they deemed her to be unfit? Either way, I had to get them away from her. My wife needed her rest.

They hadn't gotten to my end of the house yet, and thankfully from what I could see, Martin's door was still closed and locked. He's done so well taking care of us. I'd hate for him to be disturbed for what had to be a misunderstanding, not to mention a blatant intrusion of privacy. My eyes burned with fever as I shuffled out of bed and down the hallway.

Horror and anger raged through me as I spotted an officer dragging Martin from his bedroom in handcuffs. His face was blank, the epitome of expressionlessness as they walked him out of the front door. Two more officers followed behind him with evidence bags, telling me I wasn't allowed in my own damn home because it was an active crime scene. I recognized Rosemary's bright green purse through one of the bags, but I still hadn't put two together yet. It wasn't until I saw the gleam of surgical tools that the wheels started to move into place. "Where's my wife, Amy?!" I demanded through labored breaths. No one answered. They hardly so much as looked my way.

Two uniformed gentlemen, along with a woman I'd never seen before, entered the house with forensics badges. Their hands flew to their noses as they sputtered in horror. However, I failed to smell a damn thing as hard as I tried.

The unnamed woman approached me gently and guided me away from the room. "Sir, we're going to need you to come with us. We're taking you to a hospital. How are you feeling? Are you experiencing any abdominal pain? Confusion or disorientation? We need to check for prion damage. When is the last time you've eaten? When was your last bowel movement?"

The questions multiplied and continued, the next coming long before I had a chance to answer the previous one. I used what remaining strength I had to shrug her arm off and start for the room Amy was kept in before going to the hospital. Swaths of light bathed the hallway from the open door. Dark blackout curtains that I'd never bought consumed every window in the room. I remember that being the first thing that caught my eye as I rounded the hallway.

Large patches of yellow and brown stains bled into the carpet at my feet. I followed the trail of stains to their origin: the bed. I gagged at the salted air wafting from the doorway, and I imagined the smell of copper must have been intense. Even after all that I know, after being told what I've been told, I still can't wrap my brain around what I saw on that bed. My soul just can't settle with it. Whatever lay on top of it looked like an animal had mauled it. Dark, almost pitch-black veins ran through grotesquely discolored skin, the chunks left of it anyway. I could hardly tell what was what.

As another coughing fit began, a fog of panic and confusion consumed my senses. Waves of black invaded the corner of my vision with each hack, making my head pound from exertion. The dark waves were replaced with a veil of white as I felt my knees give out from beneath me. It was becoming increasingly more difficult to catch my breath. It seemed to be robbed from me before the inhalation process restarted.

My eyelids fluttered open as I was greeted with a pastel nightmare. Mint greens, pale pinks, and yellow curtains cradled plain white walls while a symphony of machinery beeped around me. I was beyond exhausted, but relieved that I could breathe.

I'd almost forgotten the past hour of my consciousness when a man in a business suit and badge walked in. God, I was sick of seeing those. If I never saw another badge in my life, I'd die a happy man. I know that's a pretty morbid thing to say, especially lying in a hospital bed. I guess all the years with Amy had left their impression on my sense of humor. *Oh God*, I thought. *Amy!*

"Excuse me," I grumbled, surprised at how much it hurt to speak. "What room is my wife in? Her name's Amy Mallone."

He stared down at his feet solemnly without an answer.

"What did you guys do with my son? Why'd you take him like that? He's a good boy." I pressed.

He began to explain what happened as I sat there, attempting to absorb every detail. At best, Martin was on the hook for murder and the unlawful handling and tampering with a body. Officers came out and found what they had done. Police officers arrived after receiving a welfare call from Rosemary's daughter. Apparently, she'd been missing for some days, and our house was her last known whereabouts. I'd been cohabitating with two dead, rotting bodies for days and hadn't known it. Amy wasn't taken to the hospital. She died the last day Rosemary showed up for her shift.

As far as Martin, well ... he never was quite the same after we lost Clark. But we had thought it was for the better. They explained why I'd been asked so many questions and why they were monitoring my digestion so thoroughly as well. They explained why no food was found in the house, yet we'd never missed a meal.

Your Obedient Servant

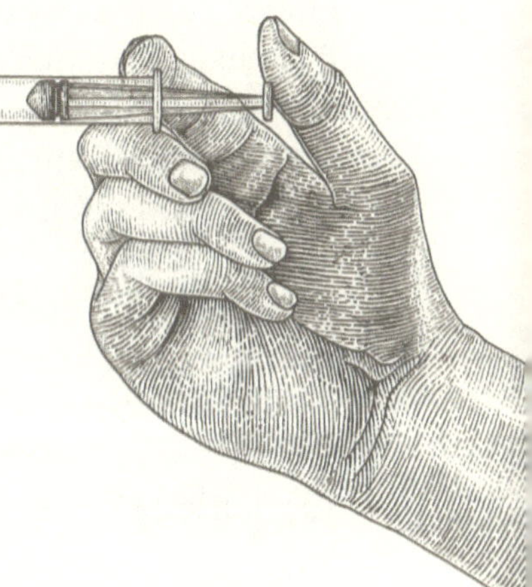

Jay Mendell

This ... *union* was coming very close to being the bane of Hobbes' existence, and considering all that his existence had been through, that was no easy feat.

Oh, the Undead Legion had done a lot of good work for a lot of people, he was sure, but Hobbes hardly found himself in need of such things. When the young representative from the union rang the doorbell and asked if he had a few moments to spare, he'd only thought to allow it for the sake of politeness.

Little did he know that the entire scenario had been a trap, designed to ensorcell him into being handed a dizzying amount of documents and signing things on clipboards without even getting a chance to fully read them through.

Now, he was part of a *network*. They had informed him of all the new 'benefits' he would be entitled to, the public services that would now be made available, and even certain avenues to take if it just so happened that he wished to break contract with the current Necromancer acting as his Master, a young man who called himself 'Malekai the Corrupted.'

Of course, he had no intention of breaking his contract—such a thing simply *wasn't done*, not by any consummate professional—but they had insisted on showing him a number of pamphlets regardless.

Hobbes had promptly booted the representative out once they began discussing things like 'vacation days' and other such nonsense. But at that point, it had been too late. Their keen eyes had noticed the way that he kept subtly shifting his left arm, and the next thing he knew, there was an appointment set up under his name at the nearest Death Clinic.

One of the perks, apparently, of joining the union.

Back in *his* day, one would rely on the Master for assistance with any such thing. But grimly, Hobbes had begun to notice that the younger generation of Servants didn't seem to put much stock in their Masters' abilities. No one of his generation had done so either, but at least they were quiet about it.

Now, he had a doctor's appointment that he had been tricked into attending, and a Master to pacify and remind that the Manor would not fall down upon them if Hobbes wasn't there to hold it up, regardless of how often it may feel that way.

As a Butler, Hobbes was meant to manage the daily happenings of the Manor, including welcoming guests, balancing the budget, and so on. In reality, Hobbes also did the laundry, the cooking, the gardening, and just about every task that was required for a living human to function.

Master Malekai claimed that Hobbes did his work so well that there was no reason to summon another servant. Hobbes chose to accept this compliment, rather than acknowledge the fact that his Master may not have the power necessary to summon any more Undead.

Less competition was always preferable, in his mind.

There was the choice to retire, of course. He could sit out the rest of his contract and decide to return to the underground—permanently, this time. Many of the servants that he had started out with on his first contract had chosen to do so eventually, but Hobbes was not like those servants.

Which was not to say that Hobbes believed himself indispensable to the world of the living—in truth, he had simply been given the kind of upbringing that left him feeling strangely bereft if he was not kept constantly busy, and as he could not recall much of his time underground, he believed that it must not have been anything of note.

Retirement, Hobbes had decided, was something that happened to other people.

Normally, he would have said the same thing about going to the clinic. Hobbes was a Butler, after all—pain did not visit him. It could knock politely upon his door, but he would just as politely send it away.

And besides, he'd never taken leave before—especially not for *medical* reasons, Lord forbid.

Of course, that did not mean Master Malekai wouldn't have allowed it beforehand. Hobbes found his Master generally good-natured and easy to please, which was a rare trait in Masters that Hobbes cultivated whenever possible. Despite his whining and often immature temperament, Hobbes knew that if he had ever asked, surely, the Necromancer would have given him anything that he needed.

But Hobbes had never asked, and it was only now, after he had committed to the whole affair in front of witnesses, that he had to begrudgingly set on his way.

This came as news, somehow, to his beloved Master, despite the fact that Hobbes had informed him several days in advance, and then the day before the appointment, and again two hours ago. Master Malekai was the sort of man who required such treatment, and this current predicament was only more proof of that necessity.

"You're leaving?" Master Malekai said, sounding vaguely panicked. He gestured toward the pile of laundry on the ground in the foyer, where dirty laundry was most *certainly* not supposed to be. "What am I supposed to do about all this, then?"

"I'm just going to discuss my options, Master, I doubt it will take more than an hour," Hobbes assured him, and pointedly made no mention of the laundry. After six years on contract, if Master Malekai did not remember that the dirty laundry was to go *inside* the laundry room, there was simply no helping him.

It was Hobbes' own fault for indulging him, he knew, but his Master was so blessedly incompetent that he often found himself bending the rules just to save them both some time.

"And you'll come back right away?" Master Malekai persisted, wringing his hands together. "No ... no detours, or distractions?"

"Just so, Master," Hobbes said gravely, resisting a scoff at the mere thought. "Though I cannot guarantee an exact time of my return, I will endeavor not to disappoint your expectations."

Master Malekai only stared for a long moment, an anxious sort of buzz settling right below his skin, before he straightened his back and nodded, his typical attitude back in full force. "Right, of course. How silly of me to question it! You have never let me down before, my good man, and why would you? A marvel of my own creation, the perfect example of my expertise! Hobbes, when you go out into the world, you represent me. I will expect your return posthaste!"

The Master then spun around, barely avoiding a stumble over the pile of laundry, and then marched, straight-backed, out of the room. Hobbes only watched him go, slightly bemused by the whole experience, but knowing better than to look a gift horse in the mouth. If Master Malekai hadn't been feeling quite so generous, the two of them could have been stuck in the doorway for the next several hours as they hashed out every little detail of Hobbes' trip.

That's how it had always been in the beginning—every grocery trip had been a battle, until Hobbes had finally figured out the 'app' that let them be delivered weekly. His disdain for these 'smartphones' was begrudgingly set aside when necessary, and in that case, it had been a dear necessity in order to stop Hobbes from doing something ... unfortunate to his newest employer.

Now, Hobbes found the mage's neuroses almost charming, in a way, much like how a pig farmer came to find some comfort in seeing the beasts rolling about in the mud and stinking up the barn, knowing that such a thing only happened when the pig was healthy and well.

It was livable, to put it plainly, and for a member of the Undead such as himself, Hobbes considered something being 'livable' to be rather high value indeed.

Turning, he moved to exit the room when the laundry caught his eye. He studied it for a long moment. On the one hand, if he kept picking up all these messes, the good Master would never learn. On the other hand, Hobbes knew that the training process for such behaviors was long and tedious, and often filled with a great deal of barking—or so he assumed, given his previous experience—and it really was easier to just do these things himself. At least that way he knew they would be done right the first time.

He dithered about for a moment, before he sighed. The car (he had ordered this as well, on another 'app') was not set to arrive for a few minutes more. Surely, he had enough time to bring everything into the laundry room, at the very least.

By the time his pocket dinged to inform him that the cab service had arrived, Hobbes had put two loads of laundry in the wash, and started to separate the cloaks (magical, covered in arcane sigils, and most importantly; dry-clean only) from the full-body pajamas (soft, non-magical, and the Master's preferred item of clothing). He swept his gaze over the rest of the laundry with a sigh, but there was nothing to be done about it. Leaving the driver to wait on his behalf would be terribly rude, and reminding Master Malekai to put the laundry in the dryer would be the fastest way for all of the linens to be forgotten in the back of some random closet until they eventually get discovered and used in another dark ritual to induce madness in any unsuspecting busybodies who came to poke their noses over the fence.

Hobbes dusted off his hands of the remains of the washing powder and made his way to the front door. In the short time it took for the car to arrive, Master Malekai had remained upstairs. Hobbes considered, for one brief moment, calling up to the man to inform him of his departure, but after suddenly recalling the way Master Malekai had managed to nobly hold his tongue from giving more unnecessary comments, Hobbes decided that it wasn't necessary this time.

After a short and uncomfortable car ride (was this what the young folks considered *music* these days?), Hobbes arrived outside of the small Death Clinic, denoted by the symbol of the Undead Legion on the door.

It was a small building, plain concrete and slightly sunken into the earth, almost as if it were a mausoleum. Hobbes had seen a number of those in his days, but at least they tended to have some sort of fanciful etchings carved into the stone. This building stood out starkly against the busy city streets, and Hobbes pursed his lips as he headed inside and gave his information to the receptionist, who pointed him in the direction of his examination room.

He'd barely had time to sit down in the provided chair before the Necromancer attending to him arrived and briskly introduced herself as Dr. Yivana. She wielded her pen and clipboard like a shield against the rest of the world.

Hobbes politely shook her hand and gave his ID information, but it seemed that the Doctor was not much one for pleasantries, as she got right down to business.

"Describe the symptoms for me," Dr. Yivana said, eyes gazing over him severely as she clicked her pen.

"Ah, yes, of course," Hobbes began. Regardless of his willingness in being here, he was hardly going to waste both their time by stalling. "As I said, it's the left arm that's been bothering me. It's rather ... tingly? The arm itself gets overheated on occasion, while the fingertips are cold and a bit numb."

"And do you experience any sharp pains during these periods?" Dr. Yivana had already made several sharp slashes on her clipboard, absentminded notes that Hobbes couldn't help but feel a bit offended by.

"Well..." Hobbes hedged for a moment, before clearing his throat at the rather unimpressed look Dr. Yivana pinned him with. "On occasion, yes. It never lasts more than a night, however."

"How about the other symptoms? Do they last?"

"A little over a week is my record, I believe," Hobbes confessed, a bit stiffly, as Dr. Yivana clicked her tongue and took a moment to record yet another note on her clipboard.

"Can I ask why you've decided to come in now?" Dr. Yivana asked with a disapproving glower.

The unspoken 'instead of when it started' hovered in the air between them, and Hobbes coughed, delicately, into a closed fist.

"Well, it hadn't been much of an issue at first," Hobbes demurred. It truly hadn't. The pain went away so long as he wasn't focused on it, and if it was that easy to ignore, he figured that it couldn't be a big issue in the first place.

"And now?" she asked, raising a brow.

Well, now Hobbes had committed to doing something about it while other people were watching, which meant he was on a strict timer until the moment someone asked him about it, and he would have to hem and haw about why he hadn't gone to his appointment yet, and it would just make the whole thing far too much of an annoyance.

"Now, I have understood the wisdom of seeking help from your betters," he smiled tightly.

Dr. Yivana sniffed, lips curled down in a faintly displeased line.

"Better has nothing to do with it," she claimed. "It's always a good idea to ensure that your body has the proper maintenance it needs. The Undead require care as much as any living person."

"Of course, Doctor," Hobbes agreed placidly. His own opinion was less complimentary, but he decided to keep that to himself at the moment.

She stared at him suspiciously, seeming to sense some sort of duplicitous intent, before looking back down at her clipboard.

"I have just a few more questions for you," she said. "Is there anything you'd like to ask of me before we continue?"

"Oh, no," Hobbes denied. Considering that he had only come here under duress, it would expressly against his desires to draw out this experience.

"Alright," Dr. Yivana huffed. "How long have you been having these symptoms?"

"Since I began my current contract," Hobbes admitted. "About six years ago, now. They've gotten worse over time, however. More frequent, when before it was rather rare."

"I see. Well, frankly, you shouldn't be feeling it at all," she said, brow furrowing in concentration. "Muted sensation is possible, of course. But something like what you've described is quite uncommon. Have you experienced this before in any of your previous contracts?"

Hobbes fought the urge to frown. Discussing the details of previous contracts was in poor taste—or, at least, he'd always been of that opinion. Younger folks had a different way of thinking about these things, and he had come to accept that, if only because it would happen with or without his approval.

"No, Doctor," he said shortly. "Not in this sense, at least."

Dr. Yivana blinked, before clearing her throat. "Yes, well. Let me explain how we're going to proceed from here. All goes well, this should be fairly simple. Thanks to the Yushis-Nyte principle, we know that dead tissue can be revitalized to a certain degree, with the reversal also being true. As such, if one uses the correct incantation, it's possible to invoke the *facsimile* of living without all of the typical requirements of such. Now, in this case both aspects will be needed—"

Hobbes felt his head spinning. For all the years he'd spent under contract, he'd never bothered to learn much about the intricacies of the practice. He had his own work and cared little about the world outside it.

Hobbes coughed delicately into his fist, politely interrupting the Doctor. "If I may ask for some clarification...?"

She glanced up from her clipboard, taking in his blank expression. "Ah. What I mean to say is, we're going to turn it off and on again. That tends to fix most small problems."

"Like a *computer*," Hobbes said, unable to help the faint disapproval that colored his tone.

He could never quite adapt to the damn things, and they only seemed to be getting more complicated over time. Telegrams had seemed a step too far for him when those had started gaining prominence. What could a telegram do that an old-fashioned letter couldn't? And now, telegrams were being sent to everyone, all the time! Just by the click of a button! Utter madness, in his opinion.

"Yes, one could compare it to such," Dr. Yivana said dryly. "Now, remove your top layers, please."

Having known this part was coming, Hobbes refrained from grumbling as he began to undo the buttons on his suit jacket, tugging off his tie at the same moment. It took several minutes to divest himself of his numerous layers, but he was soon left with just his white button-up, which he carefully folded and set to the side, leery of the various fluids and biles that could stain it. It was bad enough that he would probably have to have his pants dry-cleaned after this whole mess.

"Excellent, thank you," Dr. Yivana said, pulling up a chair. She settled by his left side, studying his arm with a critical eye.

The shadows around her flared up, taking solid form as she began to whisper ancient, arcane spells under her breath, the olden tongue falling from her lips as heavy leaden syllables.

Dark, strangely cold tendrils probed the stitches holding his shoulder together, and Dr. Yivana tutted, the sound deep and echoing with the layers of her power enveloping them both.

"No wonder you've been having issues," she rasped, a thousand more voices intertwined with her own. "Shoddy craftsmanship. Hard to believe that a trained mage was responsible. They ought to be ashamed."

Hobbes pursed his lips, refraining from commenting. Master Malekai was many things, and Hobbes truly had little complaint about their contract, but *talented* was not one of them. He had to admit, even Hobbes was a bit surprised that his body had only experienced one major issue so far.

Still, Malekai was his Master, and Hobbes' sensibilities would never allow him to comment on the man's abilities, especially to an outside observer.

Thankfully, Dr. Yivana said nothing more on the subject, narrowing her eyes in concentration as her magic began to carefully unravel the stitches holding Hobbes together.

It was a strange feeling, just on the verge of being painful. Nothing that Hobbes hadn't dealt with before, but the process of being reconstructed was not something that one could simply 'get used to'. Keeping a stiff upper lip, he refrained from flinching at the sensation. Quiet crunching sounds drifted to his ears, the echo of flesh ripping and tearing reverberating in the small clinic. There was very little blood, thankfully, as Hobbes had very little of it to begin with. But small spatters of coagulated gore dripped to the concrete floor, joining other darkened stains.

"Alright, nearly done with this part," Dr. Yivana spoke up, pulling the arm away with a swift yank that Hobbes had to brace against, neatly snapping the bones that connected the limb to his body.

That was the sharpest pain, but it dulled quickly, and Hobbes was left with the severed stump of his shoulder and its unsightly dripping.

Dr. Yivana turned toward the surgery table set-up nearby, throwing the arm on it with a meaty thump. She pulled her chair closer and began to mutter over the limb, echoes of distant voices lingering in Hobbes' ears as she worked. Hobbes politely ignored it, and stared boredly at the clinic's wall instead, taking in the number of flyers and pamphlets that plastered the concrete.

Dead or Undead, Get Tested Before You Get Busy! said one jaunty poster, showing an image of a skeletal hand popping out of a grave to display a thumbs-up. *It's Never Too Late to Seek Help!* proclaimed another, depicting a pair of smiling ghouls with patched-up, partially rotted jaws.

Hobbes humphed under his breath, turning away with a dismissive sniff. How uncouth.

Still, as he was taking advantage of these services now (though under duress), he was in no place to complain. Not that he would have done so regardless—at least, not aloud. Hobbes was a man of distinction. Such noisy actions would be beneath his dignity, and that of his Master's.

"Okay!" Dr. Yivana said, interrupting his thoughts. She sounded nearly chipper, for once. Hobbes glanced over to her, and she smiled as she approached, carrying the arm with the help of a set of dangling tendrils, and adjusting her glasses with her free hand. "I've fixed the damage done to the limb itself. As long as we can get it back on with no issues, you should be all set to go, Mr. Hobbes."

Hobbes gave an eager nod. "Much appreciated, Doctor."

The process of *reattaching* a limb was far easier than removing it, frankly, since all one had to do was take advantage of the numerous holes and assorted sundry that were already there. Taking things apart was complicated, and messy. Sewing them together was simple by comparison.

Hobbes would know—he'd had a number of less reputable Masters over the years that had required him to gain such knowledge.

He couldn't deny that it was nice to have someone else take care of the more annoying minutiae, however, and so refrained from complaining when Dr. Yivana went through all of her chanting and fancy magic rituals again.

In no time at all, the dark threads holding his limbs together wriggled out, squirming like little worms as they exited his (semi-rotten) flesh to drop down into the bucket that the Doctor had kindly put in place beforehand.

Hobbes stood slowly, rotating his shoulder blade as he felt out the limb. He hummed approvingly when there was no sense of tingling numbness, not even at the twitch of his fingertips.

"No lingering pain?" Dr. Yivana said, placing her clipboard on the side table as she began to clear the room of any more drifting shadows.

"Not a thing, Doctor," he said, feeling a sense of gratitude despite himself. "I must thank you for your kind service, it's much appreciated."

She glanced over him for a moment, a touch of amusement lingering in the corners of her mouth.

"No need to thank me. This is my job. Now, make sure you return if any more pain occurs, or if you need any other services the clinic offers. Our door is always open."

Oh, not a chance.

Hobbes nodded his head to her, gathered his coat and tie, and left as quickly as one could without it being deemed as 'fleeing.'

He had to wait, *once again*, for a car to arrive and pick him up, but by the time he had made his way back to the Manor, Hobbes found himself simply grateful that the whole mess was over and done with.

With any luck, he would never have to deal with such nonsense ever again.

"You've returned!" Master Malekai said brightly, hustling towards him as Hobbes promptly closed the door behind himself.

"Yes indeed, Master," Hobbes concurred, nodding in greeting. "Everything seems to be in order. As such, I'll be returning to duty post-haste, Sir."

Master Malekai fidgeted in place briefly, folding his hands behind his back.

"So ... You're staying around, then?" Master Malekai said, aiming for casual and ending somewhere far afield.

Hobbes bowed his head slightly, offering a smile. "Of course, sir. Until the expiration of my current contract with you, I shall remain by your side. Is that not my duty as your Butler?"

Master Malekai seemed to brighten, momentarily, before wariness overtook his face. "And after your contract expires?"

Hobbes considered it for one long moment. The blank nothingness of death was probably a relief after a long enough period of work, but Hobbes hadn't quite reached that point yet.

He pressed a fist against his chest and bowed to his Master. "I would be happy to renew it, sir."

Master Malekai's shoulders relaxed, a gust of air leaving his mouth. His relief was poorly hidden, covered by that sense of bravado that was not entirely false. "Of course. Of course! Where else would you want to go? There are no Necromancers as strong as me within a hundred-mile radius!" Master Malekai bragged, his nose high in the air.

"Just so, Master," Hobbes said indulgently. He was using his 'what a nice young man' voice, which Master Malekai normally scrambled to dispute, but the man hardly seemed to notice it.

"Good." Master Malekai nodded, lips curling up into a smug little smirk. "Now, Hobbes, I require your expertise once again. There has ... been a bit of an incident with the washing machine."

Hobbes, for a moment, considered what the inside of a grave would be like. More quiet, he was certain. And, he was equally certain, far more boring. He ducked his head once more and flashed his Master an affable grin. "Certainly, sir. I am, as ever, your obedient servant."

Patient Zero

Erika Lance

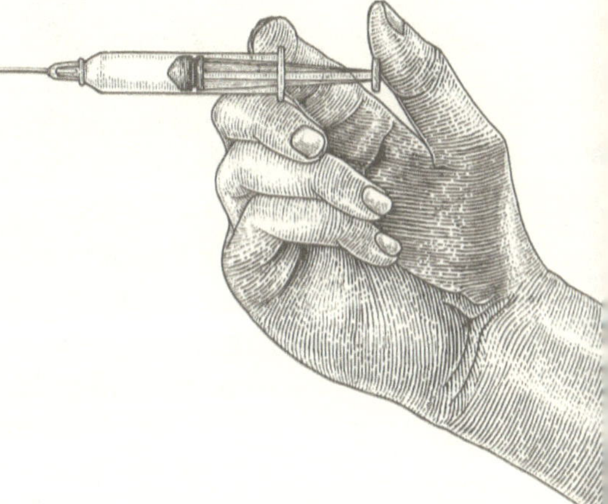

I suppose this is where the movie would begin, if in fact, there was anyone left interested in actually making movies or watching them.

When people hear "Patient Zero," they often assume the end result is zombies from the infection.

After the year 2020, people might also think it is the person who brought us COVID. Although I believe that this has been attributed to a lab or 5G cell service lines and not some random person, I don't begin to think that I understand the medical side of it.

As all of us have experienced, people are super misinformed. The internet doesn't help and might be the single largest origination point of most false information fed to you on a daily basis.

Then again, after everything that has happened in the last few months, I think most of us wish it was fake news or even zombies. At least then there would be either something to ignore or something you would have a chance at fighting.

It was a Thursday—no wait, a Wednesday—when the first reports began to hit. Actually, it was not so much a report as a viral Tiktok video showing the first signs of what was to come.

The video was taken in one of those office buildings where the 'office' is just made up of what seems to be miles of cubicles. The video, of course, starts with a male in his early twenties, who frankly looks terrified speaking into the camera. His username: LuvDaLattes69.

In his very shaky voice, he says that a woman in his office just completely lost her mind and is throwing things around. He continues on to say that he is not sure if she has a gun with her. It is interesting that everyone assumed before this began that a gun was one of the dead-liest issues in a workplace.

In the video, you can hear the crashing of things and the screams of others in the background. He lifts the camera as he appears to stand up and flips the camera in the opposite direction toward the end of a row of cubicles.

As he is panning the camera, you can see a row of cubicles on the far end of the room flip over. I know you must be thinking that it is impos-sible to actually flip one cubicle, much less an entire row. In this case, you would be wrong. In the video, you see something—or someone—appear to lift up one end of the cubicle row with ease and just toss. Because the cubicles are linked together, they all follow the first. The video gets shaky as the items on the desks go flying including com-puters, decorations, and papers. Then, as the cubicles and items crash and float onto the ground you can see a woman standing at the spot where the launching originated.

She doesn't seem like much in the video. Middle-aged, on the shorter side, close to possibly five-foot judging by the cubicle wall to her left that was still intact. Her blonde hair lands on her shoulders in a simple cut that was on the professional side. Simple white blouse, tan pants, and a pair of glasses round out her look. By all appearances, she was a typical office employee.

The only exception is the fact that she is clenching and unclenching her hands. She grabs the cubicles to her left and flips them as well.

LuvDaLattes69 is still recording with many 'Oh my Gods' and 'She's crazys' until the small, blonde office worker turns to face him. She becomes a blur as she launches toward him, and the video abruptly ends.

Many of the comments called the footage fake and made references to how that is not how it would happen in "real life."

Unfortunately, it wasn't.

The next day there were no reports on the national news. There was, however, a report from a local station in Monroe, Louisiana that said that an employee had an "episode" at work during which there was destruc-tion of furniture that caused several injuries.

What was most interesting about the report was that the news failed to release the name of the employee. It was Karlie Jacobson by the way. This, however, was only revealed in the comment section of the news channel's website and in the comments of the TikTok video.

The injuries from this event, as it turns out, were in much higher volume then the news report would lead you to believe and, in fact, two people later died from their injuries. A younger man by the name of Cole Peters was one of them. As it turned out, this was LuvDaLattes69.

This information was also not in any of the news reports.

The next incident, that was recorded and broadcast at least, took place in a museum in France called The Centre Pompidou. Unlike the first video, this one starts with a very excited bubbly teenage female, username Artislove15, showing off a painting that is her "absolute favorite in the entire world" and "she cannot believe she is standing right in front of it". Then, you can hear shouting and screams. As she shakily pans her phone camera, a man rips paintings off the walls as alarms begin to go off.

She keeps recording as the man leaps from wall to wall, tearing down the paintings as he goes. Some of the people are running around her, others look to be in shock while there are a few filming as well. This man creating the destruction lands next to the painting that Artislove15 had called her favorite. With what appears to be long black claws where his fingers should be, he rips the painting in half, frame and all.

"No!" you hear the girl holding the camera scream as the man on the wall turns to face her. His eyes appear to be a pool of swirling black and red as he tilts his head from side to side slowly, as if studying her.

A wicked grin spreads across his face as he speaks, his voice deep and gravely "You dare to tell me no, little prey?"

The camera is shaking then goes blurry as she begins to run from the monster on the wall. You can hear it laughing in the background with the same gravelly deep voice along with her heavy breathing. Then the picture changes as images whirl past; the phone seems to be knocked from the young woman's hands and then with a 'thunk,' it cuts off.

Unlike the first video, Artislove15 did not have the only footage of the event. Other witnesses uploaded videos that were taken during the incident in the museum that day. A few of the videos also showed the attack on Artislove15, her name was Valentina Monterog. When he was done destroying the painting, he jumped from the wall and onto her as she was running away, causing her to smash into the floor. Before you could see any movement from her, he grabs her by the hair and smashes her head into the floor. Blood oozes out into her hair as he leaps out of the frame.

Eventually the security feed from the museum was released, corroborating the events as well. This was done, in part, to try to find the person responsible for the destruction who they did eventually identify, but it was unlikely, given his behavior, that anyone would be looking to interact with him for any reason.

This is when the snowball effect happened.

The governments in most countries had reported that these were isolated instances at first and for the public to not worry. Of course, that fell apart soon enough with the sheer volume of reported instances. Most governments just simply fell silent; others continued to deny, but it became intensely clear that there was nothing to be done to stop the spread of information.

The genie could not be put back in the bottle.

Where both of the previous instances showed destruction and harm, the newer videos began to show different abilities emerge. Yes, there were people flipping out and breaking shit. I mean, if you suddenly found out you had super strength, you may want to do the very same thing. For others it was things like their skin strengthening to almost a kevlar-type quality. This. of course, made them harder to hurt, or kill, or get a blood sample with a needle.

Some could see in the dark as if it was daylight, while others could see great distances and could read a page from miles away when they focused. There were others that could see through basically anything they wanted. Not so much x-ray vision but the ability to concentrate and move the layers in front of them out of their line of sight.

Basically, any sort of enhancement you could think of, began to happen. New ones were being shown every day. There were abilities that had never even been thought of, and the rumors were rampant. Are you thinking that somehow superheroes were created?

In a way, I suppose many of us would want to think that was the case until you saw one of these 'heroes' decimate an entire town because they simply felt like it.

The medical community did immediately jump into action to try to find out what scientifically was happening. Although there was almost no way to run typical tests on these enhanced people. For those that were willing to volunteer information, there was a pattern that emerged for all of them. Each of them had compromised immune systems to begin with. Meaning, most were people who had an organ transplant, cancer treatment, or some kind of illness or genetic trait that left them vulnerable to almost anything.

The weakest of us, became the strongest.

Some believed this was a miracle, but after a few short months into this new reality it became clear what had caused this shift.

Religions, as a general rule, have some version of a heaven, a place where if you are mostly pure and do the proper things you will arrive in some sort of nirvana. There is always the opposite for those that are considered bad or have a transgression so terrible they cannot be redeemed. Most of these places have unimaginable terrors that await the 'souls' sent there.

In either of these places, good or bad, there are mythological creatures that reside there to make your stay either pleasurable or nightmarish. Of course, even some of the most devoted thought of these as simply representations of Good and Evil.

They were wrong.

The first creature that appeared in the Nevada desert was over twenty feet in height with skin that shifted in what could only be described as the color of darkness. If you looked at it for long, it would make you nauseous. It could be said that its form was humanoid, but this also shifted. At times it appeared to have more than four appendages including a tail or additional limbs. Its multiple pupilless eyes were a repulsive yellow color that seemed to weep a brownish pus that would fall to the ground when its eyelids closed.

The military attempted to make contact but after the first shot was fired, any life that got close simply withered and died. Those with abilities seemed to be drawn into its thrall. Each day, more and more simply arrived. There were no words spoken, or evil genius monologues. Its minions simply arrived, stayed for a time, and then left, appearing in other locations around the globe to take action or simply watch and wait.

The military forces finally decided to drop a nuke on the area where the original creature was, along with several others of varying degrees of horrid and sickening attributes. The bomb was dropped, and there was no change other than creating a radioactive crater where Las Vegas used to be.

News and information was never stopped or halted by these creatures or the changed humans which were called Daemons. They did not seem to care what was shown, letting the human race share all it wanted as the world fell apart. Entire towns, cities, and countries were destroyed mostly by poor reactions to their new occupants. Those with guns would sometimes try to gather and attack, it would always fail, and they would be destroyed.

Those of us that survived did so by creating smaller communities that were more self-sustained. Although power, water, and the internet were operational for the most part, other amenities were no longer available such as Amazon or Uber Eats. Some restaurants still operated, but these were the local ones versus the major chains.

Trade and bartering systems became more prevalent. There were, of course, those who thought they could use weapons and fear to control those around them, but they would be taken out when a Daemon arrived; it appeared they did not want a human to think they were more superior than others.

I am not sure where this movie will come to an end, but at least, for now, we don't have to pay taxes.

The Scan

Axel Kohagen

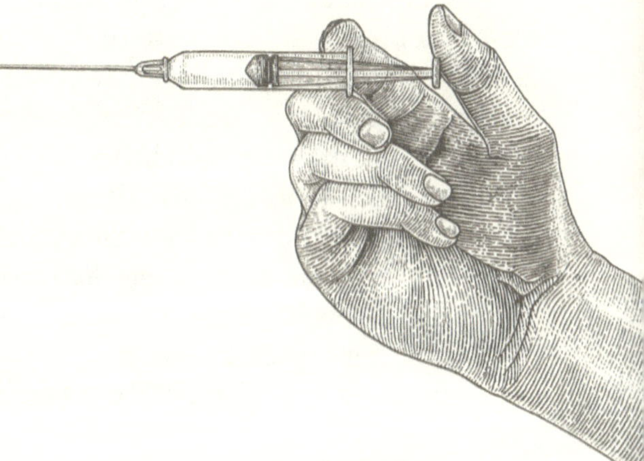

Why did they choose orange? thought Charlie.

She sat on the examining table in her doctor's office, staring at the orange walls. Was this office so old orange walls were in style when it was created, or did someone make a really poor choice? The walls were a shade darker than an orange creamsicle. They were clean, though. She had to give them that.

She had waited on the examining table for at least half an hour, spending that time either playing with her phone or studying the walls. She tried not to look at the other things in the room —the plastic gloves, the tongue depressors, the Q-tips, the Vaseline. Over the last year and a half, she'd been poked, prodded, and manipulated by all of those items more times than she cared to remember.

Just one more scan, she told herself. *Just one more scan and then no doctors for six months. Then, eventually, no doctors for a full year. And then all of this is behind me. Then I can get back to the little worries, like wondering if I forgot someone's birthday or wishing I exercised more. Stuff I'm too scared about my overall health to worry about right now. Scared for my life.*

At least she wasn't in a hospital gown or a hospital bed. They weren't planning on holding her prisoner yet again.

Her doctor told her this scan was just a formality. They wanted to make sure they got everything during the last treatment, which was supposed to get everything the surgery didn't. She was no stranger to scans, but this one had her flesh crawling. She nipped at her fingernails with her front teeth. She rubbed one foot atop the other. *Just a formality,* she repeated in her head. *Just to be sure.*

A doctor came in, except he wasn't exactly a doctor. He was a doctor-in-training. Her real doctor got her permission to have this fledgling doctor follow him around. Why would she say no? She'd already lost all pretense of pride and modesty when it came to doctors. They'd stripped her down and fully exposed her.

"How are you doing?" the doctor-in-training asked. He sat down in front of the computer and brought up a few files.

"Okay," she said. *Are we doing this now?* she thought. *Let's get it over with.*

"The doctor will be in shortly to go over your results with you," he said.

"Okay," she said again.

"Between you and me," the doctor-in-training said, "Everything looks good."

Relief filled her body. Her eyes watered. Her breath hitched slightly, then she took in one good, deep breath to reset her oxygen levels.

"Good," she said.

The doctor-in-training left again. She uncrossed her legs and kicked her heels at the side of the examining table. She breathed deeply, aware of how shallow her breath had been before.

Goodbye, orange office, she thought. *Won't see you again for six months.*

The real doctor came in next. He greeted her and then sat down in front of the computer. The doctor-in-training stood beside him, still smiling. The doctor opened even more files on the computer. He turned toward her.

"Pretty much everything looks good. We did find these two spots here, in your lungs,"

"Okay," Charlie said. She looked at the doctor-in-training. He was still grinning.

"It'll be okay," the regular doctor continued. "We can go in and take out one-third of your lung. You'll be fine, but it'll take a little bit of adjustment."

"I thought you said everything looked good?" Charlie snapped at the doctor-in-training. He nodded. Still smiling.

"I'll send the results to your primary doctor," her regular (but not primary) doctor told her. "She'll make the final decision. We'll probably schedule surgery soon."

"How long is the recovery time?" Charlie asked.

"As long as it takes," her doctor said. "We have to open you up and get inside there, so that's going to cut into a lot of muscles. You'll be really sore and weak for a while. You're going to want to take it easy."

"He told me everything looked good!" Charlie yelled.

"The nurse will come back shortly to review everything with you," her doctor said. He maintained eye contact while he was walking away, but he didn't break his stride while talking. The doctor-in-training shuffled away behind him. His smile faded when he passed by her.

I guess it could be worse news, she thought. *Maybe that's what he meant. It could always be worse.*

She leaned her head back and sighed. The tears were coming again, and she blinked hard to keep them from dripping down her face. She wanted to punch the wall but feared all she would do was break something in her hand.

One more surgery, she thought. *I'll miss more time at work. I'm going to need to take out a loan for bills. Especially medical bills ... more on the way now. I wonder if they'll find a way to fire me. I wish I was married right now. Even a husband that I hated would have a job to bring in money and keep the bills paid.*

A nurse wheeled a wheelchair into her room and left it in the doorway. He smiled and walked away.

Charlie stared at the wheelchair. It suddenly struck her that the room was very small.

The nurse returned. "We're going to go ahead and admit you today," he told Charlie. "I'll wheel you down after we get the okay that the bed is ready."

"My doctor never said anything about being admitted," Charlie said.

The nurse shrugged. "That's the plan," he said.

"I'd think I can walk myself down there," Charlie said. *If I even want to go down there. This is all happening too fast.*

"It's the rules," the nurse said. He shrugged again. "What are you gonna do?"

"Do I have to go down there?" Charlie asked.

"Doctor says so. He knows more than you or I do."

"Okay," Charlie said. She got out her phone. *I'll have to call my mother first. After calling mom, I can rest assured knowing the rest of the family will be notified in a series of short, information-packed phone conversations with her. I will have to call work. I will have to bother the neighbor again and ask* him to take care of my dog. Sometimes, I worry the dog will forget who her real owner is.

The nurse came back. He took the wheelchair and pulled it back out of the room. Then, he wheeled it down the hallway and out of sight.

So, do I get to walk myself down there or what? she thought.

The nurse left the door open, and she watched doctors and nurses pass by her room door without even glancing in her direction. Her own doctor passed by several times. Charlie got up to shut the door and paused. Is it supposed to stay open? Do they need to watch me? For signs of something? Did they find something worse in my scan that they're not telling me?

The pictures of her scan were still up on the computer screen. After peeking out the exam room door and seeing no one to stop her, she moved to the desk chair and stared at her scan. She could clearly see the two spots. What else am I looking at? she thought. All of my insides look rotten. Isn't this what they're supposed to look like? That over there looks like it moved and left some sort of blur.

Charlie touched her chest, trying to place her fingers on the spot where those two dots were located. Nothing felt abnormal. She could feel her ribcage. Will they have to cut it apart and lift it up, or could they somehow work around it while they are taking out my lung? She gently pushed against her ribs.

"Hello again," her doctor said. He knocked on the door frame and then walked through the open door to her room. "They got that wheelchair out of there, I see."

"Yeah. They're going to let me walk myself downstairs, then?" Charlie asked.

"You're not going anywhere," her doctor said. "I consulted with your primary doctor, and she thinks those spots are just scar tissue. Probably from some time where you had pneumonia or something like that. Nothing to worry about."

"Oh," she said. "Okay."

"So we're just about ready to send you home. I just came to tell you the good news!" her doctor said.

He sounds confused, she thought. Maybe he should be. I'm certainly confused.

"Okay. Sounds good." she said.

"Just hang out for, like, five more minutes," her doctor said. "Then we'll let you go."

He left the room before she could reply. *Glad I didn't call anybody,* she thought. *Now I don't have to call them back and tell them I was mistaken. I should get coffee on my way to work. After that scare, I deserve a little treat.* She stretched out her legs and yawned.

People still walked past her room. Now, it seemed to her they were looking at her instead of avoiding her gaze. One man lost his footing and tripped a bit as he passed her room. A woman gave her a timid half-smile. Charlie looked back at the ugly orange walls. The doctor-in-training walked past. He refused to look at her at all. He stared at his feet and muttered something to himself.

The nurse came back in with a long black bag. "Excuse me," he said. "Can I have you move forward on the table?"

"Sure," she said. "What's going on?"

"You know how it is around here," the nurse said. "Plans change. Doctors always want something different."

The nurse laid the black bag out behind her on the examining table. It looked like a large duffel bag. He unzipped it all the way down. "Your doctor will be right back," he said. He left the room before she could reply.

Charlie wondered what the bag felt like, but she was scared to touch it.

The doctor-in-training came back in with a small electronic tablet. He handed it to Charlie. He smiled without making eye contact.

"What is this?" she asked.

"Just a few more forms," he said. "Medical history. Organ donor."

"Why did you say everything would be okay earlier?" Charlie asked. "Before the doctor said anything. Aren't you supposed to wait to say anything until the doctor says something?"

"I'm so sorry," he said. He looked up at the corner of the room. She wanted to grab his chin and force him to look into her eyes, but she didn't want to touch him. He paused, and then he sighed. He turned and left the room.

Charlie looked at the tablet. The first section was yet another series of questions about her family of origin and medical history. She filled out one of these for every doctor she saw on her road to recovery. What have you suffered from? What about your father's side? Mother's? This information reminded her how much of her health was the result of random chance.

The next section, just like the doctor-in-training said, was all about organ donation. *Why am I filling this out now, right before I go home?* She thought. *I've already checked 'okay' on my driver's license. How many times do I have to answer the same questions? Just let me leave here and get my coffee. Maybe I'll even skip work today and go home to my dog.*

The third section was a billing invoice from a funeral home. She was listed as the decedent.

Charlie took a long look at the black bag behind her.

Her doctor came back in. This time, he was not alone. Her primary doctor was with him. There were two free chairs in the orange room, so both sat down. The doctor-in-training was nowhere to be seen.

"I came as soon as I heard," her primary doctor said.

"Heard what?" Charlie said. She crossed her arms in front of her chest. Her feet, crossed at the ankles, kicked against the side of the examining table. "What's going on?"

"Let me just check a couple of things," her doctor said. He first took her temperature by swiping a device across her forehead. He nodded. Then, he grabbed the blood pressure cuff and rolled his chair beside her. He cuffed her arm and began inflating the device. He listened with his stethoscope. Then he released the air from the cuff and nodded. "Oh-kay," he said.

"What's going on?" Charlie demanded.

"It's okay," her primary doctor said.

"Her numbers are alright," her doctor said.

"Can I go home now?" Charlie asked.

"There's no easy way of telling you what I'm about to tell you," her doctor said. "Charlie, I'm afraid you have died."

"There is no way," Charlie said. *Is this a joke? Is everybody in on this joke but me?* "I'm going to file a formal complaint against all of you and you'll never practice medicine again. This isn't funny at all."

"It's not a joke, Charlie," her primary doctor said. Her voice always soothed Charlie. She had been the doctor to give her the bad news when she began this journey into hell months ago, and it had been her voice that got Charlie through the roughest times. Charlie wanted to depend on that voice again, but what it was saying made no sense.

"We're talking. You both said the scan was fine. He just said my numbers were okay. How could I possibly be dead?"

"It's a tricky diagnosis," her doctor stated. "I apologize for almost missing it. When I saw the data, though, there was no doubt. It's very technical and difficult to explain, but you have clearly died."

"I feel fine!" Charlie shouted. "I just want to grab a cup of coffee and go home to see my dog."

Her dog. Seven pounds of Shih Tzu. All love. No malice. Always beside her, whether she watched TV, cooked in the kitchen, or slept in her bed. Named Lula.

"You'll have to find somebody to watch your dog," her doctor said.

"There's a positive side to this," her primary doctor said. "We caught it early. You'll have time to put your affairs in order. That should be a comfort to you."

"You're saying I'm dying."

"You died," her doctor said. He stretched out the word "died," annoyed she questioned his diagnosis. "I'm very sorry. You are dead."

"But I'm talking! I'm conscious! I could reach out and touch you!"

"Death is more complicated than that," her doctor continued. "Most people die the traditional way. Lose consciousness. Lose control of all motor functions. In very rare cases, a person dies without losing consciousness or motor functions. I mean, they lose those things later on. At first, they're very hard to distinguish from the living."

Her doctor perked up, excited about an idea. He re-opened her scan folder and searched for another image. He found what he was looking for and opened it up. Instead of looking at her chest, Charlie found herself looking at the inside of her skull.

"Look here," the doctor said. "And here. These areas have already reduced in size. When I noticed that, I called the labs to run another test on your bloodwork. They confirmed you were lacking in certain neurotransmitters necessary to sustain life. Enough so that we had you declared dead about five minutes ago. We came to tell you as soon as it was official."

"Is that why you made me fill out the organ donor forms?" Charlie asked. She gasped. "Are you going to cut into me while I'm still alive? I mean, whatever I am?"

"No one's going to do that, Charlie," her primary doctor cooed. "We wouldn't remove any organs while you're conscious. If you become unconscious while your body is still circulating blood to your organs, we may try to quickly remove them."

"But I need my organs!" Charlie said. "Whatever you want to call me, I'm still here."

"Not for long," her doctor replied.

"Charlie," her primary doctor began, "there are things about medicine that most people don't learn until it's too late for them. Almost all deceased people sustain some level of awareness. Brain research has come a long way. We can now determine most people experience some bodily sensation and awareness of their surroundings for up to two weeks after they die. That's why you'll never see a brain doctor getting cremated—most people maintain some sensation while cremated."

I need to change my will, Charlie thought. Her stomach felt sick.

In fact, her whole body felt different. It took a substantial amount of effort to keep her head up. Moving her eyes from one doctor to the other took total concentration. Her feet dangled lifelessly from her legs.

Am I really dying? she thought. *No. Dead. I'm really dead.*

"We're very sorry," her doctor said.

"Do you want me to ... climb into the bag now?" Charlie asked. She gestured toward it. Slowly.

"No, Charlie!" her primary doctor said. "Of course not."

"That damned nurse was supposed to wait to bring this in," her doctor said. "You can take as long as you need to reach bodily death."

"But I'll still be ... I 'll still be able to sense things? To experience things?"

"I would expect sensation for several weeks," her primary doctor said. "If you opt for burial, you'll avoid being burned while aware, but you'll still end up trapped in a casket with nothing to do but stare into the darkness. If I were you, I'd ask for an open casket funeral. It'll be your last chance to see anything."

"It's so barbaric," her doctor said. He shook his head. "Knowing what we know now, there should be more time above ground. We should go back to leaving the dead out in nature."

"I don't see how being torn apart by animals and insects is any better," her primary doctor snapped. "Anyway, now's not the right time to talk about it."

"I think I will lie down," Charlie said. She stretched out on the examining table. She could feel the bag behind her. She could not feel her fingertips.

"We'll keep checking on you," her primary doctor said. "I canceled the rest of my clients today to help you with the transition."

"If what you're saying, if it's true?" Charlie began. "Don't zip up the bag all the way. No matter where you're taking me. I don't want to be in the dark."

"I'll see what I can do," her doctor said. Charlie remembered that the nurse didn't do a very good job of following instructions. Her eyes welled with tears.

"Goodnight," her primary doctor said. They left the room in silence.

Charlie stared at the orange walls of the doctor's office. She decided this color had never been in style. Someone wanted to make a statement with these walls. Someone wanted to be noticed, to be vibrant and alive. Someone wanted to stand out from the crowd, even if they risked creating an eyesore for the world to mock. She smiled a little. These walls were beautiful.

BOOK CLUB QUESTIONS

1. Which was your favorite story? Your least favorite?

2. Medicine takes different forms in this anthology—from potions, to pills, and even voodoo rituals. Which did you find the most frightening?

3. In "A Simple Brain Scan," Judy smiles when she realizes that the parasites, which only she can see, can be killed. What do you imagine the next scene in this story would look like?

4. In "Feed Us," Alex isn't believed by her spouse or doctor, even though it is apparent that the baby is eating her from the inside. Why do you think she ultimately accepts her fate ("I think he's hungry")?

5. In "Rainbow Rock," Jack's entire perspective changes when his lump becomes a sort of third eye. What does the change in the Rainbow Rock apartments' sculpture signify?

6. Which stories did you find the most intriguing: those with fantastical elements, or those based in reality?

7. Hospitals/medicine are a common horror trope, but not all of the stories in this anthology are horror. Did any genre surprise you?

Editor Bio

Beau Lake is a tattooed, rainbow-haired, queer romance writer and editor skulking around the mountains of Virginia. She is very happily married and lives with a menagerie of children (3), dogs (2), and plants.

Her current hobbies include digital art, social/animal activism, and screaming into the void. Mostly the latter. Other favorite activities include listening to true crime podcasts, staring at empty Word documents while having existential crises, and asking herself "What Would Stephen King Do?"

Beau writes both traditional and horror/paranormal LGBTQIA romance. She edits books for 4 Horsemen Publications under the name S.L. Vargas, including the Birth of the Fae series by Danielle M. Orsino and the Realm series by C.R. Rice.

Some of her published work includes the well-received DC Pride series, co-written with Tatum West (Proud, Out, and The Space Between Us). The Wolves of Wharton is her first paranormal romance series, with more to come!

She can be found online on Facebook, Twitter, and TikTok, or at beaulakebooks.com. She loves talking with readers and can be reached at blake@4horsemenpublications.com